TO BREATHE AGAIN

INVISIBLE SHACKLES
BOOK 2

UNOMA NWANKWOR

KEVSTEL PUBLICATIONS

Copyright © 2021 by Unoma Nwankwor

All Rights Reserved. No part of this book may be reproduced in any form or by any means without proper consent of the Publisher, excepting brief quotes used in reviews. Please do not participate in or encourage piracy of copyrighted materials in violation of the author's rights.

This is a work of fiction. Any reference or similarities to actual events, real people, living or dead or to real locales are intended to give the novel a sense of reality. Any similarities to other names, characters, places, and incidents are entirely fictional.

"Broken Things", **"Blink"**, **"Sweet Mist"** are original poems written and owned by Yejide Kilanko.

First printing February 2021

Printed in the United States of America

www.kevstel.com

*To my husband Kevin, and my kids—Fumnanya & Ugo.
Their support is immeasurable.*

ACKNOWLEDGMENTS

To my Lord and Savior Jesus Christ. I thank you for paying the ultimate price that I may have life and for your grace which I do not deserve. Thank You for the gift of writing and I humbly pray I continue to be a vessel in this journey.

To my family, my husband Kevin who's my number one fan, cheering me along every step of the way. I love you and thank you. To my kids Fumnanya and Ugo, my gang, my pookies, my munchkins who keep me sane when insanity sometimes abound. I love you both more than words can express. I pray for God's continued protection over you.

To my parents and mother in-law, *Daalu*. Thank you for your constant prayers and speaking words of life, courage and hope upon me.

To my readers, author friends and sistah writers thank you. A special shout out to Sherell Denise Burns, she kept pushing me when I wanted to give up. Sometimes support doesn't always come from the people or places you expect but trust in God and He will send the right people to you.

NOTE FROM THE AUTHOR

Alas, the conclusion to my two-book series, Invisible Shackles. We started this series in 2018 with the oldest sister Itohan in TO LIVE AGAIN. Itohan got her happily ever after but due to circumstances beyond my control, I couldn't write her sister's story. For three long years I held on to hope that one day you will read about her sister Isoken.

That day has finally arrived in the form of TO BREATHE AGAIN. Each book is a complete stand-alone story. The Adolo sisters deal with emotional baggage that threaten to destroy them and the happiness they desperately desire but are afraid to have.

Being in a prison isn't always about the physical location of a 5 by 7 cell. Often as humans, we are also shackled by invisible chains that hinder our progress.

In this book, you get to meet Isoken (pronounced E- So-Ken), and Tekena (pronounced just as it is spelled). You will also meet some new folks as well as old people.

It's been a long time coming and I am so excited.

Trigger warning: This book touches on grief and makes mention of sexual abuse.

You can always reach me through www. unomanwankwor.com

Unoma

PRAISE FOR THE UNOMA NWANKWOR

"Whew! Unoma's characters were so real. They were honest, flawed, vulnerable, stubborn and saved by grace. I love when Unoma uses Africa as the backdrop for her romantic settings. Her spiritual message was clear: God's mercy and grace. Look out the Jamieson men, the Danjuma Brothers have arrived!!!" ~ **Pat Simmons, Award-winning author of the Guilty Series.**

"I love how Unoma Nwankwor weaves the distinctive, spicy flavor of West Africa into her novels. I feel right at home with the food, pidgin English, quirky expressions, and cultural norms. I'm also enjoying watching her grow as an author. ~**Sherri L. Lewis, Bestselling Author and Missionary**

Nwankwor adds more depth with the cultural nuances that could be a roadblock or a gateway to understanding. She expertly intertwines all of these elements, including faith lessons, to make a tightly woven story for a reader's enjoyment. ~ **USA Today Review of An Unexpected Blessing.**

"Unoma's writing reads effortlessly. There is the perfect infusion of faith and international flavor. Readers are quickly swept up on a romantic literary adventure. **The Christmas Ultimatum** is a great read for anytime of the year" ~ **Norma Jarrett Essence Best Selling author of Sunday Brunch.**

"**When You Let Go** is a true testament of the power of God within ourselves and our marriage. Although, we are tested every day, it is up to us to lean on our faith to get through those difficult times and offer forgiveness to those who may have hurt us in the process. Amara and Ejike's faith was tested throughout this novel but once they learned to put God at the forefront of their household, they were able to weather the storm." ~ **Diva's Literary World**

BROKEN THINGS
I'm broken,
I said with the certainty,
the fear that the pieces of me
could no longer fit together.
They reached out,
hugged all the jagged edges to themselves,
and said sometimes rest does wonders
for broken things.

CHAPTER 1

Light approaching steps alerted her to another unwanted presence. With the amount of traffic in and out of her house the last couple of weeks, Isoken Adolo couldn't begin to guess who they belonged to. Neither was her interest piqued enough to find out. Instead, she ambled to the dresser on the other side of her bedroom. Placing both hands on the piece of furniture, she hung her head.

The fragility of life.

She'd give anything to hear the heavier footsteps that made her heart flutter on approach. Anything to reverse time and not argue about her ice cream in a cup versus the waffle cone she'd requested. Anything to hear the contagious, deep laughter that calmed her world. Anything to have the hypnotic effect of his voice wash over her.

Anything.

She'd listened to the last voicemail in a loop, but the feeling was underwhelming.

Why?

How?

The well of questions were endless and the knowledge that she'd never know the answers, gutted her. So, here she was, dressed in white. He wanted white. Life was indeed cruel because it wasn't the mermaid-cut, Ziedu original wedding dress that arrived a month ago, but a pantsuit. A pantsuit with a black flower on her lapel.

White. This is the last time I'll ever wear this color.

A light rap on the door interrupted the quiet she relished. Isoken didn't bother responding because she knew the person would enter anyway. None of them had left her alone as she requested.

"Keni, it's time."

Isoken raised her head and made eye contact in the mirror with her older sister Itohan. Her hushed tone reflected the atmosphere. Tears pooled in her eyes causing her sister to close the gap between them in hurried strides. Isoken took in a deep breath and exhaled slowly. She didn't have to say much for her sister and best friend to know what she was feeling. Despite the eighteen-month age gap, they shared everything. Itohan placed her chin on her shoulder and wrapped her arms around her. They stood in comfortable silence for a few minutes.

"How do I do this?" Isoken whispered.

A tear made its way down her puffy face. She had cried so much in the past weeks that she was surprised there were any tears left.

"With your family by your side." Itohan squeezed her tighter. "Frank's mum and Mummy are downstairs waiting."

"Where's Daddy and Zogie?" Isoken inquired about their younger brother who acted more like the eldest.

"They left for the church. Ajoke is downstairs too." Itohan turned her around and thumbed away a tear. "Everyone's waiting for you."

Isoken closed her eyes. "It hurts so bad, sis. Like I can't breathe, for real. When you all return to your lives, how do I cope? How can God do me this way? I've served Him. I've worshiped Him, volunteered where I could. Followed His Word. How can He love me and do me like this? I'm supposed to be getting married and not burying the love of my life. How can this be real life right now?" More tears dropped as she looked to her sister for the answers she knew Itohan couldn't give.

"You know I'm the last person to claim to know the answers to those questions. My *wahala* pales in comparison to this. But I also asked how He could allow my heartbreak."

Maybe they weren't meant to be married like their parents. Chief and Mrs. Adolo would celebrate their thirty-fifth anniversary soon and their daughters couldn't even get to a full day. Her sister was traditionally married to who she thought was her Romeo until he sold her a dream, disappeared to America, and became Casper the Ghost. She hadn't heard a word from her so-called husband in almost a year. But her sister had closure because although he went silent, she knew he was alive, or their families would've been informed.

Isoken, on the other hand, woke up several weeks ago to top ranking officials of the Nigerian Armed Forces at her doorstep.

Frank Akintunde, the love of her life and fiancé had died in the line of duty.

He'd updated his information, naming her as the next of kin, so they came to her instead of his family. His career was dangerous, but nothing could've ever prepared her for having her life tossed like a salad two weeks before their wedding.

Nothing.

"I don't get it. Whatever I did to cause Him to punish me this way, couldn't it be forgiven? What did I do to make Him so angry? Frank was my all – my motivation, my gist partner, my protector. How do I go from planning a wedding to a burial?" Isoken shook her head and placed her hand on her chest. Her heart ached under the pressure of the clamp that hadn't let her go since she was given the news.

Itohan remained silent, and for that Isoken was grateful. She turned around to face her sister who'd been staying with her since the news hit. Her parents also flew down from Benin and accompanied her to Frank's family to break the news.

Itohan cupped Isoken's face. "You'll get through this. We'll get you through this. I read once that death leaves a heartache no one can heal, but love leaves a memory no one can steal. You'll always have the memories of your time with Frank."

"I don't want the memories. I want him. I don't want to remember old stuff. I want to make new stuff." Isoken drifted back to the bed. "I can't see him be put in the ground. I refuse." She plopped down.

Itohan kneeled before her. "Isoken Marie Adolo, you're the strongest one out of the three of us. God knew what He was doing when He had you be the middle child. You hold me up from the bottom and Zogie down from the top. For weeks, you've cried nonstop and I can't tell you when to stop mourning... But if you don't attend the service or the burial, you'll forever regret it. And what will people say when they don't see his fiancée?"

Isoken glared at her. "You were talking good until that 'what will people say' part. You know I've never given a thought to what people will say. That's you and Mummy's thing."

"Okay true. But you get the point." Itohan stood and stretched out her hand. "Let's go, sis."

Isoken's eyes traveled from her sister's outstretched hand to her face. A face that sadly hadn't held much light since her own man problems began. Isoken took her hand and stood. The sisters hugged, crossed the room, and left.

THE CHURCH SERVICE WAS A BLUR. Isoken had sat sandwiched between her mother and Frank's. It was against culture for the old to bury the young. So only her siblings were riding with her to the cemetery. The closer they got, the faster her heart raced. All through, the casket remained closed, something she was grateful for. She wanted to remember him the way he was.

She recalled the day he asked her to be his wife. They'd taken a trip to Benin for her dad's birthday. Unbeknownst to her, during one of their many talks in her dad's study, Frank asked him permission to marry her. They'd stayed three days, and on the last day, Frank got down on one knee in her father's compound.

The car came to a halt, ending her trip down memory lane. Her brother opened the door and helped her out. On wobbly knees and with her siblings on either side, Isoken made her way to the gravesite. She swallowed to rid herself of the dull metallic taste that lingered on her buds. The scorching, September sun had no mercy, even under the wide-brimmed hat she wore. Once they came to a standstill, everything seemed to move in slow motion. The military did their thing, closely followed by words from a few friends and family. The pastor then spoke for a few moments. Then it was time to lower the casket.

Isoken walked over and placed a single white rose on the closed box. Despite the heat, chills traveled down her back. She clenched her hands to stop their tremble. Her eyes remained glued to the casket that held her lifeless future. The reality of the situation, pain, disappointment, and anger hit her like a boulder.

From the pit of her stomach, she let out a guttural sound and fell to her knees in a disheveled heap as tears poured from her soul. With her hands in the soil that would soon cover her lifeline forever, Isoken continued to scream as pure agony escaped through her vocal cords. Hopelessness took over her being. She screamed until there was nothing left. Her tonsils hurt and her vision was blurred. For weeks, she'd held on to a glimmer of hope that the military was mistaken. She'd seen it in movies many times. The hero came back to life.

Frank was a hero.

Her hero.

Moments later, her brother's strong hands landed on her shoulder. He pulled her up and she leaned against him, as he led her to the car. The rest of the day was a haze.

The following day, Isoken boarded a flight with her parents to her childhood home in Benin. Everyone said a time of rest would heal her broken heart. Isoken disagreed. However, she said yes because she could no longer live in Lagos. Without Frank, the city was no longer home.

———

"Isoken, *to khian gbe mwen wa ah?*"

Isoken closed her eyes mid stir but didn't turn around. She inhaled the earthy aroma of her dark roast. She needed the caffeine high for this line of questioning so early in the morning. Why would she want to kill her mother? She contemplated ignoring Patricia Adolo, but that was never an option. Isoken covered the sugar, placed it back in the kitchen cupboard, and turned around.

"*Lamogun* Mummy. *D'evbin ne vbe rue?*"

Her mother pulled out the chair in the breakfast nook and plopped down. Her performance was complete with an exaggerated sigh for dramatic effect. Isoken struggled to keep her eyes from rolling.

"Do you know how hard it is to watch your daughter who's always so vibrant, slowly drift through life like a zombie? It's been three months."

Isoken leaned against the counter and crossed her feet at her ankles. "I'm just making coffee. I'll soon go to my room, so you don't have to watch."

Her mother's head cocked to the side with brows raised causing Isoken to shift and stand up straight. She didn't mean to be disrespectful, but she was tired of everyone setting a timer on her pain.

"Isoken, the only reason I won't slap you into the future is I know you're grieving. Don't take my understanding as a license for your mouth to run haywire."

Isoken's body relaxed. A part of her was surprised she was still standing after the comment she made. The other part would've welcomed the pain. Anything to make her feel.

Anything.

"I'm sorry," she muttered.

"Do you think this is what Frank would've wanted? For you to leave your life in Lagos and stay shut away from the world here?"

With her cup in her hand, Isoken strolled over to her mother and pulled out another chair. "I don't know how to move on."

"You have to try. Ask God for help."

Isoken chuckled. "God *ke*? Anyone but Him. He allowed this to happen."

"Yes, He did. But Him allowing it doesn't take away His love or the fact that He's good."

"Well, He wasn't good to me." Isoken blew against the hot beverage and sipped. She was ready to end this conversation. "Mummy, I'll get my life together so I can get out of you and daddy's way, but please don't talk to me about God."

"I'm not asking you to leave. You know that. It hurts my heart seeing you and your sister go through this pain." Her mother covered her face with both hands.

Isoken shook her head and mentally rolled her eyes. Her parents didn't like her sister's choice for a husband, so she wondered how genuine the concern over his disappearance was. Her mother uncovered her face and Isoken plastered on the best smile she could muster. She stood, leaned over her mother, and kissed her cheek.

"I'll do better. I promise."

As she exited the kitchen, Isoken could hear her mother sigh. As much as she'd like to reassure her mother, she had nothing more to give. All she had was her word, although she was careful not to say when. That was something she didn't even know. In the months she'd been in Benin, the pain in her heart gave way to rage.

Rage at Frank for not being careful. Rage at being stupid enough to agree to his proposal. Then rage at feeling rage. She returned to her bedroom and set her cup on the nightstand. She got back in bed and opened her laptop. When she powered it on, the page she'd been browsing for the past three weeks stared her in the face.

Up & Away Flight School.

She took a sip of the beverage, refreshed the page, then clicked on her email. Isoken swallowed the lump in her throat at the sight of the email she'd been expecting.

Congratulations...

The words jolted her heart. As she continued to read, the smile that curled her lips wasn't one of happiness, but relief. ***He provides a way of escape.*** The words from the Scriptures came to mind and she immediately dismissed them. This wasn't God; this was all her. She applied and she got in. It was her way out of this depression, and she was grabbing it with both hands. She couldn't go back to her job or flat or Lagos. Frank was everywhere. She had to get out of Nigeria.

For the next several minutes, she scrolled through the admission letter, looked for a suitable Airbnb and made a list of things she needed to get done. A knock disrupted her flow.

"Come in..."

Her mother entered with a tray. On it was a bowl of yam porridge, apple juice, and a cup of tea. Isoken attempted to stand to take the tray from her.

"Relax, I'm fine." Her mother set the tray down and sat at the side of the bed. "I know you haven't eaten anything. I keep telling you about that coffee on an empty stomach."

"Thank you, Mummy and I'm sorry about earlier." Isoken lifted the bowl and forked a piece of yam, blew on it and put it in her mouth.

With creased eyebrows, her mother asked. "No prayer?"

Isoken smiled and slowed down the chewing of her food to delay answering the question. An answer she didn't have, other than she no longer wanted to talk to God. The morning she was told of Frank's death was the last time she read His Word, went to His church, offered any tithe, or deprived her stomach of food in the name of a fast. Not that she had an appetite lately, but it was all in the principle. Her mother stood and began folding her clean laundry at the foot of the bed.

"Mummy, you don't have to do that. I got it."

"The same way you've gotten it for the past three months."

Isoken lifted the glass of juice to her lips. Her mother had a point, but she also had a counter argument. But why waste her breath on this petty argument when she knew a bigger one was ahead with the next words she uttered?

"I'm moving to La Mercy in South Africa."

Isoken's mother raised her eyes from the cloth in her hand. "To do what?" She continued to fold.

Isoken drew her eyebrows together. Her mother's calm demeanor rattled her. "Flight school."

"Hmmm. So, you're an air hostess now. No more marketing executive?"

"Errr...Mummy, are you okay?"

"Me? *Oyese o, we vbe vbo hmmm*

Isoken rubbed the back of her ear with her index finger. "I'm fine but you're acting strange."

"*Vboze*? Because I didn't shout and get your father? You're almost twenty-six and before this happened, my strongest child. If you feel you need to go to South Africa, I can't stop you."

"You can't? Since when?" Isoken set the food aside and stood. She wrapped her arms around her body. "I'm beginning to think you don't love me. What happened to your tears producing superpower?" Isoken creased her forehead. "What about my lecture?"

"I lectured your sister and she still married that nuisance. Now he has disappeared."

"Ugh, Mummy let's not go there, please. Itoh loves him and who is to say he won't come back and sweep her off her feet to America?"

Her mother laughed. "As I told her, what I see sitting down, she can't see standing up. That man is no good for her." She paused. "And now I'm going to tell you, anything you use to numb this pain you're experiencing is the same thing that will keep God from moving in your life."

Isoken waved her off. If God didn't move, she was fine with it. He moved and she lost her fiancé. So, yeah, she was good. "Okay, got it. Will you talk to daddy for me?"

Her mother remained silent for a few minutes. "Yes, I will."

Isoken hugged her mother. "Okay good, now I can get out of here. Seeing you two play love when you think nobody is watching is so unnerving. I'm sure that further added to my trauma."

Isoken found herself laughing as she dodged the towel her mother flung at her. It was the first time in three months. It was an escape, not rest that she had needed all along.

CHAPTER 2

*S*ix *Years Later.*

FOR THE UMPTEENTH time in the last hour, Isoken wondered how she had landed in the back of an Italian police car. She turned her head slightly to focus her heated gaze on the cause of her predicament. Mateo Bertarelli was talking to one of the police officers. She placed her hands over her face and leaned over. As far as she could tell, there weren't any reporters or cameras. She was grateful for small mercies because if she ended up in any publication, her career would be over. Her body prickled with fury as she reflected on the events that brought her here.

The flight she'd worked from Lagos to Milan landed several hours ago. Any time she had a less than forty-eight-hour turnaround flight, she would stay in her hotel. For the whole time, she'd veg out on food and watch pay per view movies. It was also her plan this time around. However, against her better judgment, she answered one of Mateo's numerous calls. She'd convinced herself there wasn't any harm in indulging him this last time.

Especially since, according to her schedule, she wouldn't be in Italy again for a while.

Isoken met Mateo two years ago during a vacation to Italy. She had been lounging by the hotel pool when the ball he and his friends were playing with knocked over her mimosa. When he got out of the pool, her anger dissipated at the sight before her. His olive skin glistened; his wet, silky black hair was slicked back, and his abs were ski board tight. She didn't know nine packs existed until she saw his. His body was so taunt and packaged that she almost offered to buy *him* a drink.

He'd apologized profusely. His Italian accent earned him extra points in swag. After replacing her drink, he asked her to dinner, to which she agreed. Over dinner, she got to know that he was the oldest and heir to his father's fashion empire. Their attraction was instant, but she told him up front that all they could be was friends with benefits. Intimate relationships were not her thing. Tangos between the sheets were more her jam.

In retrospect, she realized maybe he didn't know what the term meant. Over the last couple of years, he'd pursued her relentlessly, including popping up in Lagos for romantic dates. Or sending gifts to whatever city he knew she'd be in. The day he popped out a ring, she broke off their entanglement. Until now.

After much persuasion, she'd agreed to be his date to his father's dinner. The senior Bertarelli was entertaining prospective sponsors on his yacht. A yacht? Of course, she wanted to experience that. When they'd arrived earlier, her nerves were rattled at the sea of whiteness. However, Mateo kept her at his side. As the evening went on, Isoken began to relax. Everything was going great until she saw him freeze mid-sentence.

His brows furrowed, and his face looked flushed. He was always so calm and collected, so she was concerned.

"What's wrong?" She'd turned to follow his gaze.

He rubbed the back of his neck and opened his mouth to speak as an older woman who looked like him entered their personal space. Mateo dropped her hand.

"Mamma, *ciao*." He kissed her on both cheeks.

The scowl the older woman directed at Isoken prevented her from enjoying her son's embrace. Isoken's lips turned up in a faint smile as she willed herself to maintain her composure.

"Mamma, this is…"

"The *other* woman you told us about," she whispered. Her tone was terse.

Turning to face Mateo, Isoken narrowed her eyes. "Is she referring to me?"

Before Mateo could respond, his mother spoke again. "Why did you bring her here, *mio figlio*? You know Francesca and her family are here?"

Isoken placed her hand on her hip. "Fra who?"

Mateo raised his hand to her. "Hold on, Bella."

The nickname he'd given her now sounded like nails on a chalkboard. Her eyebrows lifted to her hairline at his audacity. She was practically being called a homewrecker and he was telling *her* to hold on? Granted, his tone pleaded, but his actions shushed her.

"Mamma, can we talk about this later? I don't want to create a scene."

His mother waved him off. "Send her away." Without waiting for a response, she pivoted on her heels and walked away.

Heart pounding, Isoken cocked her head to the side and crossed her arms over her chest. *Send.* "You've got two seconds to tell me why your mother thinks I'm a homewrecker."

Mateo reached out to grab her hand, but she moved away from him. His touch might set her off.

"Bella, calm down let me explain."

"Stop calling me that," she snapped.

"Come with me." Mateo's eyes implored her to move.

Isoken followed him, all the while willing herself not to slap him. With the anger racing through her body, she itched to cause a scene. But common sense ruled the day. These were very wealthy people. Even though the press wasn't allowed, camera phones worked fine. Anything she did would be in the media. Her parents already thought she was the prodigal child – a title she'd accepted proudly. However, she had no desire to go from a local prodigal to an international one.

A few minutes later, they were in what looked like a storage space beside the ballroom. "Explain. Now."

He ran his finger through his hair in frustration. Every gesture she used to find sexy now made her nauseous.

"Some months ago, my family started pressuring me to marry Francesca. Her family and mine had some sort of pact while we were still kids."

"Save the bedtime story. Tell me how I became your side chick. The other woman?"

"Calm down, Bella."

She let out an exaggerated sigh. "This is me being calm. Your mother dismissed me like a piece of trash."

"When the pressure became too much from my family, I told them you and I were already in a relationship. At the time, I thought I could convince you for us to be more."

"There are so many women you could pretend with. Why me?"

He slipped his hands into his pockets and grimaced. "One day, my cousin walked in on us talking on FaceTime. She assumed you were my woman. She told the family, and I didn't correct them."

Isoken stared at him. The family pressure she understood. Not correcting them she also understood. What had her wanting to beat him with her clutch was that he brought her here knowing she might be embarrassed by his family. If he had told her, she could've put on a good show. After all, what did she have to lose?

Now, he not only lost out on the Oscar-worthy performance she could've given, but also lost her as a friend. To save himself, he offered her on the sacrificial slab without warning. There were so many things she could do to him. But at the end of the day, she blamed herself.

"Bella, say something. I'm sorry."

"So am I. Please take me back to the hotel. Or get your driver to take me."

"Bella..."

"Stop calling me that. You left me exposed out there."

"I'm sorry. I wasn't thinking."

"Please take me back to the hotel."

"Wait, I'll clear everything up."

"I'm not going back out there."

He sighed deeply. Isoken didn't feel an iota of sympathy for him. She rolled her eyes and made her way to the door. As the door opened, Isoken was met with lukewarm liquid splashed across her face. Once she could open her eyes, they traveled down to her dress. There was a huge red stain that certified she wouldn't be wearing the dress again. The heat in her eyes landed on Mateo arguing in Italian with a younger woman. The empty wineglass in her hand gave her up as the culprit.

Isoken walked over and without saying a word, lifted her hand and connected with the woman's cheek. Isoken's hand throbbed. Mateo's eyes bugged. Tears streamed down the woman's now tomato-red face.

The events that followed happened like a tsunami and ended with Isoken in the back of an Italian police car.

Isoken's eyes popped open at a tap on the window. The door opened and one of the officers motioned for her to get out of the car. He took the plastic ties off her wrist. Mateo was still talking to the second officer. Soon after, he walked toward her.

"Can I go now?" Tears from embarrassment and anger threatened to fall. She wrapped her arms around her body to ward off the slight September chill.

"Yes, I'm so—"

"Please don't. All I want is to get back to my hotel room."

His shoulders slumped and he ushered her to a waiting car. He opened the door for her and gave the driver some instructions.

He insisted on riding with her. As far as she was concerned, he could do whatever he wanted. She was done.

Chai Isoken, you see ya life?

She wasn't hurt but bewildered that what had started so good could turn into a mess so quickly. But she'd come to expect life's gut punches.

After all she'd been through, life went on. It was a must.

———

KICKING OFF HER SHOES, Isoken tossed her key card and clutch on the dresser. Walking into the bathroom, she unzipped her dress and let it pool on the floor. Still in disbelief, she stepped into the steaming shower. The hot water relaxed her muscles, but her nerves were still charged. The tension in the car was thick as wax. She was all talked out; there was nothing else to say. In less than twelve hours, she'd be headed back to Lagos, leaving the ordeal behind.

Minutes later, she slipped between the covers as "We Ose" by Benita Okojie played from her iPad. In the last several years, Isoken didn't allow herself to get emotional or reflect on the past. The events of the evening, however, took her back to what led her to now. Tears rolled down her face as she thought about what her life could have been. Over the years, she and God had kinda reconciled. Their relationship lacked the intimacy of before, but she did communicate with Him. In spite of it all, He was her Creator.

With the solitude, Isoken sensed her mood dangerously slipping to a place she couldn't bring it back from. She sat up, scooted against the headboard, and picked up her phone. Wiping her face, she turned off the music and dialed the only person who could understand her pain. Her sister.

A lot had happened in six years. Her sister, Itohan, had moved to America. Not with her so-called husband, but on her own. Her punk of an ex-husband was now ancient history. She had married the *real* love of her life, Osaro Ikimi, and resided in Florida. They were expecting their first child and raising Osaro's niece, Eseosa, or Baby Cakes as the family called her.

When there was no answer from her sister, she dialed another number.

"Joks," Isoken said, immediately the phone was answered.

"Ah, Keni? Are you okay?" Ajoke, her sister's friend also now lived in Atlanta with her husband and son. She was more of her sister's friend, but they all hung out often.

"Yes, I'm fine. Are you home?"

It was about 5 p.m. in the U.S and Isoken knew that with them having families, they had after-work routines, but she needed to talk.

"Not yet. I'm in the car waiting for soccer practice to start."

"Oh, yeah today is Thursday. I forgot. Itoh isn't answering her phone."

"Haven't talked to her today. Maybe she's with a client at the studio."

Itohan not only leveled up with a new husband, but so had her photography studio. Hans Shots was the premier spot for professional photos. Her clients ranged from the common man to big name celebrities. Itohan Ikimi was making a name for herself and Isoken couldn't be prouder.

"Well hang on. I'm going to call her again so I can give both of you this gist at the same time." Isoken called her sister again.

Itohan answered on the third ring. "Keni? Are you okay?"

"Why is everyone asking me that? Yes, I'm fine. Are you still in the studio?" she snapped.

"Do you need to hang up and call me back when you're in a better mood?" Itohan asked. "And I ask because by my calculations, you're supposed to still be out with your Italian boy toy."

Isoken let out a sigh and rubbed her forehead. "My bad, sorry. It's transferred aggression."

"*Wetin happin*? I just got out of Walmart."

Isoken giggled. "I thought the Pregnancy Warden had you on lockdown or something."

Itohan chuckled. "Leave my husband alone. Wassup?

"*Oya* hold on." Isoken connected the three of them.

After Itohan and Ajoke briefly caught up with each other, Isoken gave them a rundown of her evening, from the time her plane landed in Italy until the present. After her story, there was no response. Isoken removed the phone from her ear, thinking something was wrong with the connection. They were still connected. "Hello? Did you hear me?"

Ajoke and Itohan burst into a fit of laughter. Isoken rolled her eyes as though they could see her.

"Are you done? I don't see what's funny. I could've been in real trouble."

"Living on the edge comes with troubles of its own," Ajoke said.

"Okay, no more laughing," Itohan spoke, her voice still laced with humor. "*Chai. Na wa o.* Sorry. You endured all that in one evening."

"Itoh, remember I didn't laugh when you called panicked because you and your hired cybercriminal almost tanked your husband's company."

Itohan immediately stopped laughing and sucked her teeth. "Why are you bringing up the past? *Oya*, sorry."

"Keni, don't mind your sister. That was bad but...but..."

"Joks, if you want to laugh, laugh and stop being the fake peacemaker," Isoken scolded. "I'm about to hang up on both of you."

Ajoke cleared her throat.

"Sorry now. But you know that you're to blame. I told you to drop that man cold turkey," Itohan said.

Ajoke cosigned with a grunt. "I don't know why you keep this string of men and play around with each of them."

"No. Nope, let's be clear. I don't play with them. I tell them the rules up front. I don't do relationships and there's a six-date cutoff."

"But this one you kept off and on for two whole years," Itohan stressed.

"That doesn't count because I rarely saw him. Then if you factor in the number of times we went out, it's not even up to six."

Itohan laughed. "You do hear yourself, *abi*?"

Isoken put her index finger to her chin in thought. "Hmm, maybe because of the language barrier, he didn't understand the rules."

"Hasn't it been English you guys have been speaking?" Ajoke asked.

"Yes, but sometimes I'm so caught up in his accent, I'll just be yessing to everything he says."

Itohan laughed again. "You sound ignorant. Very soon, you'll meet the man that'll marry you in your sleep if you're not careful."

"Stop wishing me evil. You and Joks are married. I'm good living vicariously through you. Besides, if your husbands make you angry, my house will be free for you to come hide out."

"If that's the only incentive, we pass," Ajoke said. "Seriously Keni, stop playing with these men *o*."

"And I've told you I don't play with them. I can't help that I'm fine. The correct African Butter they need in their lives. It's not in my personality to be basic."

Itohan cleared her throat. "Joks hold on *o*. Umm... Isoken my sister. You're in Italy *abi*?"

"You know that, so wassup?"

"Did you know your *real* man's race team is—"

"Okay, I see you want to get on my nerves. Let me get off this phone."

Ajoke cackled.

"I'm glad to provide you ladies with this evening's comedic relief. I head back to Lag in a couple of hours, so I need to sleep."

"Sis don't be like that now. I was only passing info."

"Info I didn't beg you for, but don't worry, you'll soon need me."

"I always need you, but it's my duty to keep you well informed."

"*Oshey o* Madam Google."

"The two of you are a mess. I gotta go, practice is about to start." Ajoke hung up after promising to catch up with them later.

"Keni, jokes aside *sha*, I worry about you..."

"Itoh, stop. I know what you're going to say and like you were, I'm tired of hearing it."

"But that's the thing. Because I went through this phase, I'm able to tell you that it's not worth it."

"We're not the same. You were after revenge. I, on the other hand, am protecting myself, so please free me," Isoken quipped.

It always annoyed her when people turned over a new leaf and suddenly developed amnesia on the struggles they'd been through.

"Okay, you're right. I can't promise I won't say anything again, but please be careful. You're my sister and I worry about you."

"I know you do. That's why I'm taking it easy on you."

"Yeah, whatever. You do know I'm the big sister?"

Isoken sighed. She knew her sister sometimes blamed herself for leading with a bad example. Growing up, Itohan being the oldest was often saddled with the blame for Isoken or their brother's wrongdoing. But they were no longer kids. Zogie, at twenty-nine, was pursuing a master's degree from NYU and at thirty-one, Isoken knew exactly how she wanted to live her life.

"How's Osa?" Isoken changed the topic.

"He's fine. I was supposed to call him when I got out of the store."

"Why didn't you say anything? *Abeg o*, I don't want him blaming me." She and Osaro had a cocky big brother and annoying little sister relationship. She frustrated him and he checked her accordingly. It was perfect.

Itohan laughed. "All right sis, love you."

"Love you too. More than you know. Stop stressing, I'm fine. Kiss Baby Cakes for me and take care of my niece or nephew."

"Will do. Have a safe flight and call me when you land in Lagos."

Isoken disconnected the call. Relief washed over her. She wouldn't know what to do with herself without her sister. She lay back down and turned on her Calm app. As she felt herself drifting off, there was a ding on her iPad. She picked it up and the notification was from the local office in Lagos – an invite for a mandatory meeting. Isoken's heart skipped a beat. She couldn't see the recipients of the email and it was too late for someone to be in the office to send it.

Had what happened tonight gotten to anyone? She quickly googled herself. There was nothing unusual or new about her.

This small peace I've managed to get; these people want to take it from me. How am I supposed to sleep now?

CHAPTER 3

Guided by the sliver of light coming from the slightly open drapes, Tekena Tamuno crept soundlessly to the other side of the hotel room. Through the blinds, he could see the early risers on the streets of Sochi, Russia. Probably getting ready to start their day as he was trying to do. He squinted at his watch as he put it on – 5:46 a. m.

He methodically began getting dressed, while glancing at the nude body tangled in the sheets. If he didn't see the rise and fall of her chest, he would've assumed she'd left the land of the living. He knew he put in work, but she had the kind of stamina that would put his average woman to shame. It never took him this long to put any woman to sleep after feeding them and laying it down.

She...

Tekena strained to remember her name. She was his celebratory gift to himself after the previous day's qualifying race. A shadow of cynicism curved his mouth. He looked at the outline of the woman lying beneath the sheets. *Adrianna, yes that's her name.* Her jet-black hair was sprawled across the pillow, hiding her face. It was ironic because he didn't have any intention of seeing her again or remembering what she looked like. She was a lot of fun, but that's all it was...fun. So much so, that he almost broke his number one rule.

Never sleep over.

He didn't start out this way. He never meant to be who the tabloids referred to as the Playboy of the Track. It was so cliché, but at thirty-one, that's exactly what he'd become. Despite public perception, there was a time he'd wanted a committed relationship. He thought his career and love could mix, but after a mistake that almost cost him his life, he knew better. Love and his career were like oil and water. Cynthia taught him that. So, until he achieved every goal he'd set for himself, attachment to any woman was taboo.

Tekena freed his mind from the gloomy musings and looked around the room to ensure he wasn't leaving anything behind. Satisfied, he took out a couple of Rubles from his wallet and tossed them on the nightstand. She wasn't a prostitute, but he at least wanted to pay for the dress he ripped and an Uber to wherever she lived. He paused at the door, and as always, pushed down the feeling of disgust at the war between his physical needs and the disappointment the sleeping woman would feel when she woke up. Tekena was always up front about not wanting anything more than an enjoyable time. But he wasn't callous or oblivious to the fact that women had selective hearing.

After a split second, he turned the knob and slipped out of the room. As he sauntered down the hallway, his mind shifted to race mode. The Formula One season was coming to an end. He and his team driver, Andreas Piero, had won good grid placement during the qualifying, however, their total points for the season wouldn't be enough to clinch the championship. That didn't mean he was planning to be at the end of the final standings either. His plan – use his grid position to increase his overall standing.

It was show time. Time to let his engine roar.

"Forty-one, forty-two…"

The next day, Tekena counted the sit-ups as "I am Champion" by Steven Furtick blasted from his headset. He didn't listen to the good pastor, but Andreas had put him on to this spoken word recital and it was dope. Every race day, like clockwork, Tekena woke up by three a.m., said a prayer of blessing, and did a hundred sit-ups.

For the past five years, he lived and breathed the Formula One Circuit. Tekena's love for cars and speed began when he was in high school. He started as a wide-eyed kid, ready to push the boundaries of what was possible. It was his escape from the reality of his pain. He had started from GO Karting. Between that and a college education his mother insisted he must have; he worked his way to Formula Three. Then, his only aim was speed. After winning numerous races in the Formula Three Circuit and finally the Euro Series Championship, Tekena left that circuit. Now he was a Formula One driver signed with Veloce Ferrari which was headquartered in Italy.

With a career spanning over a decade and a couple of accidents, no longer was speed his sole goal. Over the years, he had mastered skill and precision to become one of the most respected, black drivers in a white dominated sport. Despite all his hard work, one thing still eluded him. The world championship.

Tekena finished his sit-ups and made his way to the shower. His phone chimed. He knew without a doubt it was his mother. He had to remember to give his little cousin a beat down for getting his mother a WhatsApp account. If she wasn't forwarding a prayer, she was sending the verse of the day or worse, some unwanted research about anything. He told her that he had YouVersion on his own device, but that fell on deaf ears.

"You may have it, but I don't trust you to read it every day. Tekena, you need Jesus in your life. Since you've refused to put Him there, I'll put Him there for you."

"Mummy, how you gonna force Jesus into someone's life? Besides, I do know Jesus."

"But does Jesus know you?"

"I don't know. You have his direct line. Ask Him."

"Stop being smart. You're my only child. Until you find a wife, I can do anything in your life."

Tekena grinned. "Is that right? Then do what you must, my queen." He had nothing else for her because the wife thing wasn't happening any time soon.

"Those little, blue checkmarks tell me you've read my message. That way, I know you've read His word for the day," she'd justified.

Tekena chuckled, remembering the conversation they had months ago. He could never win with Loloba Briggs, so he didn't bother arguing. Locating the phone in his pants pocket, he saw he was right. It was his mother with the verse she sent every race day for the past couple of years. Psalm 16:1, **"Keep me safe, My God, for in You I take refuge."**

Tekena typed back a greeting and an Amen. As a rule, he never talked to anyone before his race. Placing the phone on the charger, he headed to the shower. Right before he stepped into the bathroom, his phone buzzed again, causing him to retrace his steps.

My love, you're awake. I wasn't sure of the exact time zone. I know you should be getting ready but before I forget, I'm going to a symposium.

How are you & Pops? Symposium? Do you need me to do anything?

We're fine. No, I wanted to know your type.

Type of?

Lady. It's a woman empowerment event. There'll be many beautiful, educated nice young ladies there.

Tekena narrowed his eyes at the phone and regretted indulging her. He shook his head. Without bothering to reply, he tossed the phone on the bed and headed to his intended destination. His mother was constantly putting in work to get him to settle down. He'd given up on telling her he wasn't ready and ignored her altogether. But he was definitely going upside his cousin's head. WhatsApp was the worst thing to happen to his mother.

AN HOUR LATER, done with pictures and pre-race promos, Tekena fist bumped Andreas before they headed to their cars. By the fourth lap, the voice of his crew chief came over the head-phones in his helmet.

"Tex, how is she doing?"

"She kinda tight, but I'm gonna keep going." Tekena's fingers gripped the steering wheel as he maneuvered the curve.

"Are you sure you don't want to bring her in?"

"Nah, I'm in a good place. Let's win this thing." Tekena straightened the wheel and sped past other cars.

"If you think you're good, then okay."

"Ai—"

The loud explosion of a blowout muted what Tekena was about to say. The next few seconds blurred by. There were panicked voices in his ear. Something was wrong. He heard the collision and saw the blazing flame and smoke ahead. Cars piled upon one another. And the medical car sped by to get to the driver. Tekena muttered several curses under his breath as he tried to get his steering wheel to turn to avoid the chaos.

It was stuck.

No, I can't go out like this. His heart rate quickened as he yanked the steering wheel in time for the car to turn and avoid the pile up. He looked through the rearview mirror, adrenaline coursing through his veins at the disaster he'd dodged. His relief was short lived as he saw his teammate's car run off the rails and head straight into the retaining wall.

TWO DAYS LATER, the elevators opened and Tekena sauntered over to the nurse's station. The overwhelming mixture of sterility and stifling antiseptics attacked his nostrils. A few hours ago, Elle, Andreas's wife, called to say he had been taken out of his medically induced coma. They had a two-week break before the next race in Japan. Normally, Tekena would've flown back home to New York. But since Andreas couldn't be moved to Italy, he was staying with the family until he could.

"Hello, how may I help you?"

Tekena pulled out his phone and went to the text thread where Elle had sent him the room number. In haste to get out of his hotel room, he'd only read the name of the hospital.

"Hi, I'm here to see Andreas Piero in room 2584."

He waited while the nurse clicked and moved her mouse around. She looked up at him intermittently. Her eyes told him immediately what she was after. Motorsport was huge in Europe, so she probably knew who he was. The gleam in her eye when she looked up at him again confirmed his assumption.

He allowed his eyes to roam over the part of her he could see. Pretty nice. He didn't discriminate in creed, color, or size. Any other day, he would've flirted and told her to come to his hotel room. However, he had a lot of things on his mind and a wanton roll between the sheets seemed less appealing at the moment.

Seeing that he wasn't biting, she clicked a few more screens before she directed him to where he needed to go. Tekena mumbled his thanks and turned left. He approached the door and took in a deep breath before he knocked gently. When he heard Elle's voice telling him to enter, he did. The bed was empty and for a moment his chest constricted. He looked at Elle. Her face was red and swollen, evidence of tears and sleep deprivation.

"Where...when." Tekena couldn't get the words to form.

"Oh no, I'm sorry. I should've told you. They took him down for X-rays. He'll soon be back." She walked over to him.

Tekena drew her in for a hug. From the way she clung to him, he could tell it was one she desperately needed. Having a condo in

Italy kept him close to the Andreas family. Any time he was in town, Elle always invited him over. He was the Black uncle. From dinner to their kids' recitals or functions, he was part of the family. Before his boy, Osaro Ikimi, got married, the Piero family was like a unicorn to him. He never had family growing up and he admired it. For others, not him. Definitely not now. He released Elle and looked down at her.

"How are you doing? Do you need anything?"

She wrapped her arms around herself, lowered her head and shook it. Tekena took the room in. Stark white walls, a small television mounted above, and dimly lit machines. There was a huge sling from the ceiling, which he assumed was to keep Andreas' leg elevated.

"The team is handling everything." Elle sniffed and went back to her seat. "They paid for the kids to fly down to be with my mother since we'd be here for a while."

Tekena nodded and stood near the window. Soon after, the door opened, and Andreas was wheeled in on another bed. Tekena stared in disbelief as he watched the nurses and male tech transfer his friend from one bed to another. His upper body was wrapped in bandages, so were his head and lower right arm. His other arm and left leg were covered in full casts. After the nurse made him as comfortable as could be and hooked him to the machines, she left. Elle walked over and kissed her husband on his lips.

"*Tesoro*, Tex is here. I'm going to the cafeteria. I'll be back."

Tekena's eyes connected with Piero's, who held his gaze for a minute before returning it to his wife. The look he gave her was one Tekena had seen so many times before. Pure love and adoration. She squeezed his hand and let it go. When she left the room, Tekena walked over to the bed.

"I'm so sorry, man," Tekena said. He honestly didn't know what else to say. He felt like a punk when his eyes began to water.

"Don't tell me big bad Tex can get emotional," Piero teased. His speech was slow and weak.

"Man, there you go. Nobody's being emotional. Something got in my eye. I don't know what's in this hospital air." Tekena swiped the side of his eyes. "But I see you got jokes."

"No jokes. I'm thankful I get to see another day."

"Yeah true. I'm so happy about that. Elle and the kids would've been through if your punk behind had gone bye, bye."

Piero attempted a chuckle, an action that caused him pain. Tekena watched as he drew a shallow breath to get himself together.

"You want me to call the nurse?"

"No, I'm okay."

"Okay isn't how I'd describe it, but hey, whatever you say."

"I may not be good physically, but for what matters most, I'm good."

"How you figure that?"

"When the car was spinning, all I could think about was Elle and the kids. That scared me. Then I remembered they'd be okay financially and I was assured of where my soul was going, and I knew it'd be okay."

Tekena shifted in his chair. He knew exactly where this talk was going, and he wasn't beat for it. He had nothing against God. They just didn't rock like that with each other. After all the stuff he had done, there was no way the same God everyone close to him raved about would fool with him.

He wasn't a complete heathen, and neither was he crazy, so in the morning and at night, he gave God His props in prayer. Sometimes before he ate, he said thanks. It really depended on how hungry he was. If his stomach was hitting his back, the likelihood of God getting thanked diminished. All in all, Tekena tried to stay in his lane.

"Hmmm..." Tekena finally responded.

"I know you don't like hearing this but give me two minutes."

Tekena contemplated. "I guess I can. Not like you can run after me like before if I try to leave. So, go ahead. You got two minutes, then we're changing topics." Tekena sat back in his chair, looked at his watch, and crossed his arm over his torso. "Your time is ticking, Andreas."

"All I'm trying to say is, it's best to live every day with heaven in mind because you don't know when."

"So, you saying you were happy because you've earned your entry into heaven?"

"That's the thing. I earned nothing. All I did was accept the salvation of Jesus. I let Him in my life and work daily to change my habits according to His word."

"Well, I'm happy for you, man. I was scared there for a minute, but now you're telling me I shouldn't have been 'cause you were good regardless. I feel like I wasted a good portion of the last two days."

Andreas stared at him and Tekena lifted his brows in challenge. He came to see about his friend, not get a Bible lesson.

"I'm trying to tell you, like I've been doing since we met, let Jesus in."

"What are you talking about? He is in. We talk. I do good deeds. We're good."

"That's not letting Him in. That's religious performance."

"Are you high? You're saying words I ain't never heard you say before. Anyway, your time is up." A beat passed between them. "Seriously, the things I've done in my life, God won't want to touch with a ten-foot pole. I didn't grow up like you. I had a rough life."

Andreas frowned. "I thought your parents were research professors and you spent your life traveling the world."

"I never said we were poor. But you'd be amazed at what happens to an only kid whose only parent is drowning in work and a new lover. You end up with a lot of time on your hands."

"But Tex, no matter..." Andreas placed his semi-good hand on his chest, his discomfort visible.

Tekena wished he'd stop talking. "Okay man, I'm about to leave if you keep exerting yourself. I don't want your wife on my case for tiring you out."

Andreas coughed. "I know, but if after all I went through, I don't say something to you..."

Tekena saluted him. "And I got it." He leaned forward in his chair. "So I'mma be here for a couple more days fulfilling endorsement obligations. You sure you don't need anything?"

Andreas shook his head. For the next several minutes, they chatted about lighter topics until he began to feel pain. Tekena called the nurse who returned with Elle in tow. Once he was given his medication, Tekena left. He told Elle to call him if she remembered anything they needed.

Tekena strolled down the hospital corridor. Nurse flirty was still on duty. She called out to him as he approached the elevator. He waved his hand to her without turning. As he waited for the elevator doors to open, his phone buzzed with a text. It was from Andreas. He quickly swiped it to read, but his hand mistakenly clicked on the link. It was a Bible verse.

May God himself, the God of peace, sanctify you through and through. May your whole spirit, soul and body be kept blameless at the coming of our LORD Jesus Christ. The one who calls you is faithful, and he will do it. 1Thessalonians 5:23-24.

Tekena read the verse again, then closed out of the thread without a response. The elevator opened and he walked in.

"How will He do it when He hasn't called me?" Tekena muttered to himself as the elevator took him to the ground floor. As the doors opened, he heard in the air, *I've called. You're not listening.*

CHAPTER 4

After countless trips across the world, arriving back in Lagos was always bittersweet for Isoken. She loved the city, but that adoration also made her want to escape it. She wasn't among the lot that complained about the hustle and bustle of the city or the traffic. The city's fast pace was what drew her to it after graduation from the University of Benin and was now exactly what she needed to survive. Her job as an air hostess took her on a whirlwind of new cities, experiences, sights, and sounds. She wasn't sure where she'd be from week to week and like the pace of Lagos, she needed the whirlwind to survive.

"Don't forget we have to be at the main office Monday morning," Captain Adere tossed over his shoulder as he passed her on the walking escalator in Murtala Muhammed International Airport. "Have a great weekend."

"You do the same. Greet your wife for me. I'll see you Monday."

"Will do."

Isoken moved to the right to give those who wanted to speed walk on the moving sidewalk room. Unlike the Captain, she had nothing to rush home for or to. What was once a sanctuary, was now a pit stop before the next adventure. After eighteen months in South Africa, she'd returned home, and in the last several years, had perfected the art of avoiding the hodgepodge of memories it held. Some good, bad, and even downright ugly.

The chime from her phone interrupted her musings. It was a notification from her car service. The driver was waiting outside. She didn't complain about Lagos traffic, but also never drove in it if she could avoid it.

Minutes later, she stepped out of the airport and was immediately attacked by the heat and mugginess of the atmosphere. Thankfully, soon the coolness of the Harmattan breeze would be rolling in. She took the short stroll to where the cars always parked. On her approach, the driver popped open the truck and got out of the car. He reached for her luggage which she quickly handed over.

"Madam, welcome. I hope you had a good flight."

"Yes, the flight was smooth. Thank you." Isoken settled into the back seat and leaned her head against the headrest. She tuned out the blaring horns as the driver maneuvered to merge into airport traffic headed for the freeway. She took off her heels and exchanged them for slippers from her oversized handbag. Her stomach growled.

"*Oga*, before you take me home, can you stop by Wak 'n' Roll so I can get something?"

"No problem, Madam."

She called the restaurant to place her order. Pick up, bathe, eat and straight to bed. That was the plan for the night. The sooner she went to bed, the faster the next day would arrive, then the day after that the head office meeting, then off again. Before she could put the phone down, a series of texts came through.

W. Port: **Hey Keni, are you in town? I got into Lagos this morning. Let me know.**

F. Sapele: **Hey Keni, I passed by ur parents' house and thought of you. Hit me up sometime.**

B. Abuja: **Hey beautiful, give me a call. I've been trying to reach you.**

A. Ikeja: **Have you made it back?**

A. Ikeja: **Give me a call when you're settled.**

A. Ikeja: **Or I can call you. It's your world, baby girl. Let me know.**

A. Ikeja: **We're still on for tomorrow, right?**

Isoken rolled her eyes and cleared all texts, except the one from A. Ikeja. She'd forgotten Akin was supposed to take her to Eleko Beach this weekend. But he shouldn't be blowing up her phone like she owed him money. She specifically said, "Don't call me, I'll call you."

She let out a deep sigh. *I'm gonna have to cut him off. I'm not built for this clinginess. Too bad this was only the second date.*

Isoken contemplated whether she had the energy to respond to him now. She tried to recollect his last name since she only saved her male friends by first initial and the place they met, deciding last names weren't important since they wouldn't be around long.

She sent her parents, brother, and sister a What's App message that she was back in the country. Aimlessly, she scrolled through her Facebook and Instagram feeds, trying her best not to like or comment on anything that would indicate she was online. The familiar melancholic feeling crept upon her as she stumbled on a post from a couple whose wedding she was a guest at some years ago. Being a sucker for punishment, she followed the picture to their page. Unwanted tears rolled down her cheeks when she saw the different stages of their life from then to the present. New job, house, the second baby, and family vacations. She swiped the tears away and smiled at a silly family video she came across.

Happily, ever after.

She'd wanted that for herself. She dreamed of it since she was a little girl. She and her sister played house with their dolls and imagined it would one day be them. Nobody told them that while playing house, they were supposed to factor in this thing called life. So, when her late fiancé proposed to her, she was on top of the world. Until that world came crashing down. In a few days, it would be another anniversary of his death. She blinked her eyes a few times, glad she wouldn't be in Lagos then.

The car coming to a stop brought her back to her surroundings. Isoken checked her face with her phone's camera and opened the door.

"I'll be right back."

Minutes later, she stood in line waiting for her food. Her eyes caught the celebration of some bikers on the muted television. Narrowing her gaze, she noticed it was a feature of a group who were part of the Female Bikers initiative – a group of all women whose tactic was to ride bikes to draw attention. They then used the audience as a tool to educate the average Nigerian woman on things such as breast cancer awareness. It was genius.

Isoken moved up the line and let out a breath. Things like this always drew her mind to her brother-in-law's arrogant best friend, Tekena Tamuno. Since she met him on a flight she wasn't even supposed to be on, her senses were heightened about racing, races, bikes, and cars. Against her will, she thought of him when she saw the commercials, in airports, hotels, or restaurants. They were everywhere.

She paid for her food and headed out. A smirk crossed her face as she thought about what she'd save him as in her phone if the opportunity ever arose.

J. Inflight.

She chuckled and got back into the car. His name started with a T, but the name jerk fit better. No man had been able to get under her skin like him. Twice they'd been in close proximity and it didn't go well both times. It was a good thing she didn't have a reason to run into him often. But he was attached to her through her sister, so he was bound to pop up whether she liked it or not. She shuddered and redirected her mind to the piping hot food she was about to devour.

Two more sleeps and she'd be out of Lagos.

MONDAY MORNING, coffee in hand, Isoken made her way to the large conference room. The weekend had dragged by. It was further ruined by her mistake of a date. Akin, like Mateo, had forgotten the rules of engagement. The minute the dude asked where her sister lived so he could "greet" her during his upcoming visit to Florida, she knew it was time for her imaginary headache to make an appearance. One of two things needed to happen – either she dulled her appeal or upped her "no strings attached" radar. Since the first option might never happen, she needed to reevaluate the second.

"Do you know how long this is going to take?" Isoken took a vacant seat near Elizabeth. They often were on the same flight.

Elizabeth shrugged. "I don't know, but they need to make it quick."

Isoken took another sip of her coffee. "*Abi o*. I don't want to be here all day on my day off."

Elizabeth glanced at her, a smirk adorning her face. "Hot date?"

Isoken shook her head. "Madam nosey, no. Laundry and packing to jet back out." Her eyes darted toward the door as more people entered. Then she returned her focus to Elizabeth. "But even if that was the case, somebody has to brighten up the lives of single Lagos men."

"I envy you *o*. I've been married now for fifteen years. Right out of university. My husband is all I know."

Isoken gave her a weak smile. "Nothing to envy, I promise you."

Elizabeth was about to respond when Isoken raised her hand to return a wave from across the room. She was grateful for the distraction because nothing bothered her more than people belittling what they had because of the life they perceived another was living.

Their division manager entered with a couple of other people. Isoken's heart sank when she saw the Human Resources Director.

God, please, I don't ask for much. In fact, I've left You alone mostly, but please, this job is my lifeline.

"Ladies and gentlemen, thank you for being here today..."

As the stocky, potbellied man spoke, Isoken's thoughts wandered to the circumstances that made this job her lifeline. Her degrees in Marketing and Mass Communication were thrown to the wayside as she charted a new path for her life, desperate for survival.

"...we've had to cut down the number of flights. We tried offering deals and specials, but the market hasn't been the same. However, based on the assurance from the head office, plans are underway to get the airline back on track. But in the meantime, we need to put in place some measures to stop the bleeding. With that being said, today, we sadly announce that the company has decided to lay off and furlough some of you as mitigation methods to survive the economic strain on the airline."

Murmurs and loud gasps took over the room. Isoken's heart thudded and the hollow feeling in her stomach ached as she digested the meaning of his words. The HR director took over the podium and tried to bring order to the chaotic gathering. Isoken took in deep breaths, chiding herself. Why was she rehearsing for a misfortune she wasn't even sure was coming her way? God knew what she had been through and there was no way He would snatch her job from her. At least she hoped He wouldn't.

A couple of hours later, Isoken walked into her house. After a forty-minute meeting explaining her status, effective dates, and other human resource matters, Isoken had left her supervisor's office.

She had been laid off.

Her security blanket was gone. She had to stop several times on the drive home to get herself together. How she made it was a blur. On autopilot, she climbed the stairs. Powering off her phone and tossing her keys, Isoken undressed to her undergarments and got in bed. She opened the bottom drawer of her nightstand and retrieved a frame. It had been housed there, face down for years.

Her chest tightened as she traced Frank's face with her index finger. Tears streamed down her cheek as she remembered the day they took the picture a few months before their wedding. He had her in his arms bridal style, their eyes locked on each other. Nothing else in the world mattered.

Frank was what the books would describe as tall, dark, and handsome. More like lanky. But what he lacked in build, he made up for it with a well-toned physique. One day, she was leaving her favorite coffee shop and he was walking in. Not paying attention, she bumped into him and spilled coffee on his immaculate white shirt. She expected a tongue lashing.

Instead, he stood dazed for a few seconds, then said, "If you're trying to tell me brown is my color, I don't think this was the way to do it."

It was the corniest thing she'd ever heard, and she didn't hesitate to tell him so between her numerous apologies. That was the beginning of their love story. Isoken chuckled, remembering the only reason she'd given him her number was she felt bad. He hadn't been in uniform because if she knew he was in the military, she would've politely declined his offer to allow her to make it up to him. They survived two short deployments and were engaged soon after. They planned to do a traditional wedding, court, and church ceremony all in one weekend. Thursday to Saturday. All of that was interrupted when he was called away. That was the last time she would lay eyes on him.

Isoken placed the picture over her heart and lay in a fetal position in the center of her bed. She drew the covers over her head as the grief poured out in uncontrollable, gut-wrenching tears. She tried to think of what to do next. How much more could she take? The life she wanted; God took away. The alternative she created, He also interrupted. What had she done? Who did she offend?

Fix your eyes on Me.

Isoken heard the whisper. Deciding to ignore it, she racked her brain for options.

I will provide a way of escape.

Isoken raised her index finger to her ear and pressed down on it. She closed her eyes and reopened them to rid herself of the illusion she was having. If her sister wasn't a newlywed, Isoken would've been out of the country on the next available flight. Several minutes later, exhaustion took over and her eyelids drooped. As she drifted off, she remembered she had to cancel the car service she'd scheduled for the morning.

Isoken powered on her phone and navigated to the site when a text came through. It was an international number. She aborted her initial mission and opened it. Her eyes bulged as she jolted to a sitting position. Her heart knocked rapidly against her rib cage as she read the message a second time.

Someone who you encountered has tested positive for HIV. We recommend you contact your doctor and get tested immediately. More at HIVspa.com/alert.

The text was from Spain, so she knew exactly who it was. But that had been a while ago. She blew an exaggerated breath through her lips. "I lost my job and now I'm about to die. Well played God. Well played." In under twelve hours, her life made its way down the drain.

She'd come to expect life's gut punches. What she didn't expect was a knockout.

CHAPTER 5

A few days later, Tekena boarded the United flight headed to Japan for his next race. He placed his carry-on in the overhead cabin and plopped down in his seat when his phone vibrated in his pocket. It had been doing that nonstop since the accident. Apart from his parents, he hadn't been in the mood to talk to anyone. Looking at the Caller ID, he braced himself.

"Hey Ro, what's up?"

"Whatchu mean, what's up? I've been calling you for days," Osaro roared. Osaro was the closest thing he had to a blood brother. They'd been friends since middle school. Malcolm "Mac" Bryson completed their trio, but Tekena met him through Osaro later in high school.

"I'mma need you to bring it down a notch. I ain't Baby Cakes. My bad, but I sent you a text."

"Man, get outta here. You sent me a two-word text. I swear, your moods be giving me an itch."

Tekena laughed. "I said my bad. Whatchu want? A check?"

"Ion even know why I bother..."

"Cos you my boy, that's why." Tekena paused. "And why Mac not on three-way? He doesn't care about me?"

"Ol' attention-seeking knuckle head. He's on the road and we saw you on the podium, so we know you okay. I wanna know what's really up witchu."

Tekena ran his hand over his head. In the past few days, he hadn't been still enough to fully process what happened. From the hospital to meetings with team executives about the next steps since their two-man team was now down a player, he had been busy.

"Man, Ro, Ion know." He gave Osaro a brief rundown of what he did know. Tekena had to step up as driver number one and a new guy that the team would pick would take his old position as the second driver. This brought on a new level of pressure that Tekena wasn't sure he was ready for. He'd had accidents in his career, had also seen numerous pile ups, but none had affected him as personally as Piero's crash. He was now out indefinitely.

Osaro grunted. "Da—"

"Is that Uncle Tex?"

Tekena smiled hearing Baby Cakes in the background. "Put my Baby Cakes on the phone." His eyes met the air hostess who signaled him to wrap it up.

"Hi Uncle, are you okay?"

"Hi, my princess. You know I'll always be okay for you."

"Okay, I was scared."

"Why? Remember I told you not to be."

"Yeah but one boy in my class said you were going to die."

"Next time I come to see you, take me to him so I can punch him in his throat."

"Man, don't tell her that," Osaro interjected in the background. "She had no business bragging on you in school in the first place."

"Says who? She can brag on me all she wants. And I will punch that kid in the throat."

"No, you won't," Itohan shouted. "But I'm glad you're okay."

"Hey, sis. Can I at least smack him?"

Itohan giggled.

The air hostess walked by him again, smiling. "Ro, take me off speaker."

Osaro did as he asked. "Wassup?"

"This fine air hostess signaling me to wrap up. She did it all nice and professional, not like your nappy headed sister-in-law."

Osaro chuckled. "You shoulda talked about her sister while it was on speaker. You scared?"

"Nah, but sis pregnant. Why upset her for no reason?" Tekena snickered. "You should be thanking me."

"Why?"

"Because she'll carry out her vex on you while I'll be wrapped up in another warm thang on the other side of the world."

"Man, get off my phone."

Tekena laughed. "You called me, and I was being considerate. I'll hit you up when I land. Be easy." Tekena disconnected the call and was about to put it on airplane mode when a text came through.

They agreed to the new terms. Hit me up when u free so I can give you details.

Be easy man.

Have a safe flight.

Tekena quickly replied. **Bet.** And turned the device off.

Once the plane was in the air, Tekena put on his Beats headphones, reclined his seat, and relaxed. The text he received from his business manager, Eze Chindu, was good news. He knew better than to contact him if things weren't on the up and up. When he signed his five-year contract, he knew it would be his last in motorsports. So he started to invest in his future and passion – driver education and safety.

In the last couple of years, he'd built a successful driving school located in Lagos. TSquared Driving Academy was a fully functional facility that sat on about two thousand acres of land. Tekena had instructors that taught classes to everyone from truckers, bikers, cooperate car services to first-time personal or professional drivers. Eze was based in Lagos and managed the day-to-day operations of the school.

Early last year, the body that governed international races wanted to expand to Africa. To create awareness, they had pegged him as the Nigerian to help with the effort. The goal was to get motorsport wider recognition in West Africa before a Grand Prix could be held there. It was a huge investment opportunity, so Tekena decided to invest some of his own money in conjunction with the Lagos State government. The new terms Eze confirmed was the request for his driving school to be the official school for driver training.

The next step was a meeting with his team to ensure the terms on paper were mutually beneficial. Tekena knew that the next few months would be tedious, but he was up to the challenge. For now, all he wanted to do was enjoy the peace of the next few hours. Adjusting his music to "Ire" by Adekunle Gold, he buckled in and braced for takeoff.

THE CREAK of the opening door snapped Isoken out of her horrible vision of looming death. In walked Dr. Ted Gooden, her gynecologist. She massaged her temples and made a mental note to call her sister the second she left this office.

"Before we get into what has you looking so rattled, you're clean. However, since you were exposed over three months ago, I'll suggest you wait a couple of weeks for another negative result to be sure."

Isoken placed her hand on her chest and let out a huge sigh. He handed her a piece of paper. Isoken read through the list of all the other STD tests she had him carry out. After getting the heart-stopping text some days ago, she sat in denial. She was already at a low point with the loss of her job. Did she really want to know if she was dying? Rocked with disbelief at how her perfect life shattered to the point of joblessness and the possibility of a terminal illness, she contemplated waiting for the symptoms to appear...or not.

She wanted to pray. Ask God to do this one thing for her, but He'd likely decline. After wallowing in defeat, she summoned up the courage to take the test. She opted for a small, by-the-way clinic. In case of unfavorable results, she didn't want anyone she knew to recognize her. Once she got her negative result, she decided to do the test again. This time with every other test included and done by her regular doctor.

"Did you hear me?"

"I'm sorry doctor, what did you say?"

Dr. Gooden had been her doctor since she moved to Lagos.

"I was giving you the options for a baby. IUI or IVF. Since you're in perfect health, I'll recommend the IUI. Without hormonal drugs first." He took out his writing pad and scribbled something down. He handed her the piece of paper and she looked at it. "That's the fertility clinic we talked about in Ikoyi."

"Okay..." Isoken looked at her test results again and smiled. "I'll check them out."

"Let me know what you decide, and we'll go from there."

Entering her Toyota Highlander minutes later, Isoken put the key in the ignition and leaned her head back. When she got her first result, thoughts about the one thing she'd wanted more than anything flooded her mind.

A baby.

She and Frank had plans for so many things, a family to enjoy being one of them. All of the dreams died with him, except this one. The first thing she did when she got to the doctor's earlier was discuss her options. Adoption was an option she considered but for only a moment. She wanted a part of her in her baby. Now that she'd confirmed she wasn't dying; she was going for it. No holding back.

She was going to have her baby. And all the other dreams she had for herself.

First, she needed a secure, stable job. She couldn't wait to see if after nine months, the airline would be willing to reinstate her. Even if they did, her baby would come first. She couldn't be in a new city every other night. She put the car in reverse to go to her next destination. God might indeed be turning toward her again.

Later that evening, Isoken stretched out on her couch with the numerous brochures she'd been given. Dr. Gooden made a call to the fertility clinic for her and they had an opening. Isoken settled the empty plate of *amala* and *ewedu* by her side and dialed her sister.

"Hey," Itohan answered.

"Where are you? Why is there so much noise?"

"Uhm, hello to you too. I'm fine, thank you for asking."

Isoken chuckled because she could imagine her sister rolling her eyes. "*Ehen*...my bad. How are you? My niece or nephew? Bros is good and behaving, *abi*?"

"I knew you had manners underneath it all."

Isoken ignored the underhanded insult. Let everyone tell it, she was brash. She called it witty and straight-shooting.

"We're all good and to answer your question, I'm at a photo shoot."

"Anybody I know?" She flipped through the channels. "I'm still vexing for you. You photographed those sexy gospel singers and didn't even give me a heads up. I could've accidentally been there."

"Nobody you know. And what are you talking about?"

"My crush now. Niyi DaSilva from the 891 Crew."

"Oh them..."

"Ah, it's not your fault. See as you're dismissing them because you have a man. Fine African Kings."

"I only have eyes for my man who's my king."

"*Chai*! Educate me, I'm your student."

"Something is wrong with you. But even *sef* if the Niyi approached you, you wouldn't even give him a real chance."

"I said crush, not man. Been there done that."

"Your future husband will have his hands full." Itohan sighed. "Moving on, wassup?"

"Well since I'm never having one of those, there's no issue."

Isoken knew Itohan was about to hit the roof because she hadn't told anyone what happened. In her mind, not talking about it made it not real.

"Isoken..."

"We'll gist later. Go back to your photo shoot."

"Nice try. We're on a break. Spill it."

Isoken took in a deep breath, exhaled, and told her sister everything that had happened since she landed in Lagos. When she finished, there was silence. Isoken stood, picked up her dirty dish and walked to her kitchen. "Itoh..."

"I'm hurt, honestly. That you can be going through something so deep and stay quiet. All my aches, pains, fears, insecurities I share with you. Why can't you do the same with me?" Itohan's octave increased with every word she spoke.

"I don't need anybody fixi—"

"I'm not trying to fix anything. I want to be there for you like you were for me. Is that so bad?"

A beat of silence passed between them. Isoken gave her sister time to calm down. Truth be told, she'd be angry too if Itohan kept something so deep from her.

"Itoh, it has nothing to do with you. All my life, I've been the one that helped others. I guess it's my middle child thing. The attention was either on you as the first or Zogie as the last. To be noticed, I had to have a role. I ended up being the strong one that never gave our parents trouble but helped others."

A beat passed between them.

"When were you laid off, again? And how much Netflix have you been watching since then?"

"Huh?"

"Because what you just said is a load of crap. You probably crammed it from one of those shows you binge on. You? Not give trouble... in what universe?" Itohan sucked her teeth. "Say you didn't want to tell me and apologize. Instead of this story you're telling."

Isoken cupped her mouth with her hand to stifle her laughter. Maybe she mixed up the lines when she was watching Brené Brown's special on vulnerability the previous night. It wasn't all crap. However, it would be easier to apologize than try and convince her sister otherwise. "Okay, my bad. It was a lot and I had to process."

"I'm glad you're okay. I would've worried to death." Itohan sighed. "Moneywise do you need anything?"

"No, I'm good. Another reason I didn't tell you. You can't fret with the baby."

"I'm only ten weeks along, so cut it out. I've already accepted your apology."

Isoken's strolled back to the living room and her eyes met the brochures on the coffee table. She might as well come clean. "Moneywise, I'm good, but that brings me to the next thing I want to tell you."

"Jeez Keni, you're full of news today—"

"Well, this is a doozy, for you, not me. I want to have a baby."

Itohan started to choke. Isoken shook her head at her sister's dramatics. As she waited for the drama queen to calm down, Isoken plopped down on the couch. "Are you done?"

"I don't know what to say…"

"Then listen. You have a beautiful family. Zogie is in a relationship. I have nobody and now nothing—"

"A baby isn't something used to fill a void. Sis, you can have a family too, but you refuse to give anyone your heart," Itohan pleaded.

"I did that! Love comes with loss and I refuse to go through that again! What part of that is so hard for people, especially you, to understand?" Isoken found herself yelling at the brink of tears. She didn't choose this path. It was handed to her and she was going to live it the best way she could.

"I'm sorry. I'm so sorry. That came out wrong. I'm not trying to dismiss your pain. I was you not so long ago. I understand."

"I know you mean well. You're trying to stop me from wallowing, but I'm not. I'm just not putting myself in the same situation twice."

"Okay. So, give me details. Who are you having the baby with?"

"I don't know."

"Huh? What do you mean you don't know?"

"I'm going to a fertility clinic to get artificially inseminated. After that health scare, my body is closed."

Isoken had saved herself for marriage. She'd prided herself on being a virgin. With Frank's death, the desire to hold on to anything she wasn't saving for any other man died too. So, she'd been active...very active. She practiced safe sex, but her motto was sample and move. She'd thought she was being cautious, until recently. Although she hadn't talked to God in a while, she vowed that if her results returned negative, she'd keep her legs closed.

"For real, so no more sample and move?"

"Yeah, but dates are allowed. As usual, I'll let them know up front that along with no commitment and no clingy, there's also a no trespassing."

"You're special. I have to ask Mummy if she dropped you as a child." Itohan clicked her teeth as though she remembered something. "Did you tell your mother about your decision?" She chuckled.

"Nope and I won't until I'm about three months. Did I tell you that while I was mourning, that woman threatened to slap me into the future?"

"Yes, Keni you did. Every family gathering, we hear the story."

"That shows I'm still traumatized."

Both sisters laughed while Itohan grilled her some more. After her consultation today, her next step was to pick out a donor. When they disconnected, Isoken felt the boulder roll off her back. She was thankful her sister now knew. She would hit the proverbial pavement in the morning. It was time to prepare for her baby.

CHAPTER 6

Sunday morning, Isoken's sneakered feet hit the gravel in rhythmic steps as she completed her second lap around the park near her house. She glanced at her Fitbit that told her she needed about five thousand more steps to complete her goal. "Broken & Beautiful" by Kelly Clarkson played through her ear pods. It was the perfect soundtrack for the current state of her life.

Three weeks had gone by and there was no sign of a job. She hadn't expected it to be easy, but that didn't make the reality any less worrisome. Once upon a time, she loved her job as the Strategic Marketing and Corporate Communications coordinator for Upward Solutions – a position she held for several years. Helping clients develop ideas to effectively communicate and bring awareness to their products was her jam. Presented with any product, she and the team she led could come up with different ways to sell it to them. Brainstorming and entering the psyche of potential customers to anticipate their buyer behavior gave her an adrenaline rush.

Mr. Gambo, her former boss, had empathized with her plight and reassured her that she'd always be part of the Upward family. After all this time, she didn't know if that was a true statement or a nicety in the moment of her pain. Over the years, she'd made sure to keep the lines of communication open, but never with the anticipation that she might need him one day. That day seemed to be upon her.

For someone who had been on the road for several years, being idle was killing her. The issue now was, if she were offered her old job, could she endure the memories of that time in her life? Some days, her own home was unbearable. As soon as she got a job, she was changing her furniture.

Isoken jogged in place for a few minutes, then stretched. She opened her car door, grateful she got to the park before sunrise, as people were now trickling in. She tossed her phone and water bottle on the passenger seat and started the engine.

"I was in so much pain. I mean my heart literally hurt," a female voice came through her speakers.

Isoken lifted her hand to change the station. She must've turned the station to talk radio by mistake. She stopped with the next words.

"I mean I had waited eight years. How? Why would God do that to me?"

Isoken grunted. *Yeah tell me about it. I wonder what He did to her.*

Isoken put the car in reverse as who she assumed to be the host continued.

"For those of you just joining us, this is the "Pressed Not Crushed" show, where we share stories from people who've struggled with dark life challenges and how they overcame those seasons."

Isoken scoffed. She'd heard all these types of stories before. However, curiosity kept her from changing the station.

"With me today is Oge Zora and you guys must hear this amazing story. So Oge, after eight years, God gave you a son...then what?"

The woman continued. "Yeah, after eight years of treatments, prayers, fasting, you name it. But not only that. There was the ridicule from everywhere. People even carried rumors I was a witch and came to my husband's house with bad luck. I was in hell. But then, I conceived."

"Praise God. I'm sure everyone was happy, and you were relieved."

"Oh yes. There was a huge Thanksgiving. Five years later, my world was shattered.'

Isoken reached over to increase the volume. This was what she was waiting for. There was a pause and Isoken could hear the guest sniffing and the host asking for Kleenex.

"I'm sorry."

"No, take your time."

"When our boy was five, he was diagnosed with a rare illness. After many months of once again praying, fasting, pleading, it wasn't in God's plan for him to live. We lost him six months later."

"You see that's not right. He knew what she wanted, gave it to her, and then took it away," Isoken muttered to herself.

"Wow... I'm sorry. We heard about this story through your organization, Refined Pain. Tell us about that."

Isoken brought her car to a stop under the canopied car park in front of her house. She unbuckled her seatbelt and leaned the seat back a bit. She was sticky and desperately needed a shower, but the desire to hear how the story ended kept her still.

"After you lose all you've ever dreamed of having or your plans don't go accordingly, you find yourself in a valley you couldn't fathom. I went through the motions, mourned, grieved, and was angry. I was disappointed with God..."

Isoken thought about that word disappointment. That was exactly what she was feeling, but she had never been able to articulate it that way. Her anger at God had dissipated, but there was still resentment. Although she used church attendance to deny the existence of bitterness and anger, deep down, she nurtured it.

"Then I got to acceptance and surrender. Because at the end of the day, I knew God's character. That helped me pull myself out of despair. I wasn't going to let my pain define me, rather I was going to let it refine me. And as the Bible tells us, nothing comes to us that is not common to man."

"That's in 1 Corinthians 10:13?"

"Yes. If it happened to me, I'm sure there are others out there with a similar experience. That's how Refined Pain was born. An initiative to help that community."

"That's a blessing because you and your team are doing so much. I'd like you to speak a word to anyone out there who's gone through a rough season, but instead of passing through, they remain stuck in it."

Isoken shifted in her seat. She gathered up her phone and water bottle and was about to turn off the engine when the guest spoke.

"Pain and disappointments will come. But nothing changes how good God is. He's such a loving Father that He welcomes the intimacy with you – for you to pour out your pain like David. Ask Him questions without questioning His character. That never changes. Instead of running from Him, because that's what the enemy wants, hold on to Him. The Bible tells us that He is close to the brokenhearted. Don't get stuck in the valley, grow through the pain."

Overcome by a pull she hadn't felt in years, Isoken set her water and phone back down and leaned her head against her steering wheel. The words and emotions she wanted to express were caught in her chest.

She opened her phone and read Psalm 142. She knew there was no way with her own strength, she could free herself from the shackles that had her bound. If she could, she would've done it years ago. She'd heard stories like Mrs. Zora's so many times before. Why this one had her arrested, Isoken didn't know. Maybe it was the reckoning of her life with recent events or maybe this was the time. Whatever the case, she was now too tired to fight. She needed help. She knew that God heard the murmurs of her heart and right now that was all she had.

Tekena was awakened by the buzzing of his alarm. Groggily, he reached over and silenced it. It took him a few minutes to get his bearings. Being on the road nine months out of the year made it hard to keep up sometimes. It was finally good to be in his own bed in New York for a change. From Japan, he'd gone to Mexico. Currently, he was on another brief break before heading to Austin, Texas. His friend, Andreas, had been moved back to Italy, but he was at a rehab center.

In both races, Tekena had assumed the place of driver number one and they were in good standing for the finals. Contrary to his expectations, the new driver was pretty good. But the pressure was still on. Although Tekena loved his job, he was so ready to get to the end of this season. He desperately needed the break. One more month to go.

As much as he wanted to, Tekena couldn't lounge in bed all day. He had stuff to do, starting with a Zoom call with Eze. He sat up and gave a prayer of thanksgiving. Picking up the remote, he turned on the gospel station on Pandora. After all, it was Sunday. Grabbing his phone, he headed for the bathroom.

Bobbing his head to "Hallelujah" by Funbi, he brushed his teeth and trimmed his beard. Moments later, leaned against the sink, he scrolled through Instagram, liking and commenting on pictures from his team's fan page, his driving school page, and any other thing he found interesting. He and social media had a love-hate relationship. When he was painted in a good light by the press, he loved it. When he wasn't, he hated it.

Tekena went to the explore page and watched a few mindless videos. Then he landed upon what seemed to be a parade in Italy. Tekena smiled when he realized it was the day they'd won in Melbourne. After a few more pictures and videos, he landed on a party being held by one of the wealthiest Italian families – the Bertarellis. He did a double take when he saw someone that looked like Isoken. He grunted and knew it was in his best interest to keep it moving, but curiosity got the best of him. It was her. Something in his gut tightened when he saw Mateo Bertarellis' arms around her.

I guess she don't discriminate either.

He knew he had no business worrying about who or what she was doing. He hadn't seen her in almost two years. When they were around each other, it was always a war of wills, so he wondered why he cared. He wasn't going to spend time analyzing the thought. The tag on the picture took him to her page.

"African Butta?" he muttered to himself at her username. Careful not to mistakenly like any pictures, he glanced over her posts. Selfies from places she'd been across the world, inspirational posts, and what appeared to be poems. Her last post was a couple of weeks ago. It had a black background with the words "Life comes at you fast." For a few seconds, he contemplated her meaning, then dismissed the thought. He set the phone down and resumed what brought him to the bathroom in the first place.

Sometime later, with the television on ESPN showing the sports highlights, Tekena lay on the couch listening to "Born A Crime" by Trevor Noah on audio. Books and racing saved him from himself. For a long time, he related to what Trevor wrote about. He felt like his birth was an inconvenience. Growing up with a mother who remarried soon after his dad died, then decided to become a traveling professor like her new husband, he tended to feel out of place. Unlike Trevor, who was close to his mother from a young age, Tekena and his mother only patched up their relationship in his early twenties. Nana Rubi, the nanny who traveled with them, was who he looked to as a mother for a very long time. She was his heart.

Tex, I'm not home yet, give me 15

Eze's text shifted his agenda back a bit. With his phone in his hand, he went back to Instagram and headed to Isoken's page again. Ignoring the warning of his mind, he sent her a message.

@t2_minus_rearview: Hey big head. Life kicking ya behind?

Since they weren't following each other, he knew it might be a while before she got it, so he set the phone down.

@africanbutta: really? That username ugh

Tekena laughed at the green sick emoji she put after her message. Just like her to come out swinging. He paused the book to give her his full attention.

@t2_mius_rearview: U c dat smart mouth is why ur life ain't going right.

@africanbutta: What do u want? I'm busy

@t2_minus_rearview: What u doing?

@africanbutta: It's Sunday. I'm reflecting.

@t2_minus_rearview: You reflect only on Sunday? Another reason...

@africanbutta: Who told u life is kicking my behind?

@t2_minus_rearview: Ur post. So, what has u reflecting? Ur life?

@africanbutta: No. I'm reflecting about urs.

Tekena chuckled. She was something else, but he had time today. Frankly, her sass was the main reason they couldn't get along. Unfortunately, that was the same reason she intrigued him. She was the only woman who came close to matching his wit.

@t2_minus_rearview: I'mma have to do something about that tongue.

@africanbutta: Tekena Tamuno what can I do for u? Is there no chicken wing for u to bother?

@t2_minus_rearview: My whole government name tho? And I do my extracurricular activities in the evening. It's not even noon Goldie. Is that how u get down?

@africanbutta: Don't tell me it's becos of ur near death experience you're reaching out to everyone you've wronged. How many more hundreds of pple do you have to call?

He hadn't laughed this much in a while. The laughter was a welcome relief from his recent stress. He was going to respond 'no', but another thought occurred to him.

@t2_minus_rearview: So, u follow my races? U worried abt me?

@africanbutta: goodnight.

He was about to respond when Eze's call came through. Money was calling so they'd have to continue this chat later. He answered the call.

"Hey man, my bad. You ready?"

"It's cool. Gimme a sec."

Tekena stood and walked over to his MacBook. He sat at the kitchen island and powered it on.

"I'm sorry to hear about Andreas. How's he doing?"

As his business manager, there'd been times when Eze had to meet him on the road. On many of those occasions, he'd met Andreas.

"He's got a long road ahead of him. But he's in good spirits."

"Good to hear. You got the document open?"

Tekena answered in the affirmative and for the next hour, they went over what was expected of him in Nigeria for the ten weeks he'd be there. The racetrack was set to open in six months, and as the face of the new venture, he was required to be available to attend several events with sponsors for promotion.

"Did you run this promo schedule by the agency?"

"Yes, I sent it to Brandi before I tentatively agreed to the dates."

Brandi McIntyre was the personal assistant assigned to him by his management company. Tekena wanted to make sure no events were planned for him from November to mid-January.

"Good. I don't want Amara on my neck."

Tekena had changed management companies twice since becoming a professional racer. The current company used Amara Dike of Collab Relations as their public relations firm.

Her being Nigerian was a bonus. She was by far the best representation he'd had. The down part of that decision was, she was always in his business. She'd become like a big sister to him, so he allowed it.

"When are you getting in?"

"Hopefully three weeks."

"Cool. We gotta see the Commissioner of Sports as soon as you get in."

"Bet." Tekena closed the laptop. "I'll send the contract to my lawyer to look over the legalese, then I'll sign. And he'll get it back to you."

They chatted a few more minutes before Tekena disconnected the call. He saw he had an IG notification. Isoken had followed him. Beaming, he returned the gesture. He went to his DM and read her message.

@africanbutta: Anyway, glad your rude self is okay. Can't have Osa crying on my sister's shoulder this early in their marriage.

@t2_minus_rearview: I'mma let you have that. 'Ppreciate it. Be easy and stay outta trouble.

Tekena was sure with the time difference, she was either in bed or preparing to go to bed, so he didn't wait for a response. Instead, he ordered lunch to be delivered. He didn't feel like cooking; neither did he feel like calling over one of his regulars to whip something up for him. That would entail him listening and playing nice and he wasn't in the mood for it.

As he contemplated what to eat, a strange albeit unwanted feeling came over him. He knew immediately it had to do with Isoken. She was a potential distraction he couldn't afford. He tightened his resolve to maintain his distance from her. He still had a whole new season ahead of him next year and she was too close to home to play with. Not only physically, but figuratively speaking. His boy, Osaro, was still a newlywed and Tekena didn't want to do anything that would cause strife between him and his wife. Because whatever he'd do with Isoken wouldn't be serious.

Women and his career didn't mix. And it was guaranteed that he'd choose his career every time. And the upcoming season was the most important one.

CHAPTER 7

Wednesday morning, Isoken walked into the building that housed the Upward Solutions offices. After a lot of reflection over the weekend, she did something she hadn't done in a while – trust God to work out her dilemma. Monday morning, she stepped out in faith and contacted her former boss. Surprisingly, he responded and asked her to see him this morning.

It was the last week of October and the building was already decorated for the holiday season. Isoken made her way to the familiar elevators and rode to the third floor. Upward Solutions occupied the entire floor. After meeting the receptionist, a few minutes later, Isoken was headed to Mr. Gambo's office.

"Ms. Adolo." Mr. Gambo walked over to her and extended his hand.

'Good morning, Sir." Isoken shook his hand. "How is the family?"

"Everyone is well. Can't complain. How are you?" He walked back behind his desk. "The last time I saw you was in Amsterdam about a year ago."

"Yes, it was. I'm good sir, thank you for asking."

"Although I missed having you on the team. I'm glad you had options."

Isoken shifted in her chair. "Actually, sir, that's why I'm here."

"Tell me."

Isoken sighed and spend the next several minutes explaining to her former boss what happened to her employment. She reminded him of his offer some years ago. And finally, she let him know what she needed.

Mr. Gambo searched through some papers on his desk. "Hmm. That's quite unfortunate. I'm sorry to hear that."

Isoken waited with bated breath. She needed this job. She had her real first appointment with the fertility clinic in a couple of weeks. She wasn't broke, but there was no way she could stay idle.

"You do remember Lara Olu – well she's now Johnson?"

Isoken nodded. "Yes, sir I do." Lara had started at Upward a year after her. They weren't exactly friends but had a good working relationship. They also kept in touch via social media.

He looked up from what he was doing. "You're in luck. She's due to go on maternity leave in three months. I was about to approve the candidate for her temporary replacement."

Isoken clasped her hands together and looked up at the ceiling. *Father God, thank you for Your favor.*

"You were one of my top employees and no one has come close since. However, I'm not able to offer you permanency right now. I'll have you shadow Lara, so she can show you the ropes for her projects while preparing you to step in while she's on leave."

"Ah thank you, sir. Thank you so much."

"You're welcome. Remember it's not permanent. Any permanency will depend on the board and your performance." He smiled at her. "I hope your skills aren't rusty."

Isoken smiled. "No sir, they're not." Even if they were, she wasn't telling him that. Depending on the projects, she'd brush up on the latest trends. The basics always remained the same.

Hours later, done with the Human Resources paperwork, Isoken rounded the corner to Lara's office. Isoken tapped on the door and entered when given permission. Lara looked up from her laptop, smiled and closed it.

"Hey, Lara. Is this a good time?"

"Yes, yes come in. Sit down." Lara walked around her desk and sat in the chair next to Isoken. "Oh my gosh, Keni, I've missed having you here."

"I missed you too." She did miss the people. It was the memories she couldn't deal with. Surprise lunches, random flowers, pop up visits. Walking in earlier, she wasn't sure how she'd feel. So far, so good.

"So, you and Stanley? Wow?"

Lara gave her a shy smile while strolling over to the small fridge to retrieve two small bottles of water. "Yep, one day I couldn't stand him, the next we were walking down the aisle. The facts of life. What about you?"

Isoken shook her head. "Nah. Not for me." She didn't want to expound further and was grateful when the topic changed to the business at hand.

Lara spent the next several minutes updating Isoken about what had changed and what remained the same around the office. Later, Lara showed her the office she'd occupy. After that, they went over the current projects.

"Right now, I have three extremely high-profile jobs. The one with the government, I'll still handle personally. For the other two, I'll definitely need your help. You'll begin sitting in on both client meetings, starting next week. One of our rising stars, Ben Ade will assist you with everything you need."

"Got it."

Lara proceeded to give her a detailed rundown of the clients she was going to handle. Isoken took notes and asked questions. Soon after, Lara left for a meeting and Isoken worked with IT to get her computer and everything else she would need set up. The pace at which everything was going was somewhat overwhelming. She did ask for this, but she expected to be eased into it.

If she was being honest, on some level, she expected a gut

punch. God was moving and she was there for the ride. It wasn't permanent, but there was no doubt in her mind that her status would change. If it didn't, that would be fine too. This would serve as her steppingstone while she prepared for her baby. Things were indeed looking up. She hoped there wasn't another whammy around the corner. She'd taken enough punches to the gut.

A COUPLE OF WEEKS LATER, Tekena got off the treadmill and walked over to the bench for his water. The chime on his phone solicited a smirk when the caller id told him who it was.

"My favorite publicist."

"I'm your only publicist," Amara said. "I might not be your favorite after you hear what I have to say."

"Then don't say it, because I'll hate to fire you."

"You know I'm your lifeline."

"Don't let your husband hear that. I gave dude a pass the last time he tried to size me up." Tekena wiped the back of his neck with a towel and sat.

Amara laughed. "Jokes aside. I know you'll be busy when you get to Lagos, but I have to squeeze in an additional event for you."

She paused and he knew he wasn't going to like what she had to say next.

"It's black tie—"

"Nah, why? You know I relax when I go home at the end of the year."

"I know, but one of the owners of the sports drink, UME, is also a huge Formula One fan. One of his subsidiary companies is hosting an end of year charity event in Lagos."

"I'm not seeing why I should be interested in this."

"Because he has major money and a corporate sponsorship from them will help put you in front of more African countries. The man is even toying with the idea of starting an all-African team to compete in the Grand Prix."

"I'm not planning to still be a driver when he starts his team, and I can do without one sponsorship."

"A portion of the money raised will go to a deserving charity. That's a good cause."

"Not for me."

Amara gasped. "Tex!"

"Come on, Amara. I do my fair share for charity through my foundation."

Tekena tugged on his beard, stood, and exited the gym. Although necessary, he hated hobnobbing with rich, boring people. He did enough of it during the season and was desperately looking for some downtime. He didn't want to add to a schedule he already anticipated would be heavy.

"I know, but you need to be there. Come on, it'll help with what you're trying to do back home."

"Amara, this isn't the move *o*. I got things to do." Tekena stepped to the side as an elderly couple got out of the elevator.

"Then add this to the list. I'm not the one who needs the exposure, or her reputation to remain sparkling."

Tekena chuckled as the elevator stopped three floors before his. "You're so wrong, but okay. You're lucky I like you."

His eyes roamed the body of the melanin goddess who got on the elevator.

"No, you're the lucky one. Have a Merry Christmas and please, please be on your best behavior."

"I got it. You swear I'm too much to handle." His attention returned to the lady riding with him. The good and bad Tekenas on his shoulders were having a debate on whether he should make a move.

"You *are* too much to handle. But I do what must be done. When it comes to my countryman, I do extra. Now don't make me regret it. Talk to you after Christmas."

"*Not happening. You're off until the New Year.*"

Tekena chuckled, hearing her husband lay down the law in the background. She and Ejike were a cute pair with an almost teenage son and a young daughter. Tekena shook his head. They might be cute but being accountable to another human being was for the birds.

"*Oga* has laid down the law. Tell him I said wassup and I'll talk to you in the new year."

They disconnected the call and the elevator opened. Good Tekena won and the goddess walked off without him saying anything. Another woman had been on his mind lately.

Since that first time they'd communicated on IG, they'd only communicated one time after that. Yet he thought about Isoken often. And he was still trying to determine if he liked it. He'd be in Nigeria in a couple of days and didn't know anything about her except that she stayed in Lagos. He dared not ask Osaro who would give him a whole lecture. He also didn't want to ask her because her mouth was sharp, and he could do without the sass. But then maybe it was a good thing. Not knowing would help him fight his intrigue for her. Because he knew for a fact, she was a distraction he didn't need.

A few days later, Tekena made his way downstairs. He hung his sports coat across the chair and a smile covered his face as his second favorite lady came into view.

"Good morning, Nana Rubi."

She had her back to him as she prepared breakfast. His flight had landed late last night from New York. He hadn't expected to see her so early in the morning but knew there was no way she would stay put knowing he was back in Lagos. Nana Rubi lived in the guest house at the back of his five-bedroom Lekki home. She kept his place cleaned and well stocked for when he returned. His mother would've loved to play that role, but she and his stepdad had since retired and settled in Port Harcourt, their home state.

"Ah my son. Let me see you."

Tekena met her in the middle of the kitchen and walked into

her embrace. She was a petite, slender woman who didn't look a day over her sixty-two years of age. Tekena kissed her on her forehead.

"I told you not to worry about me. I would've grabbed something to eat since I'm on my way out."

Right before he went to bed, Eze messaged him that the Commissioner of Sports for the Lagos State government had an emergency scheduling conflict. The meeting that was planned for later in the week was now scheduled for mid-morning.

"And you know I can't do that. Now sit." She returned to the stove and Tekena did as he was told.

She was preparing boiled yam and egg sauce. As she cooked, they caught up on the happenings in their lives.

His phone beeped and he looked down to see a text.

Eze: Hey man, hope you had a good flight. U wanna drive or U want me to come get you?

Although he had a fleet of cars, the only time he liked getting behind the wheel was if he was getting paid.

Come get me in 2 hrs.

"Have you called your parents?" Nana Rubi placed a cup of black coffee and a plate of food before him.

"Thanks, Nana." Tekena said a quick grace over the meal. "No, I haven't. I'll do that when I'm done." He took a couple of bites, engrossed in his phone. A memory crossed his mind and he looked up at her cleaning the kitchen. "Nana, have you been taking your medicine?"

"Yes, I have. Stop worrying."

He shuddered when he remembered the time that he'd walked in on her in a diabetic coma. "Okay, don't make me get you a caretaker, because I will."

"You think you're so big now, ordering me around." She smirked with her hands on her hips.

He laughed at her. "I am big."

"Call your mother. I'm going back to my place. Do you want anything for lunch?"

"Nah, I'm good. I'll stop by later."

Minutes later, Tekena put his earbuds in and dialed his mother.

"Hello? Tekena?"

"*I ba te.* Good morning, Pretty Lady."

"Good morning, my love."

"Why were you sounding confused? Isn't my number locked in your phone?" Tekena's brows furrowed together.

"This new phone you sent is difficult for me to transfer all my contacts. *Aha...*" The frustration in her voice solicited a chuckle from him, one he dared not let her hear.

"What are you talking about? Upon all the degrees you have?"

"Tekena, did you call to harass me this morning?"

"You know I'm a lover, not a harasser. But I had to ask?"

Tekena heard movement in the background as his mother laughed. He loved hearing her laughter. After all his years of rebellion and their subsequent reconciliation, it was a comforting sound. He and his mother chatted for a few minutes then he asked to speak with his stepdad.

"Hello, Son."

"Good morning, Pops. How are you doing?" Tekena walked to the trash, emptied his leftovers, and washed his plate.

"I'm fine, but you won't be if you keep harassing my wife."

Tekena cackled. His stepdad was so protective of his mother. Tekena had once despised that with every bone in his body. After his dad died, that was supposed to be his job. Before he could settle into it, this man appeared on the scene. He uprooted them from their normal and in Tekena's eyes, his mother was wrong for going along with it.

"She's good. She can handle it." He wiped his hands and walked out of the kitchen.

"When are you coming to see us?"

"Pops man, don't put me out there like that. You know once she hears you, it's on."

"As it should be..."

"I got a tight schedule because of that thing I told you about, the Speedway, but I'll be there. Or I'll have you guys fly down."

His stepdad grunted his displeasure.

The doorbell rang. Looking through the peephole to ensure it was Eze, he opened the door. They gave each other a brotherly dap.

"Okay Pops, I gotta go. I'll call later." Tekena disconnected the call.

"Hey man, *how far?*"

Tekena shrugged. "Nothing as important as making this money. How your side?"

"I *dey*. Let's do this then."

Tekena picked up his phone and keys as they headed out.

CHAPTER 8

In hurried strides, Isoken rushed into the restroom. She pulled out her phone and dialed...again.

"Lara, are you okay? I just got your text. What's going on?"

"Keni, I'm so sorry but I'm cramping badly," Lara grunted. "I won't be able to make it. With Mr. Gambo out of Lagos, I need you to handle this presentation."

Her heart thumped widely. *No now Father, is this a test?* She'd been at Upward Solutions for a month and although she got back on the saddle effortlessly, this was the government they were talking about.

"Hold on, you want me to give the Gidi presentation? I'm only here to observe."

"Yes, I know but you've been with me while I prepare it. You've read it, I really need you to present it."

"But—"

"Isoken, you can do this—"

"Do what? I know the facts and figures but if I had known I'd be talking, I would've researched the company." She rubbed her sweaty palms along her dark blue jeans.

"The guy's name is Mr. Chindu. He—" Lara groaned.

The sound decreased Isoken's apprehension. She knew what she was going through, but the timing couldn't have been worse.

"I can't reschedule because the Commissioner has some scheduling conflicts. That's why we had to move it to today."

Isoken struggled to take control of the spiraling carousel of worst-case scenarios going through her mind. "Okay, the company is TSquared *abi*? I'll research it real quick."

"Yea. Don't worry, marketing is in your blood. Ben has the presentation, and he should be there already."

"I don't know how you have all this confidence. If anything happens, nobody should blame me." Isoken tapped her nails against her temple.

"Nothing will happen. I've sent you my notes."

Her phone chirped, alerting her to the arrival of the notes. Instead of opening it, she and Lara went over the highlights. Once she disconnected the call, Isoken took in her appearance once again. She straightened her belted, striped navy and cream top. She checked her teeth to ensure they were lipstick smudge free and that there were no telltale signs of the donut she had earlier.

"Okay, Isoken, you got this. Motorsport..." She put her phone in her back pocket. As she washed her hands, she thought of the sport and the one person she knew that engaged in it. She had no time to dwell on Tekena. She dried her hands, left the restroom and pulled out her phone. Opening Lara's email, she got on the elevator. Isoken closed her eyes and blew out a heavy breath when the attachment refused to open. Neither could she pull up the website. In her hurry, she didn't remember that the Wi-Fi would be spotty in the elevator. There was nothing she could do now but act like she was familiar with the people she'd be talking to.

Isoken got off the elevator and with her black pumps hitting the ceramic tiles in quick strides, she rounded the corner to the conference room. Blood rushed through her ears as the possibility of her making a complete fool of herself haunted her. Although she had warned Lara no one could blame her if anything went wrong, she knew she couldn't afford for anything to go wrong.

The government wasn't a client to joke with and she wondered again why Lara felt so confident.

She said a quick prayer and entered the room. She closed the door quietly and turned to face the room. Her heart thudded against her rib cage as she perused its occupants. She used the doorknob to steady herself when her gaze fell upon the proverbial thorn in her flesh.

Tekena Tamuno. Now it made sense, he is TSquared.

I'm going to kill Itohan.

Tekena's slightly opened mouth and bugged eyes comforted her in the seconds that followed. Judging by his expression, they were both caught off guard by the other's presence. The last thing she wanted was for him to have one up on her. She withdrew her gaze from him, greeted the room, and found Ben sitting opposite of Tekena. She walked over to him and took her seat. She whispered the update from Lara to him and he immediately went into action pulling out papers for her.

The Commissioner, done with the sidebar with his secretary, smiled at her. If not for the additional people in the room, she would've rolled her eyes. She'd met him earlier and the extra-long handshake and sheepish smile raised her predator antenna. She'd dated her share of older men, but she wasn't into married ones. Ever.

"Ah Ms. Adolo, I'm told you'll be walking us through the pitch," the Commissioner said.

"Yes, unfortunately, Mrs. Johnson can no longer make it. Give me a few minutes and I'll be ready to start."

Soon after, she met the Commissioner's eyes alerting him to her readiness. Isoken didn't know what it was, but something about not falling on her face in front of Tekena put an extra pep in her step. She glanced over at him. He narrowed his eyes at her and returned to viciously typing on his phone. If she could guess, he was texting Osaro. She didn't blame him because she had some choice words for the newlywed couple herself.

"Thank you everyone for being flexible to the schedule change. Before we begin, let me make the introductions."

The Commissioner's voice kicked her thoughts to the background. He started with Kamal Danjuma. Isoken loved soccer, so the reformed bad boy was no stranger to her. He was finer up close. His wife was one lucky woman. From the introduction, he had an architectural firm and was responsible for the design of the speedway. The next man was Abayomi Rice. He was the developer of the land at Ibeju-Lekki where the facility was being built. He was mixed, but she had no idea with what. His hard face and posture oozed sex appeal. Her eyes traveled to his hands and the wedding band told her he was off limits. She made a mental note to head over to good old Google to tell her who the lucky woman was and more about him.

"Lastly, this is Tekena Tamuno."

Isoken met Tekena's eyes. She tried to gauge his reaction. If he acted like he didn't know her, she was going to follow his lead. His expression was blank, so she trained hers to mirror his.

"He's a race driver for Formula One and the CEO of TSquared Driving School. He's one of the stakeholders in the project and the face of Gidi Motor Speedway. All promotions will be centered around him."

Tekena smiled. "Nice to meet you, Ms. Adolo."

Oh, so he wanted to play this game. "Likewise, Mr. Tamuno."

Isoken tried not to ogle him but she couldn't help but appreciate his good genes. His chestnut-colored eyes were framed by dark brows and lashes she envied. The apricot-colored sports coat he wore over a crisp white shirt contrasted perfectly against his butterscotch skin. His hair was no longer in a fade but cut close to his head. His thin mustache connected with his full beard. The Big Guy took extra time with him, but he'd never hear those words from her lips.

"Mr. Danjuma and Mr. Rice are here because they are interested from an investment perspective and your presentation will help in shaping their decision. So, without further delay, you have the floor, Ms. Adolo."

She could have done without the extra pressure. Pushing the thought to the back of her mind, Isoken picked up the clicker and began. She started with relevant facts about the sport that Lara had pulled together. The history of the sport in Africa. Morocco and South Africa were the two countries that had hosted international races before. She went on to highlight the growing interest in motorsports with one speedway already located in the central southern region of Nigeria. She discussed the creation of the Nigerian Auto Sport Association and its aim at holding a Nigerian Grand Prix in Abuja. She also highlighted some races being held, but on closed roads. These were all things Isoken had no idea about until now.

Her confidence increased as she spoke. Isoken made sure she made eye contact with everyone in the room. Each time her eyes landed on Tekena, she couldn't tell whether he was impressed or indifferent. His expression remained stoic. She knew his mouth couldn't remain indifferent, so she'd hear his opinion soon.

Later she talked about the challenges and advantages they'd have in Nigeria and how Upward planned to tackle them. She ran down the planned events for promotion. She went through the targeted demographic and incentives for each group. Finally, it was time to go over the budget.

"The detailed breakdown of the figures should be in the folder before you. I'll give you a moment to look over them and I'll answer any questions you have." She twisted the cap off the bottle of water before her and sipped.

"We all know that the sport is not as popular as soccer in this part of the world, but it is fast growing. An increasing number of Nigerians watch Formula One races and travel to Dubai to watch the Grand Prix." Isoken glanced at Lara's notes and cringed at the bolded last line. Her eyes went to Tekena and she plastered on a smile.

"The sole aim of this campaign is to create awareness for a

successful opening of the Gidi Motor Speedway. To do that, we'll make Mr. Tamuno and motorsport the talk of every Nigerian household and business." Isoken concluded and opened the floor for questions.

Over the next several minutes, Ben who was closer to the raw research, fielded most of the intricate detail questions. Isoken jotted down the questions she wanted to take back to Lara. She wanted to make sure there was no reason for her to sit in on this project again. The remainder of the meeting ran smoothly with Isoken noting a request for a detailed schedule of how Tekena's time would be spent. She learned that he would be in Nigeria for a short period, so things had to run tightly.

Next, there were presentations by two sports ministry employees. There were very few questions and the meeting ended. Isoken was under the impression they had another meeting, but she had other things on her mind. Like a sister to fuss at.

HOURS LATER, Isoken still hadn't gotten any real feedback on how she did. After the presentation, the Commissioner had a smile on his face. Isoken wasn't sure if it was a testament to the job she did or a polite gesture. She called Lara to see if she'd gotten any feedback. All she got in return was a text with a thumbs up and a promise to fill her in the next day. This left her with twenty-four hours to obsess over the outcome of the meeting.

Her mind traveled back to the last hour. When she opened her eyes in the morning, seeing Tekena wasn't anywhere on her radar. The last contact they'd had was when they chatted several weeks ago. Since then, the thought of him moved in and out of her mind, but not so much as to conjure him up. All through the presentation, his magnetic gaze sent unwanted electrifying currents through her, almost knocking her off balance. The reaction she had to him cemented the warning she felt the first time she met him. He was bad news.

After running a few errands after the meeting, it was time to go home. Before she put the car in drive, her phone dinged. She reached for it, thinking it was the office. Isoken furrowed her brows when she saw it was an IG message notification. She should've tossed the phone to the side, however, considering who it was, she decided to open it.

@t2_minus_rearview: u havin' a career crisis?

Isoken rolled her eyes.

I need to disable these notifications.

She was about to respond to him when there was a honk behind her. She set the phone to the side and shook her head. He knew how to get under her skin, and she had no idea why she reacted to him the way she did. He was arrogant and thought the universe revolved around him.

Hours later, showered and dressed in her loungewear, Isoken made her way to the kitchen with her laptop under her arm. As time went by, she convinced herself that although she had unique suggestions for his campaign, she couldn't work with Tekena. Now she was torn between keeping her mouth shut or telling Lara about her ideas. There was a strong possibility that if she said anything, she'd be stuck on the project. She placed her laptop on the kitchen counter and lifted her eyes to the ceiling.

"Father, you know I'm trying to turn over a new leaf. Since we're working on this relationship thing, do me this one favor *abeg*. If I give these ideas to Lara, like a good Christian, don't let her try to stick me with the project."

Isoken heard her phone ring. She picked up her things and walked with hurried strides to the living room. Setting down her laptop, food, and drink on the coffee table, she went in search of her phone and remote on the mantle. She turned on the television and answered the FaceTime call.

"Before you say I don't have manners, how are you, the baby, Baby Cakes, and your man?" Isoken asked her sister as she leaned the phone against the vase on the table. She removed the carry-out dinner she'd picked up earlier from the bag.

Itohan chuckled. "If I say you're touched, you'll vex. They're fine. Wassup?"

Isoken peered into the camera and smiled. Her sister was dressed down and ironing, but her glow was so evident. She looked so happy and content. Isoken was about to speak when her brother-in-law entered the frame. She was sure he didn't know she was on the phone. He wrapped his arms around his wife and nuzzled her neck. Itohan began to giggle, causing Isoken to roll her eyes. They were sickening. She was their number one cheerleader, but they still got on her nerves.

"I'm here *o*."

Osaro turned in surprise. "Sis? What's going on?"

"As if you don't know."

He raised his shoulders. "Know what? You love giving me a hard time, *abi*?"

Isoken narrowed her eyes trying to decipher his confusion. She couldn't believe Tekena hadn't called him. But in case he hadn't, she didn't want to tell him first, so she wouldn't look bothered. She was never one to play games, but she needed to talk to her sister first.

"Nothing, you know I'm messing with you."

They chatted for a few minutes before he kissed his wife, telling her he was going to play basketball with Baby Cakes.

"So, what has you so bothered?"

"Why didn't you tell me Tekena was coming to Lagos?"

Itohan cocked her head to the side. "Tekena is in Lagos?"

Isoken tossed a plantain cube in her mouth and nodded.

"But how am I supposed to know his itinerary?"

Isoken furrowed her brows and shrugged. "Don't you and Osa talk?"

"Tekena is the last thing on my mind when I'm with my husband." Itohan winked.

"Ugh, stop being nasty. I'm serious."

"For real though, what do I look like asking my husband about his friend's whereabouts?" Itohan put the cloth she was ironing on a hanger. "But I don't see the issue. He has a house in Lagos and it's Christmas time." She shrugged. "Maybe he's there for the holidays. Surely both of you can co-exist in that big Lagos."

"Well, sister dearest, that's where you're wrong."

For the next couple of minutes, Isoken filled Itohan in on the events of the day. As she narrated the story, she could feel the perspiration on her forehead as her heart raced.

Itohan remained silent before she broke out in giggles. "Are you kidding me? Ha! This thing might be fate *o*."

"*Abeg* stop it."

"No for real. The coincidences that have followed both of you are uncanny. You met on a flight you shouldn't have been on. Then ended up at the same Thanksgiving table, now this." Itohan counted on her finger.

"Whatever. After I meet with Lara in the morning, I'm sure I won't see him again."

"Okay then, problem solved. No *wahala*." Itohan clapped her hands together.

Isoken took a sip of her drink and swallowed. "You know I can't stand you." She chuckled.

"Admit it, you like him."

"No, I don't. He's so fine, no one can dispute that, but I do not like him. We barely said anything to each other at your wedding and that was the last time I saw him."

"You know why?"

"No, teacher, but I'm sure you're going to tell me."

"A blind man can see the chemistry between the two of you. And I know you feel it too. You don't play games, so the only conclusion I can draw is that you're afraid of what might happen with Tex. And that has you running scared."

Isoken sucked her teeth. "You should've studied psychology in school—"

"I did, child psychology, but the same principles apply."

"On that note, my show is about to start, and I still have some work to get done."

"And I love you too with all my heart. Call Mummy. The woman is bad mouthing you..." Itohan laughed.

"It's not funny. Your mother thinks because I'm no longer traveling, I should be calling her every single morning and night."

Itohan continued to laugh. "When did you talk to her last?"

"Yesterday morning *o*."

@t2_minus_rearview: Don't like being left on read.

The message came across her screen. She remembered that she hadn't responded to Tekena's message. So much for Lagos being big enough for them to co-exist.

The sisters switched topics discussing other things before landing on Isoken's baby plans.

"After my first appointment. I settled on an artificial insemination with the clinic, so I've been taking some meds prescribed."

"Any donor yet?"

"I haven't looked through the book yet, but I still have time. The procedure won't take place until the end of the month."

"Do you need me?"

Isoken smiled. They fought like normal siblings but when it came to dropping everything to be with the other in the time of need, nothing and no one stood a chance.

"No sis. I know you'll be here in a heartbeat. But you're married now and pregnant. I don't want you flying."

"You and Osa act as if I'm handicapped. I'm only three months. I can still fly if need be."

"There's no need." Isoken winked at her. "I love you, but I gotta go. Oh, and yeah, pray for me."

"Always, but anything specific?"

"That I don't end up back on the dark side."

Itohan laughed as Isoken disconnected the call. Itohan thought it was all fun and games, but something in the pit of her stomach told Isoken that co-existing with Tekena in Lagos, as big as it was, wouldn't be easy.

CHAPTER 9

Of all places... The odds of seeing Isoken in his meeting still spooked Tekena. Wasn't she supposed to be an air hostess? How did she go from that to marketing? To the best of his knowledge, there wasn't a relationship between the two. He'd made up his mind that entertaining any thoughts of her was a bad idea. Then lo and behold, she walked her fine, sexy self, right into his business.

Gone were the golden tresses she had when he first met her. They were replaced by a black silky, wavy mass that fell below her shoulders. Her deep mahogany skin glowed against the light colors of the wrap-around shirt she had on. He had to make several adjustments to keep his concentration from lingering too long on the way her tight jeans hugged her curves. The forced smiles she threw his way played on her lush lips and drew attention to her defined cheekbones. Her dark brown eyes were filled with the mystery and mischief he knew her for.

Tekena sat on the carpeted stairs of his home and refreshed his phone. Curiosity got the best of him, so he'd hit her up to find out her angle. She had yet to respond to his DM. He could ask Osaro, but that had to be his last resort.

If she was going to be working with him, he wanted assurance she knew her stuff. He had a lot of money riding on this. Granted the government had already signed a contract with the firm she represented. But it would be nothing to get her kicked off the team if she was an airhead. No matter how much it pained him to admit it, even through visible nerves, she handled herself. On the other hand, he had to question her knowledge since she kept consulting the nerdy dude next to her.

A couple more minutes went by and nothing. No response. He hated being ignored. It reminded him too much of his childhood. He went into the kitchen. He smiled when he saw Nana Rubi putting some food items away. Although the kitchen was already stocked, he needed things more aligned with the diet laid out by his trainer.

"It's late, young lady. Shouldn't you be home by now?"

She rinsed some fruit under the running tap. "I wanted to get these here today, so I can have them handy in the morning."

He pulled out a stool near the island and sat. "You do know I can cook for myself."

"I know. I also know you work so hard during the year. The only time I can take care of you is when you come home."

Tekena grunted and looked at his phone again. He knew he couldn't convince her otherwise, so he decided to save the fight for another time.

"You know what I want for Christmas?" She put the last fruit in the bowl and lifted a mango to him. He nodded and she retrieved a knife and plate.

Tekena was about to ask what she wanted when his phone buzzed.

@africanbutta: Mr. Man, hw can I help you?

@t2-minus-rearview: y u mean all the time? Ur man must not be doing something right.

He looked up at Nana Rubi as she placed a plate of sliced mangos in front of him. "Thank you, Nana. So, what is it? I aim to please."

She crossed her arms over her chest and a grin crept over her face. The grin was the giveaway, and he shook his head immediately.

"Nope. Anything but that."

@africanbutta: my man is none of ur business.

@t2_minus_rearview: oh, u must not have one.

"But Tekena Tamuno, you can't go through life with only meaningless relationships."

He frowned at her. "I have meaningful relationships."

"Osaro and Malcolm don't count."

"Why?"

She hit him with a dishtowel. "Stop giving me a hard time. You need a woman. A family to carry on your legacy. You need someone to grow old with."

@africanbutta: I hv plenty of them. Thank u very much. Now what do you want?

Tekena chuckled. He knew she was mean and hardheaded, but she had the right one. Deciding to leave her on read and give Nana Rubi his full concentration, he put his phone in his pocket. "I'll have that. You know I hated being an only child, but not now."

"You know it's arrogant to put off what you can do today for tomorrow. God isn't on your timetable."

Tekena laughed. "I've heard that saying, but marriage ain't what they were referring to."

"Speaking of God—"

"Hold up, I didn't speak of Him. You did."

"Then let me continue. You fly around so much that before I know it, you'll be gone again."

Tekena took a bite of his fruit and shook his head. "Nah, you got me here till February."

"Oh, that's good, but as I was saying..."

Tekena glanced up at the time. If he didn't get her off this topic now, he'd be here all night. As much as he loved her, he wasn't in the mood. He hadn't had any rest and he needed it if he was going to be dealing with Isoken Adolo.

"Nana, I love you, but I gotta hear this God talk another day. I promise I'll even open the Bible with you. But your boy is really tired."

She studied him for a few seconds then slumped her shoulders in defeat. "Okay. If you need me, you know where to find me."

Tekena walked over to her, drew her in for a hug, and kissed her forehead. "Yep, I do and that's why I love you." He picked up his plate, bit into the last piece of the juicy fruit, and washed the dish before heading up the stairs.

A few minutes later, after he was settled in for the night, he picked up his phone.

@t2_minus_rearview: What's up Goldie, so you gonna answer my question?

@africanbutta: Why r u calling me Goldie & which one?

@t2_minus_rearview: First impressions. U going through a career crisis?

@africanbutta: Uphm... (eye roll emoji) Not that it's any of your business but my original career is mkting

Tekena furrowed his brows. Original? Then why was she an air hostess?

@t2_minus_rearview: U went to school for it?

She sent him several eye roll emojis

@t2_minus_rearview: Roll 'em again and watch 'em fall out

@africanbutta: Whatever. Yeah, I went to school for it.

@t2_minus_rearview: So, u quit being an air hostess?

@africanbutta: Anyone tell you that u r nosey.

@t2_minus_rearview: Don't flatter urself sweetheart. If you gonna be working for me, I need to know you know whatchu doing.

She sent him some laughing emojis.

@africanbutta: First, I'm not ur sweetheart, and two, it's a good thing I'm not going to be working for u.

@t2_minus_rearview: With me.

@africanbutta: Nope, not with u either.

@t2_minus_rearview: See I knew u were confused. U going back to d air hostess thing?

@africanbutta: Wrong again. I only stood in for a colleague today. I would've said it was nice seeing you, but the verdict is still out on that. But I wish you luck with your campaign.

This woman.

He didn't know what to make of her. Then why did the thought of her not working on his campaign have his stomach in knots? *What is that?* He rubbed his stomach, chucking the strange feeling to the mango. He hadn't had one in ages.

Going to his text thread, he asked Eze for the following day's schedule. It was Friday, and he wanted to make a trip to see his parents then be back Monday morning. Eze responded. Turns out they had a noon meeting at the Upward Solutions offices. Tekena contemplated briefly if he wanted to tell Isoken he would be in her office. He nixed the thought, opting for the surprised look on her face instead. So, he responded.

@t2_minus_rearview: 'appreciate it Goldie

THE NEXT DAY, Abayomi and Kamal met Tekena at his driving school for a tour. After the meeting, they had expressed interest in investing and wanted a tour of his facility. Like Isoken, Tekena was also surprised to see both men at the meeting yesterday. He knew of their involvement but didn't know they'd sit in on the promo meeting.

Tekena was introduced to Abayomi when they broke ground on the project a year ago. He and Kamal went way back. They weren't exactly close friends but ran in the same circles in Europe years back.

"This is a really good set up you have here," Abayomi Rice said.

"Thanks, man." Tekena parked the tour cart in its spot after returning from a drive around the practice grounds. He'd already taken them through the three-story facility, starting with the offices on the top floor, then the classrooms and lobby on the second. They ended with the garage on the ground floor. The three men alighted and walked back into the building and went up the elevator to his office.

"I'd like to come on board, but I think it will make more sense if my family is game. For that, I gotta talk to my brothers about Danjuma Group investing." The shrill ring from his phone interrupted them. Tekena observed him looking at the phone and smiling.

"I gotta take this." Kamal slipped away to the other corner of the room.

"The offer looks good, but I report to a board. Send me the investment packet and I'll get my assistant to tee it up for the next meeting," Abayomi added.

Tekena leaned against his desk. "I appreciate it. The more local and Africa-based investors that come on board, the more attractive it looks to foreign companies. I mean we're good now, but the more the better."

"E, come on babe. I said I'll be there—"

Abayomi and Tekena turned and looked at Kamal, who rubbed his forehead. After murmuring a few more words on the phone, he disconnected and walked back over to them.

"You in trouble?" Tekena laughed. Hearing that Kamal had gotten married stunned everyone who knew him. He was almost twice his wife's height, but from the look on his face, she ran things.

"Yeah, man. I've been in Lag for almost a month. Should've been home yesterday but the schedule change kept me here. She's about to have my head because we're opening up her second location tomorrow."

"You better get moving then." Abayomi looked at his watch. "I need to get moving too. We recently relocated to Cape Verde from LA. I can't let the Mrs. set up the house alone."

"You won't hear the end of that, man," Kamal chuckled.

"I know."

They laughed.

"I don't see how y'all do it. But respect it," Tekena said.

The men walked out of the office.

"That's because you haven't met your one yet. You'll move mountains to lock her down. No one will tell you twice," Abayomi said.

"Facts. When I met E, I was in a situation, but I still wasn't letting her go," Kamal said.

"Me neither. We were married, divorced, then remarried. When you know, you know."

Eze approached them and they exchanged greetings. "Tex, we have to leave now if we're going to make it."

Tekena nodded. After exchanging personal contact information, they men left. Minutes later, Tekena was back in his office to send a few emails. There was a brief knock and Eze entered.

"You ready?"

"Yeah, give me a second."

Moments later, he packed up and exited his office. "Please, coordinate with the Commissioner's secretary and get investment packets out to Rice Holdings and the Danjuma Group."

"Okay. I'm glad they switched up our contact at the firm."

Tekena looked up from his phone. "Whatchu mean?"

"The lady that presented yesterday seemed far more knowledgeable than the one I've been meeting with."

"For real?"

"Yeah, the one I've been meeting with knows her stuff, but something about the lady yesterday...her confidence. I can see people bending to her will...man." Eze rubbed his chin.

The inflection in the other man's voice sent Tekena on high alert. It was more than admiration of Isoken's knowledge...but her personality. "I'mma have to stop you there, playa. She's off limits."

Tekena walked ahead to his car. He could feel Eze staring at him, but that wasn't going to change his mind.

"Why? That's you? You know her?"

"She just is. No. And yeah I do."

"Can you hook me up then?"

"The only place I'll be hooking you to is a pole if you make a move on her. Now, let's roll."

Tekena got in his car to follow Eze. The agitation he felt at Eze's suggestion was foreign, but so was everything else when it came to Isoken. He knew she'd be trouble for him, but he wouldn't stand around and let anyone he knew get to her. Selfish. That was a name he was gonna have to own with his chest because it wasn't happening.

CHAPTER 10

With her laptop cradled against her chest, Isoken entered some notes on her phone as she strolled down the hall to her office. The end-of-week staff meeting had just concluded and there were some additional things she needed to update Lara on. Poor thing still couldn't make it into the office. Mr. Gambo gave her feedback on the presentation and suggestions he had based on the questions asked. According to him, the Commissioner said she was, "very in tune with the market." Isoken was thrilled with the compliment, but glad it was over. Now all she had to do was type up comprehensive notes for Lara and then she could get back to her own assigned project.

She walked behind her desk, set her stuff down and picked up her mug. She leaned against the counter in the breakroom as the Keurig brewed her favorite blend. The hazelnut aroma wafted up her nostrils, calming her raging thoughts. Her cheeks burned as images of Tekena flooded her mind. Their conversation the night before irritated and excited her at the same time. When she gave him the time of the day, he always evoked conflicting emotions in her. Those emotions, coupled with her sister's words, played in a loop in her mind. It was driving her to insanity. She straightened herself from the counter, added creamer and sugar to her coffee, and left the room.

Did she like him?

How could she when she really didn't know the man? What she did know was that she wouldn't be able to handle him. Not like she'd handled all other men since Frank. She acknowledged their forbidden attraction. Forbidden, not only because they were too much alike, but his career was death wrapped in steel. Like Frank, he had a profession that could have him killed. There was no way she could ever put herself in a situation to even be friends with him. She'd made a big mistake engaging with him in the first place. Now she had to regroup and go back to hating him.

ISOKEN STRETCHED her neck and leaned back against her white, leather chair. She closed her eyes to rest them from staring at the monitor for the last couple of hours. Reopening her eyes, she took in the lemongrass and sage scents emanating from her diffuser. Even though her position was still temporary, human resources allowed her to put her own touches on the office she occupied. The décor didn't need much help as its warm gray and earth tone minimalistic style resembled a set up straight out of a magazine. Her eyes roamed to the passage reference from Luke 2:52 that sat in the corner of the glass desk along with some family photos.

Wisdom. Stature. Favor. With God and Man... In that order.

Isoken whispered an amen, then glanced over the pitch she'd been working on. Satisfied, she emailed it to Ben to go over before their meeting Monday morning. She rubbed her growling stomach. Remembering she hadn't had anything but toast and coffee, she pulled open her drawer for a menu. A yawn escaped her mouth as there was a brief knock on the door. Before she could respond, Mr. Gambo's secretary peeped her head through the open doorway.

"Isoken, *Oga* wants to see you in his office."

Isoken struggled to hide her displeasure. She needed to eat something. Her brain needed food to have an intelligent conversation. *I should've gone when Ben asked earlier.*

"Do you know why?"

The woman shook her head.

"Okay, tell him I'll be right there."

Isoken clicked on her mouse to save her file again. Out of habit, she took out her compact mirror and checked herself, running her tongue over her teeth. Since it was casual Friday, she had her hair in a plait down her back. She tucked a loose tress behind her ear, then straightened the company t-shirt. Picking up a notepad, Isoken left the office.

After being permitted to enter, Isoken strode into Mr. Gambo's office. He was standing behind his desk while two men sat in front of it. They had their backs to her. For some reason, the hair on the back of her neck stood, goosebumps took over her arm.

"Ah Isoken," Mr. Gambo started.

"You wanted to see—"

The men stood and turned causing her steps to falter. There in her boss's office stood Tekena and the guy she saw him with the previous day. Her heart knocked against her chest when Tekena winked at her. Something in his eyes told her he was up to no good. She hoped he wasn't crazy enough to mess with her where she earned a living.

"Yes," her boss continued. "You met Mr. Tamuno and Mr. Chindu yesterday."

Isoken plastered a smile on her face and nodded. She accepted the outstretched hand of both men in a firm shake.

"Although we aren't supposed to meet and kick off the campaign until next week, Mr. Tamuno here was so impressed by your presentation that he wanted to meet before then to discuss a few things he came up with."

"So impressed that I couldn't wait to get my ideas to you," Tekena added effortlessly.

Isoken ignored him and diverted her eyes to her boss. "But Sir, you remember this is Lara's campaign. I was only standing in."

"Let's sit down," Mr. Gambo urged, ignoring her.

Isoken twirled the pen she had between her fingers. She reminded herself of the reasons she needed this job. Repeating them to herself would be the only thing that kept her from going off on Tekena right now. She wasn't making any promises for later.

"Mr. Tamuno here, like the Commissioner, has reiterated that time isn't a luxury he can afford. So, Lara will take over your campaign and you'll take over this one."

Isoken gaped over at Tekena and back to Mr. Gambo. "But Sir, I know nothing about this campaign."

"Yes, that's why I expect you and Lara to get together to exchange detailed notes and all the contacts she has lined up."

"But Sir..."

"No "buts" Ms. Adolo, you've always been one of the best. Besides, I told you what the Commissioner said about you."

"Based on yesterday, I also think you know enough to handle what I'll need before next week..." Tekena crossed his ankle over his knee and leaned back into the chair.

Dismayed by his audacity, Isoken narrowed her eyes at him, but forced a smile. Wasn't this the same man that insinuated she might not know what she was doing? The glint in his eyes told her that he knew he had her stuck.

"Sir, Lara will be back Monday..."

Tekena turned his gaze to Mr. Gambo. "Every hour is precious where I'm concerned. If it'll be a problem, I could let the Co—"

"Oh no, it's no problem at all." Mr. Gambo hastened to reassure him. "Miss Adolo here will be your contact from now on."

He then turned to her. "She'll make this campaign her utmost priority."

Did Tekena just threaten the contract they already had with the government? There was no way Mr. Gambo believed he had that kind of power. But then, one could never be too sure. A smooth American accent and loads of money could make anything happen in Nigeria. Especially from a famous son of the soil. But no matter how smooth he was, she had the antidote.

"Good." Tekena met her eyes. A smile lingered on his lips. He looked at his watch. "If you're free for lunch, we can get started on what needs to be discussed."

"Now?" Isoken shook her head. "I was gonna run across the street and get something quickly since I have a few more meetings today. Besides, I haven't gotten myself acquainted with the campaign yet."

This man already had her out here telling tales. In all honesty, she'd spent a considerable amount of time the previous evening getting acquainted with the project so she could pass the ideas she had to Lara. Still, she didn't want to give Tekena the satisfaction of knowing that. She would rather eat sand.

"Don't worry about it. I'll have my secretary move your calendar around." Mr. Gambo picked up his phone to give his secretary instructions.

Isoken glared at Tekena who gave her a thumbs up. She felt like a prostitute whose pimp was offering her to the highest bidder. "Okay, that's settled. Lara should be forwarding her files to you as we speak."

"Great, I'll go get my purse." Isoken turned to leave. She hoped Lara wouldn't think she had hijacked her project.

"Oh, Isoken, you can also take the remainder of the day off."

She turned to face both men. With clenched teeth, she responded. "Thank you."

I guess I'm having sand for lunch.

Isoken walked ahead of them to her office to retrieve her things. She didn't say a word to Tekena until they were outside.

"Are you insane?" she demanded. "What are you up to?"

"Right now, I'm trying to eat. Come on." He sent her a lazy glance walking to his car.

It was the latest Land Rover Evoque SUV. *Impressive,* she thought, but quickly cleared her mind to get back to the matter at hand.

"Didn't we establish that I'm not working with you?"

"You established. I thought about it and decided otherwise." He pressed on his key fob to unlock the car. He shrugged and opened his passenger door.

Isoken scowled at him. "I'm not riding with you. Where are we going? I'll meet you there."

"I won't want you to get lost. So, get in and we'll come back for your car," he ordered.

"I don't take orders from you."

"Mr. Gambo says otherwise. I'm your number one priority."

"Your campaign, not you."

"In case you haven't caught on, I am the campaign." He smirked.

Isoken grumbled. "Whatever and I'm paying for my own food."

"Yeah right, Goldie. Now get in, this Lagos heat isn't playing today."

She entered the car and folded her arms across her chest. He shut the door and chuckled before walking to the other side of the car. So much for her plan of avoiding him. They knew they didn't like each other. He was trying to punk her. As the car engine purred to life, Isoken straightened her back. He thought she was going to cower. Well, she had something else for him.

TEKENA GLANCED OVER AT ISOKEN. The initial victory he felt was now hollow as heat oozed off her skin. When she gloated about not working with him, he was disturbed, but made peace with it. That all changed when Eze started raving over her.

"What do you have an appetite for?"

"Oh, you didn't plan that out as well?" she seethed.

"As a matter of fact, I did, but I'm being nice and asking for your preference."

"You can be nice and take me back to work. Let's act like this never happened."

"Nope. Seafood, *Naija*, English or Chinese?" he offered. Learning that her office was not too far was a plus for him. As intriguing as she was, he wasn't driving any great distance for anybody.

"Anything except seafood."

"Why?"

"I'm allergic, nosy." She turned her body and stared out the window as though the streets were strange to her.

Tekena laughed and decided to let her be. Hopefully by the time they got to the restaurant, she'd be done sulking. He navigated the midday traffic with skilled ease until he arrived at their destination. It was one of his favorite restaurants in the heart of Lekki. He loved coming here any time he was home for their quick service, great ambiance, and mouth-watering food. Tekena pulled up to the valet. He opened his door and smiled when he saw who was on duty.

"Ah *Oga* Tex, you *don* come back," one of the regular valets greeted.

Tekena tossed his keys to him. "Yeah, man. How you been?" He walked around and opened the door for Isoken. He offered his hand which she completely ignored.

"*Fine o. We dey manage.*" The man looked over at Isoken. "Ah madam, welcome."

She mumbled her greeting and started walking to the entrance. Tekena told the attendant he would see him later then warned him to take care of his baby. With hurried strides, he caught up to Isoken and within minutes they were seated. Tekena watched her eyes take the place in and although he knew she'd never say it, he sensed she was impressed.

Minutes later, a waitress came over to take their orders. Once she left, Isoken lifted her brow to him.

"Yes Goldie, you got something to say?"

"I've told you to stop calling me that."

"Sweetheart...is that better?" He teased.

"No, it's worse." She tucked her hair behind her ear and rolled her eyes.

He shrugged. "Why? I like it."

"I don't. It's condescending. My name is Isoken or Ms. Adolo."

Tekena threw his head back and laughed. "I ain't calling you no Ms. Adolo and the best I can do is Goldie."

"Then call me Keni like everyone else."

"I'm in a league of my own."

She shook her head. "A league that's determined to get on my nerves."

"I aim to please." He rubbed his hands together. "Now we got that settled. Whatchu 'bout to ask me?"

She gestured around the restaurant. "Must be nice to get into a place I know firsthand needs a month in advance for reservations."

Tekena observed her. "This is the second time you've referred to money. Does mine intimidate you?"

She furrowed her brows and shifted in her seat. "No. Why? I'm just saying."

"Are you? I work hard and can afford the finer things in life. I make no apologies."

"I'm sure you don't, but I'm paying for my meal."

"How much did you earn last year?"

She narrowed her eyes. "Huh? That's none of your business."

"Humor me." Tekena waited. When she didn't say anything, he leaned toward her. Hearing her breath hitch, he smirked. She leaned back. "Me? I made a few million Euros. I'm paying for lunch."

Their stare down was interrupted when the waiter returned with their drinks and appetizers. Tekena watched in amusement as she ignored the spring rolls and went straight for her drink. He raised his to his lips and took a sip.

"Tell me about yourself."

"Why?"

"Come on. Are you gonna be a brat throughout our meal? It messes with digestion."

"Says the bully that uprooted me from my job."

"If I'd asked you nicely, would you have come?" he challenged her.

"No, but why do you want me to? We don't like each other, remember?"

Tekena nodded. "Yeah, I remember clearly. But since you gonna oversee a campaign that's connected to my brand, I need to know about you."

"What part of I didn't ask to be in charge are you not getting?"

"None. Now answer my question. All I know is you're the middle child that for sure got dropped on her head. You're fine and disrespectful. Oh, after today, I'll add bratty."

"You think I'm fine."

He frowned at her. "Of course, you're fine. A blind man can see that. Don't tell me you have esteem issues."

"I don't. I never expect anything good to come out of your mouth."

"Very funny. Yeah, you're beautiful, but you know that. It's why you're mean and disrespectful. But I know your sister, so you must have some redeeming qualities." Tekena swept his gaze over her.

"Tekena, shut up calling me mean and disrespectful. I'm a genuinely nice person."

"Ha! Let's see, on the plane, you rudely walked out on me.

You then had the nerve to question my mental state and sexuality when you saw me with Baby Cakes' pink plaything around my neck. During your sister's wedding, you refused to hold the door open for me even though you saw my hands full carrying drinks into the reception. That's not all, you purposely closed the elevator on me when I clearly told you to keep it open. Now I'm trying to feed you, your stomach has been speaking in tongues and you're being a brat."

Isoken stared at him speechless.

"Yeah, so I rest my case. Now convince me otherwise. Starting with why you no longer fly." He folded his arms across his chest and leaned back.

She opened her mouth to speak when the waiter arrived with their main course. After he left, Isoken said grace. For the next few minutes, the only sounds that could be heard at their table was the clanking of silverware on their plates. They were both famished. As they ate, Isoken filled him in on the events that led to her not being with the airline. What amazed him was that she had a double major in Marketing and Mass Communication. He had judged her unfairly. He shouldn't have done that, considering what most people thought of him when they first met him.

Most people assumed he was an uneducated race car driver. But he had a bachelor's in accounting from Clark Atlanta. Then over the years, taking evening classes, he obtained a master's in business. Being the son of academics, it was kind of written in his DNA. It was a good thing he didn't have an aversion to books and learning. His years of rebellion were a way of getting his parents' attention, one that backfired in a way he never expected. He shook his head dismissing the bad memories.

"What's wrong with you?"

Tekena straightened up at the sound of her silvery voice. He must have worn the expression of displeasure on his face. "Oh, nothing, I'm amazed. Now I have nothing to fear."

"Hmm..." She eyed his plate, then reached over with her fork and cut a piece of his moi-moi.

Tekena watched her lips close around the fork and shifted to adjust himself. Although he knew she was aware of her looks, he wasn't sure she was fully aware of her sex appeal.

She opened her eyes and stared at his that held amusement and intrigue. "What? I wanted to see how it tasted. This still doesn't mean I like you."

"People that don't like me can't eat off my plate. And I don't like you either."

"So, what are these clarifications or suggestions you had about the campaign?"

Tekena picked up his glass and took a long sip. "There weren't any."

Isoken shook her head and blinked her eyes. "I must have heard wrong. I thought you said there weren't any."

"Your hearing is perfect."

She gave him an incredulous look. 'I can't believe this. Did you even read it?"

"Yes, I did, and everything is doable. I fly out later today to see my parents in Port Harcourt. I should be back on Monday, Tuesday tops." He paused to gauge her reaction. "Eze is talking about traveling out of the country to see an investor, but that has nothing to do with the campaign. That's something between the State and me."

"I can't believe you. But more importantly, it's five weeks to Christmas. We have events up till Christmas, a small break in between, and some after. How are you going to pull all this off?"

"Speed is my thing."

"Please be serious. Mr. Gambo expects me to run a successful campaign and unfortunately, it hinges on your availability."

"And I'll be available for whatever you need." He winked at her.

"You can't possibly be flirting with me, now. And I'm serious. You can afford to mess this up. I can't."

"I can flirt and talk business at the same time. I leave for Morocco right after the new year for a few days. I didn't see anything planned for that week. Then I'm back for the whole of January, and a little bit of February before I head back to New York. But there goes the reference to my money again."

She waved him off. "Nobody's thinking about your money. I'm thinking about my future." She rolled her eyes at him.

"Stick with me and your future will be bright."

"Oh jeez. You're insufferable."

"My mom has this saying, the expectations of the righteous shall not be cut short." He held her gaze. "Do you know what it means?"

"Of course, I'm not a heathen."

"Could've fooled me."

"I could say the same thing about you. But what's the point of your story?"

"My point is, if you keep expecting the worst from me, you'll get it."

"Now can I expect you to pay the bill 'Mr. A Few Million' and take me to my car?"

"Your wish is my command. Come on, Goldie."

They stood. Tekena paid the bill and ushered her out of the restaurant. The valet brought his car around. Tekena paid, adding a generous tip. He tossed the keys to Isoken which she surprisingly caught.

"Quick on your feet. I like it." He walked over to the driver's side to open the door.

"Why are you giving this to me?"

"I'm tired of driving and I saw the way you were lusting over my ride." He saw her eyes light up as she scurried to the driver's side and got in.

She adjusted the seat. "I wasn't lusting."

"Yeah, right." He made sure she was buckled in then went around to the passenger's side. He was about to get in when she moved the car forward. Tekena raised his brow, chuckled then walked up to where she stopped.

He opened the door. "Keni, I promise you don't wanna play with me now. I'm full and I got time, baby."

She laughed. "Oh, so I'm Keni now. Get in big baby."

Tekena got in, reclined the seat, and placed his sunshades over his closed eyes. "You better not scratch my baby."

The melody of "Case" by Teni came through the speakers as Isoken merged into traffic. She sang along to the popular track. Her voice was surprisingly good, but he'd never tell her that.

"Aye, stop all that croaking, let the lady sing the song."

He chuckled when he heard her cursing him out under her breath. The next several weeks were going to be quite interesting and he was looking forward to it.

CHAPTER 11

The next afternoon, loud voices from downstairs stirred Tekena from his slumber. Prying open his eyes; it took him a few seconds to get his bearings. The previous day, once he dropped off Isoken, he headed to the airport to catch a charter flight to Port Harcourt. After getting out of bed, Tekena strolled into the adjoining bathroom to wash his face and brush his teeth. Judging by the time on his cell, he'd been asleep for five plus hours. He stretched his body and pulled on a white tee to pair with his grey sweats.

He made his way down the stairs to the living room, but almost turned around when he saw his mother's childhood friend and her daughter. The look he gave his mother was one he knew she recognized. And unfortunately, cared nothing about.

"Ah Tekena, you're awake." His mother's friend jolted from her relaxed position. "We almost left."

I should have stayed in the room longer.

"Yes ma. Good evening." He walked over and stood by his mother. "Where's Pops?"

"He's in the back." His mother soothed the back of his hand with her thumb. She knew she'd messed up, but that wouldn't stop her from ambushing him again. This was the fourth friend he had to greet, and he hadn't been home a full twenty-four hours yet. The only problem was this one came with her daughter. The same daughter he had a two-hour thing with back in the day. How two sticks of *suya*, a movie, and some fooling around branded him her potential husband still amazed him.

"Nengi, don't you see Tekena?" his mother's friend asked.

Tekena glanced over at her daughter. Her lips turned up in a sheepish smile and she giggled and covered her mouth with both hands.

His eyebrows pulled together and he rolled his shoulders to stop his skin from crawling. He was thirty-one so he knew she was about twenty-eight. How was she acting as though she was in high school?

"Mummy..." She giggled. "I did see him, but you guys were talking." She waved at him. "Hi Tex."

He gave her a head nod "Hey. Wassup." His mother was the only reason he didn't say what was on his mind.

Nengi giggled again. "I'm fine. How are you?"

Tekena turned to his mother. "Really?" He narrowed his eyes at her. "I'm about to go hang out with Pops for a bit."

He turned back to his mother's visitor, completely ignoring her daughter. "It was nice to see you again."

He left the women and headed for the back. As he strolled away, he heard his mother's friend tell her daughter not to forget to say goodbye before they left. He hated to hurt her feelings but that's exactly what would happen if she took her mother's advice. *Giggling like she's on crack.*

"What's going on, Old Man?" Tekena took a seat opposite his stepdad. "They chased you out here too?"

His stepdad chuckled. "No. I came out here to provide an escape for you when they chased *you* out."

"Good looking. I've told your wife I'm not ready. She keeps trying to push her friends needy daughters on me." Tekena reached over for the Ludo board. "You wanna play a game?"

"Yes, set it up. And your mother only wants what's best for you."

Tekena set up the board and placed the seeds in their positions. Shaking up the dice, he rolled. "But I've told her what's best for me. Nothing is happening until I reach all my goals and retire from the track." Rolling a six and five, he moved his seed.

"You're her only child, and she wants grandchildren."

"How come y'all never had other children?"

His stepfather shrugged. "I already had a child, and your mother didn't want anymore. I loved her enough to be okay with that. I have you and I'm fine."

Tekena had only seen his stepsister once in all the years his parents had been married. The divorce between his stepdad and his ex-wife was an ugly one. From what Tekena gathered, the girl's mother kept her away. He was dealing with his own trauma then, so he never gave it another thought.

Tekena's biological father died when he was six and in a little over a year, his mother up and married his stepdad – a man who also happened to be his late father's friend. He despised his mother for forgetting him and his dad. She tried for a long time to tell him that she knew his stepdad first, but miscommunication took them on different paths. A story Tekena didn't buy or cared about.

"Well, that wasn't a wise decision because now she stays on my case."

At the end of his rebellious years, his stepfather took an interest in his racing. Especially when he realized he wasn't giving it up. He got him his first Go-kart and the rest was history.

"Indulge her. You know she feels guilty. I feel guilty. Every time we stay up at an ungodly hour to watch your race, she prays and cries the whole time."

Tekena frowned. "Then why do you let her watch the races?"

"You know nobody stops Loloba from doing what she wants to do."

"Nah, Pops. My mind won't be at rest knowing my mother

cries while watching my races. I'mma teach you how to disconnect the cable so she thinks something is wrong with it."

His stepfather laughed, but he was dead serious. He needed her prayers, not her tears. They continued to play as he filled his stepfather in on the details of his trip.

"I'm so proud of you son, securing your future."

"I appreciate that, Pops. Thank you for believing in me."

"All we want is what's best for you, son. I know your mother can be worrisome with this marriage topic, but don't be like me and let the perfect woman slip away." He paused. "I know your dad is a sensitive subject, so I'm not talking about him. I'm talking about me. I let your mother slip away, thinking she would always be there when I was ready. When she got married, I was devastated. My anger made me marry a woman who became a nightmare. For ten years, it was torture. I'm sure I wasn't the easiest to live with either. Under not so perfect circumstances, we found each other again, but that rarely happens."

Tekena nodded. For some reason he couldn't quite understand why he thought of Isoken. They had already established they didn't like each other. "Okay Pops, I got you. You gonna play or we going to continue this kumbaya?"

His stepfather laughed and they continued the game. They played two rounds of Ludo with each of them winning a round. Tekena looked out into the massive yard. The orange and red skies indicated the sun was setting. It was such a beautiful sight. Tekena pulled out his phone. "Come on Pops, let's take a picture."

As Tekena took the pictures, he heard that skin crawling giggle behind him. He shook his head, studying the picture to ensure she didn't bomb it.

"That's how people get shot. Next time announce yourself. Don't be sneaking up on folks."

"Tekena..." his stepfather warned.

"Sorry, I wanted to tell you I'm leaving."

Tekena stood observing her incredulously. "Okay...be easy. Pops, I'm about to go lay it down." Tekena walked back into the house while he posted one picture to his IG stories and one to his feed with the caption *"Tales at Sunset with the Old Man."* He closed out of the app when he heard ol' girl on his trail. He kissed his mother on her cheek, said goodbye to her friend and headed upstairs.

"Tekena, don't forget church in the morning."

He grunted but didn't respond. He loved his parents, but them showing him off was always exhausting. He understood they were proud of him. Even understood he was their only child. However, he longed for a day with them minus the show. Hopefully, he would get that before he left on Tuesday.

CHAPTER 12

Tsoken shoved another spoonful of butter pecan ice cream in her mouth as she scrolled through Instagram. Because of time constraints, she and Lara had agreed to use the weekend to go through everything she had on the speedway campaign. It had been a busy Saturday so far and they were winding down at her favorite ice cream parlor. Their day started mid-morning when she picked Lara up. In addition to going over the details of the campaign, they'd visited a few vendors. One for custom t-shirts and the other an event planner they wanted to hire.

"Are you sure you're not upset?"

Lara lifted a spoonful of vanilla ice cream. "Hm...no! This campaign is so top notch that I couldn't even talk about it to my husband until everything was signed and secure. I'm seriously not up for that kind of *wahala* or pressure." She put the ice cream in her mouth. "You wouldn't believe the number of meetings I had to have with that Eze guy to make sure everything was perfect. This is my first child. I don't need the stress."

"Okay. I'm glad."

"My *dia*, me too. I can't be held responsible if—"

Isoken held up her hand. "Okay. I get the picture. Wow, the pressure." She took another spoonful.

She was sure Tekena hadn't shared with her boss that he knew her personally. So, she didn't tell Lara either. She wasn't sure if that knowledge was grounds for removal due to a conflict of interest. Tekena would never believe she didn't intentionally get removed from his campaign. And she'd be the laughingstock of their circle. He would never let her live it down and would taunt her about being a coward every chance he got. Osaro and Itohan had already asked them to be godparents to their unborn child so there was no getting rid of him.

"I know you can handle it. Besides, I'm not trying to struggle with understanding that Americanah accent. The one time we had to be on a Zoom call together... half the stuff he was talking, I didn't even hear."

Isoken laughed and shook her head. "When he slows down, he isn't that bad."

"Then you should have no problem. Since you almost sound like him. *Me I no fit.*" Lara lifted her eyes when her phone rang.

Isoken nodded in understanding as Lara stepped away to answer it. She picked up her phone and aimlessly scrolled her social media accounts, starting with Facebook before hopping over to IG. Twitter was too much for her, so she never bothered. The first photo she saw in her feed was Tekena's. He was with an older man. His arm was on the man's shoulder while he bit on his lower lip. They didn't look alike, but he called him pops in the caption.

This man is too fine abeg. And he knows it. That's the problem.

She was certain drawing attention to his full lips was intentional. She squinted her eyes at the picture, zooming in on acrylic red nails and bangle on a hand touching the chair he was seated on. She was careful not to like it. The last thing she wanted him to think was that she was pressed. She then noticed his outfit. White t-shirt and grey sweatpants. *The male thot outfit.*

"Sorry, that was my husband. He's worried. We've been out all day."

Isoken closed out of the app and stood. "Yeah, I'm tired too. I have one day to rest before I take on this campaign I'm not ready for."

"I told you, you'll be fine. Besides, I'll still be available in case you need anything."

Both women threw away their trash and left. As Isoken got in her car, her phone buzzed indicating a text coming through.

T2: You can like my pic but can't ask if I arrived safely.

Isoken's heart slammed against her chest as she opened the IG app. True to his word, she had liked the picture. It was probably in her haste to close out of the app before Lara noticed what she was looking at. She typed back.

I can see you're not dead. Thot uniform and all.

T2: LOL! How am I thoting in my parents' house?

You're the one that said you're a man of many talents.

T2: If you had come with me, maybe I won't have to thot.

Goodnight Tex. I need to get on the road.

T2: Where u at?

Went out with Lara. She frowned. Were they really having this conversation?

T2: Call me when you get home.

Why?

T2: What you mean why? Because I asked.

No

T2: A'ight don't call me and see what happens.

Isoken tossed her phone in the passenger seat and made her way home. A smile crept across her face. The man aggravated her to no end with his demands.

THE NEXT MORNING, Isoken reached out and silenced her alarm for the second time. She shifted from under her pillow and peered at the time. *Oh great, I've missed church.*

"There's still time to Live stream the second service," she muttered to herself.

She'd started attending regularly since the day she rededicated herself in her car some Sundays ago. She'd also joined a small Bible study group made up of women from her church. They were seven of them. Married, divorced, widowed, and single.

Isoken rubbed her eyes, then yawned. She reached for her phone, then she remembered she'd left it on the charging dock in the living room. Isoken said a quick prayer then made her way to the bathroom for her morning routine. She changed into some tights and a sports bra, then picked up her yoga mat. Walking into her second bedroom, she spread her mat, lit some candles, and started her "Way Maker" playlist. For the next hour, Isoken listened to gospel music play through her iPod while she did her stretches and poses. She tried to clear her mind and focus on her breathing, but the upcoming week and the man it was centered on kept invading her thoughts.

After meeting with Lara the day before, she had a chance to look at the detailed project plan. To make it easier for her, Isoken transferred them to her own format in Google docs. She then synchronized the times and dates on her phone. She also made notes to call the promoters of the festivals where Tekena would make appearances to ensure they had sufficient security. Granted Tekena's celebrity status was not as prominent in Nigeria as it was in Europe and America, still, he was under contract with his team and she had to make sure he stayed intact. It was year-end, and although there were enough activities in Lagos for fun, there was also the propensity for crime and she wanted to make sure for his sake and hers, they were safe. By the time she'd made it to bed, it was way past midnight.

Several minutes later, Isoken was showered and dressed, and walked into the kitchen to make brunch. She opened her laptop and went to her church's website. Clicking on their live stream, she walked over to the pantry to see what she had a taste for. She decided on a plantain and egg frittata, got out the ingredients and walked back to the counter.

While cutting up her plantains, tomatoes, onions, sausages, and peppers, Isoken listened to the pastor preach from Ruth1:11-12. He talked about how even in a hopeless, painful situation, God still placed people around Naomi that would help her deal with her loss – her daughters-in-law that she tried to push away. He went on to say that the natural human instinct when we've been hurt is to hide from God and people. But God didn't create humans to live in isolation.

Isoken took in his words that seemed to be directed at her. For months after she left for South Africa, she had cut everyone off. It took her dad threatening to fly over and drag her back home to straighten her up.

Isoken was drawn from her thoughts by her phone ringing. She dried her hands, lowered the volume of her laptop, and walked into the living room. Picking up her device, she smiled and answered.

"Oh, sister of mine, how are you?"

"Uh oh, you're in a good mood," Itohan said.

"Why will I not be? This is the day the Lord has made." Isoken walked back to the kitchen.

"Well, then let's bless His name."

Isoken chuckled. "Hold on a second." She placed the onions, peppers, and sausages in the hot oil and sautéed them. She added spices, stirred, and picked up her phone.

"So, what's up? How are my people?"

"They're all good, but I'm worried about you."

"Ah, why? I've been behaving, praising the Lord, and living my best life." Isoken cracked two eggs in a bowl and whisked.

"Ok, so I'm going to assume you haven't been on IG yet."

Isoken frowned retrieving a pan to fry her plantains. "No, I haven't. Missed church, so I did some yoga and I was listening to service..."

"Didn't mean to interrupt that."

Isoken could feel her sister stalling. "No *wahala*. It was at the end anyway. "What's going on?"

"When did you talk to Tex last?"

Isoken rolled her eyes when she remembered their conversation last evening. She gave her sister a brief rundown of their last encounter. She folded her sautéed mix into her eggs and poured it into a casserole dish, placed the plantains on top and put it in the oven. She was true to her word and didn't call him. Who did he think he was?

Itohan laughed. "Okay... I'm gonna hang up now. Go check IG and please don't do anything crazy."

"Itoh, what's going on?"

"I'll call you back, sis." She kept laughing and that annoyed Isoken, so she disconnected the call.

Clicking on the app, Isoken's eyes bugged at the number of comments she had. She had only a thousand plus followers and wasn't obsessed with social media, so who were all these people? Her followers were now ten thousand. She clicked on the tag she had, and her body heated up in rage. The tag took her to Tekena's page. Her heart slammed against her chest as she read the caption. This man had her on his page and told his 12.9 million followers to tag her and ask her to call him.

This dude is really crazy.

She paced the kitchen while running her fingers through her hair. Immediately, she stopped and made her page private. Next, she dialed him.

"Tex, take me off your page now!"

"Hello?"

"Can't you hear me?"

"No, only someone yelling at me."

Isoken took in a deep breath. Then exhaled through her mouth. "Tekena, I'm not playing with you."

"I'm not playing either. Didn't I tell you to call me when you got home yesterday?"

"I was busy, and I don't answer to you."

"Busy doing what? One of your boy toys?" He chuckled. "I saw the way your phone was ringing off the hook at lunch the other day."

"And that concerns you how? But if you must know, I was working on your stuff."

"And I appreciate it. But next time, don't test me." He paused and Isoken could hear him talking to someone in the background, asking the person who was probably his mom to add some more pieces of goat meat to his rice.

"You see I don't like the word no. I'm allergic. And if you gonna be working with me, you shouldn't be using it."

She put her phone on speaker and placed it down on the counter. She checked on her frittata. How many people had seen his post? She wasn't up for any social media frenzy. Already, she had all these people following her based on his stunt. People she would have to block.

"Tex! You're not the only one that is crazy *o*. Take me off your page now."

"Ask nicely."

"No."

"There goes that word again."

"Tekena, you're testing my patience. I just got the Word in me and I'm trying to have a peaceful Sunday—"

"For real? I went to church too. Haven't been in a while. It was good. What did they preach on your end?"

All the time she talked her phone kept beeping with notifications. "Tekena, please take me off your page," she said softly. The harshness in her voice wasn't getting her anywhere.

"Better. Now, I'm going to hang up, take you off and call you back. You better answer, Goldie," he warned.

At this point, she was done fighting him. There was no telling what he'd do next. He disconnected the call. Isoken plated her food, went into the living room and plopped down on the couch in front of the television. The next couple of weeks promised to be crazy so she wanted to catch up on her shows. First *Money Heist* and then *Queen Sono*. Several minutes later, her phone rang again.

"Hello, Tekena," she said.

"Don't be calling my name like I'm getting on your nerves."

Isoken chuckled. "Shouldn't you be spending time with your parents? Why are you on my phone?" She then decided to mess with him. "Your dad is one handsome fox. I might want to get his number."

There was silence on the other end of the line. It took all Isoken had to stifle her laughter.

"You don't wanna go there with me." The chuckle he gave had a sinister tone to it. "You were about to tell me what they preached about in church."

"Didn't you say you went? Isn't that enough for you?"

"Aren't you supposed to willingly share the gospel with all? What kind of Christian are you?"

"One that is tired and wants to watch my show."

"What show is that?"

"*Money Heist* on Netflix."

"For real? That's my show."

Over the next several minutes, Isoken settled on her couch as they discussed the show, dissecting the characters they liked and hated the most. They even made predictions on how the show would end. Later, she gave him a rundown of the things planned for the week ahead, the first being an interview with Lasgidi TV.

"You get back Tuesday, right?"

"Yeah, you miss me?"

"Err... no. I need to make sure you're going to be at the TV station by eight a.m. Our interview is for nine."

"Goldie, if you don't leave me alone about this dang interview. You sent me an email, a text and you reminded me a second ago. I'll be there."

"Well, excuse me. I'm not used to working with a celebrity. I don't know your level of divadom."

"Divadom? Really?" He chuckled. "I'll be there. If for nothing but to see your beautiful face."

"Do you flirt like this with all your colleagues?"

"Nope and you and I know you're more than a colleague..."

"You're right. We're family."

"Nah. I won't go that far."

"This is why I don't like you." A smile crossed her face. She had been doing a lot of laughing and smiling while they've been on the phone.

"And? I don't like you too, but that ain't got nothing to do with anything."

"I've always known you're abnormal. Who flirts with someone they don't like?"

He barked out a hearty laugh in response. "You gonna come get me from the airport?"

"Tex, you're not about to make me your driver while you're in Nigeria."

"Why? You can keep a leash on me that way."

"I don't need to keep a leash on you. I gotta go. Don't let me hunt you down. Be at the station at eight sharp."

"Yes, baby."

"Ugh...stop that. Bye."

Once they disconnected the call, Isoken stared at her phone for a few moments. This wasn't going the way it was supposed to. They were only supposed to be working together and he go on his way in a couple of months. Now she was faced with a dilemma. How did she stay cordial with him without defeating her goal of staying detached? One thing she learned early was never to deny a problem. Tekena was one she couldn't afford and unfortunately, he refused to be placed in the box she'd kept him in.

CHAPTER 13

Tuesday morning, Tekena picked up his luggage and walked toward the door. He had about half an hour to get to the airstrip to catch his 6.30 a.m. flight. He walked downstairs and chuckled when he saw his mother waiting.

"Good morning, ma." He hugged her. "I told you not to get up this early. I called a car service."

She waved him off. "Good morning, my dear. How do you expect me to sleep? I don't know when I'll see you again." She pointed to a chair. "Sit down, let me pray for you."

Tekena willed himself to ignore her shaky voice. He drew her close and kissed her temple. "You'll see me soon." Then he did as she asked. After her prayers and blessing over him, his stepdad came from the back. He was dressed and Tekena frowned.

"Good morning Pops, where are you going?"

"Morning Son, are you sure you don't want me to take you to the airport?"

Tekena chuckled. "You guys act like I'm not a grown man. No, I got it. The car service should be at the gate. I appreciate it though."

"You'll always be my baby." His mother leaned into him.

"And you're my favorite lady. But I gotta go." *I know another lady that will have my head if I'm late.*

They hugged and minutes later, he was at the back of the black SUV on his way to the airport.

Buckled in and waiting for the plane to take off, Tekena pulled out his phone.

Good morning Goldie.

She must've been waiting on him because seconds later, he saw the three dots signifying she was sending a response.

Morning. Are u on ur way?

At the airport now

Tex!

Relax. I'll be there even if I have to come funky.

You better not!

Relax woman. See you soon.

Tekena mused over the change in dynamics between them. There were a lot of surprising things he had found out about her. One thing that was still true was what he knew from the beginning – she challenged him like no other. Every woman he had been involved with was ready to bend to his every demand. Isoken danced to her own tune. That drove him insane and intrigued him at the same time.

"I TOLD you I'd make it." Tekena locked the car and walked towards Isoken standing outside the station. As he got closer, he could see the worry lines disappear.

She rolled her eyes at him. "Thank God."

He stroked his beard. "O ye of little faith. Nerdy ain't with you today?" he asked, referring to the guy he now knew as Ben.

"Stop calling him that. He's inside. *Oya* come on." She turned and headed towards the entrance of the station.

"I don't get a hug first?" he hollered after her.

Without breaking her stride, Isoken glanced at him. "No, but I got you a macchiato. Now come on."

"Look at you, being all considerate and stuff." He sauntered behind her, distracted by the sway of her hips.

Once inside, she introduced him to some key personnel and the anchor of the morning segment, Aduke. Isoken walked away to take a call leaving Tekena and Aduke to themselves. He licked his lips, pleased with what he saw. She was petite, beautiful, and stacked. She too must've liked what she saw because their handshake lingered. They were lost in discussing nothing in particular when Isoken cleared her throat. Aduke blushed, visibly embarrassed, and excused herself to go check on the crew.

Isoken squeezed her nose pushing a covered cup toward him. "Take *ashawo*." She walked to a pair of chairs and sat.

Tekena chuckled at her calling him that and followed suit. "Why I gotta be all that?" He looked at the beverage. "Hope this ain't got—"

"No, I told the barrister almond milk."

She'd learned he was lactose intolerant during Osaro's wedding when he didn't partake in the buttermilk wedding cake. She'd derived great pleasure in telling him that he was weak like his organs. Tekena shook his head at the memory. He sipped his hot beverage. The almond milk tasted funny, but he dismissed the thought. He observed as she typed away on her iPad. Determination and drive were sexy on her.

"You worried about me and ol' girl?"

Isoken glanced over at him. "Why should I be worried about what you do with your little thingy?"

Tekena scoffed. "Ain't nothing little about it. You can find out."

His remark got her full attention. She tilted her head and drew her eyebrows together. "Are you okay? Heck no. Did they spike that drink?" She closed her iPad.

"What? Don't tell me you're allergic to men."

"No, I'm allergic to you."

"Very funny. No, you ain't. I saw how you were giving ol girl the evil eye."

"If I was, it's because both of you were wasting my time."

"A'ight Goldie, I'mma let you rock."

The presenter walked back over. "We're ready."

Tekena and Isoken stood. He finished his drink, thanking her before following the morning host to the other part of the studio to handle business. After the makeup chair, which he always hated, he was wired with the mic and it was show time.

"Today we have the pleasure of having Tekena Tamuno with us in the studio. He's a Nigerian-American race driver currently competing in the Formula One Circuit. He has won multiple races and championships in local European races. Not only is he a force to be reckoned with on the track, but he's also business savvy. Mr. Tamuno is the owner of TSquared Driving School here in Lagos and founder of the TSquared Foundation." Aduke beamed at him and he nodded at her. "Mr. Tamuno, welcome to the program."

"Thank you for having me. And please call me Tekena."

"Okay. Let's get straight to it. We have you in the studio today to talk about the new initiative you're working on with the Lagos State government."

"Yes, we are working together to bring Nigeria one of the first and biggest Speedways in West Africa. In addition to promoting the sport on an amateur and professional level, we hope to attract tourism. This will lead to international recognition and encourage the international circuits to hold a Grand Prix in Nigeria. There are existing associations that govern local races. What Gidi Motor Speedway provides is a safe and controlled environment for these races."

"That's a great segue. There's a division of Motorsport in the Nigerian Sports Ministry, but the sport still isn't well known. There are festivals and special events where races are sometimes featured... more bikes than actual stock cars, so there is growth potential. What's needed for the sport to grow?"

"Another reason I'm here. I want to use my platform to draw attention to the opportunities we have here at home. We need more corporations to believe in the vision of the sport. This will increase their willingness to sponsor local races. These small races will eventually turn into big ones. My ultimate desire is for us, here in Africa to start our own circuit. With a governing body and everything without foreign validation." Tekena felt his stomach bubble.

Something's not right. He shot his eyes at Isoken. She was standing behind the cameras showing Ben something on her iPad. "So, partnerships, investors the possibilities are endless."

"Sounds quite interesting."

"It is. This will also allow African youth the opportunity to learn and build careers in different fields related to motorsport. That's something my driving school does today on a smaller scale."

"There are promising careers in motorsport?"

Tekena discreetly rubbed his stomach. *If she put something in my drink, I'm going to kill her.* Despite the discomfort, he plastered on a smile. "Of course, not only is the industry a multi-billion-dollar one, but there are also careers in engineering to produce professional mechanics for the cars. Management, driving, and hospitality. We need Africa, especially Nigeria, to offer its own contribution to global technology, engineering, and innovation."

"Well said." Aduke looked through her notes. "So, tell us, what can the people of Lagos expect?"

"The fully equipped speedway located in Ibeju-Lekki, is built to international standards and is set to open in six months. I'll be hosting and attending a slew of events up until the opening. A full schedule can be seen on the website." As he spoke, his stomach clenched, confirming dairy in his system.

For the next few minutes, Aduke reiterated the website address and contact information for her audience.

I guess this is how we doing it because I had a couple thousand people follow her. I should've known not to take anything from her. This chick needed to hurry up or I'm about to funk up her whole studio.

"I can't let you go without asking the question I'm sure the ladies want to know," she blushed.

Tekena mustered up a smile. "And what's that?"

"Is there anyone special?"

He grinned. "That would be a negative."

"That means you're available for the ladies—"

"That will also be a negative."

Aduke smirked and hiked her brow. "Why? Are you—"

"Nah, let me stop you right there. I'm for the ladies, but I'm not ready for one now."

"There you have it, ladies, there's still hope."

Tekena masked his displeasure with that statement. None of what he said was a signal of hope for anyone. Minutes later, the interview wrapped up and Tekena scurried toward the exit. He didn't wait around for small talk. He heard Isoken calling his name, but he didn't stop. His stomach was hurting, and if he spoke to her, he was sure to say something he'd regret. For both their sakes, he needed to get away from her. He pressed the key fob to unlock the car and got in.

Isoken tapped on his window. "Tekena, don't you hear me calling you?"

An idea popped in his head and he lowered the window. "My bad. Get in for a second."

She narrowed her eyes at him. He could tell she was trying to decipher his intentions. He trained on a blank expression.

She opened the door and entered. "What's wrong with you?"

He engaged the child locks. "You into poisoning people now?"

"What?"

He lifted his buttocks and released the gas he had been holding in.

Her eyes bugged. "What? Oh heck no." Isoken pulled on the door handle. "Oh my gosh. Let me out. Are you crazy?"

"You put milk in my drink to mess with me and I'm the crazy one?" He deadpanned her. "In fact, hold on." He let out more gas.

"Tekena, I promise if you don't let me out of this car. I'm going to make the rest of your stay miserable." She frantically pulled on the lever to get the door open.

"Here I thought we were making progress and you pull this stunt?"

"You think I tried to harm you on purpose? The girl mustn't have done what I asked her."

"I don't believe you. But then it was your job to make sure she did."

She rolled her eyes. "My job? You've really lost your mind. Let me out of this car. All I tried to do is be nice to you."

"If your nice gives me bubble guts I wonder what your bad will do."

"You'll find out if you don't let me out of this car. Then I suggest, go directly to jail. Do not pass GO. Do not collect $200 and head straight home."

Tekena narrowed his eyes at her. Her flustered look had him reevaluating his conclusion. Was this an honest mistake or did she try to take him out?

"For real. I didn't set out to hurt you." She was fanning herself with her notebook. "Let me out, please."

Tekena disengaged the locks. She hurried out and slammed the door. She looked frazzled and gave him a nasty look. He smirked and started his car. He would've tormented her some more, but he needed to get home now. Not giving her another glance, he sped off.

ISOKEN CLOSED her laptop and chucked it into her portfolio. She picked up her handbag, phone, and keys then left the office. She stepped into the elevator, pressed the button to the lobby and checked her phone again. It was now the end of the day and she hadn't gotten a single text from Tekena. After the earlier fiasco, she went to pick up the t-shirts for their appearance at a festival next week. But not before the nosy television presenter inquired about Tekena's hasty exit. Her thirst was long and wet.

Isoken had the pleasure of telling her he had somewhere important to be. She wondered why she cared but decided not to give it another thought. While she was at the custom t-shirt designers, she sent him a few texts to see how he was doing. None of which he responded to. A little after lunchtime, she went back to the office and still no word from him. If the situation weren't so serious, she would have been dying of laughter. But she was upset that he even had the nerve to accuse her. She needed him to be well and present because her job depended on his appearances. When she got to the office, she was told that his appearance garnered the highest ratings that the show had ever had. This was only the beginning.

He had more press, photoshoots, and public appearances in the weeks ahead. Lara had put together some solid events. Over the weekend, Isoken called in some of her favors and got some additional promo slots. She was surprised he didn't complain when he saw the updated schedule. He needed to ask himself why she would spike his drink if she needed him well to do what she had planned.

As she cruised the highway, she thought about how she was going to reach him. They had to be at a radio station in the morning and she wanted to make sure he'd be there. Her Bluetooth rang.

"Hey, Itoh. How far?"

Itohan was laughing. That could only mean one thing. She knew about what happened and since Tekena wouldn't have called her, that left one option...Osaro. Who then told Itohan.

"Itoh, I'm about to hang up on you."

"No, wait hold on…"

She laughed some more before quieting down. "Keni, you tried to harm the man?"

"All of you are getting on my nerves. First, if I were seeking revenge for the stunt he pulled, I would have had a more sophisticated plot going. Then two, unfortunately, I need him to keep my job, so why would I want to harm him?" She took a breather. "That I'll leave until after my project ends."

Itohan laughed some more. "You need to see the way he was carrying on and Osa was laughing so hard."

"Oh, so he can call the U.S to report, but he can't answer the phone when I call."

"You have his number?"

"I work with him remember. I'm bound to have his number. Don't start any useless rumors."

"I'm saying, if you have his number, go check his location and pull up since he refuses to answer the phone."

"That's a great idea—"

"You can't go there empty handed, *sha*. Take a peace offering and you guys should stop. Next thing you know you'll be on a billboard with a special message attached."

Isoken didn't doubt in the least bit that he would probably retaliate. "What can I get him for an upset stomach?"

"Pepper soup, crackers, ginger ale, coke…"

"I can't show up with soda and crackers."

"Pepper soup it is. I know you hate cooking, so good luck."

"I can easily buy it…" Isoken stopped when she realized he'd probably not eat anything he didn't see her make. She would have to go to the supermarket and pick up some ingredients then pull up on him. "Okay sis, I gotta go. I'm going to stop on my way now to buy the stuff and take it to his house."

"Please behave yourself."

"Hmmm I'll try. I can't wait for him to go back to where he came from." The sisters chuckled together. "I'll text you when I get there. If I don't, know that Tex has killed me. Make sure he's prosecuted to the full extent of the law."

Itohan laughed and Isoken hung up on her. Her sister could laugh all she wanted to but celebrity or not, if he harmed her, they better do the needful. Or she would haunt all of them.

CHAPTER 14

L ater that evening, Isoken walked up the gravel pathway to Tekena's front door. She'd been at the gate for ten minutes before the gateman allowed her inside. Now she knew why. This house was fabulous. She could only imagine what the inside looked like. Pressing the doorbell, she shifted the nylon bag that held the foodstuff she bought from one hand to another. After shopping, she sent Tekena a text that she was coming over. Like all the other texts, it went unanswered.

The door opened but instead of Tekena, it was an older woman. An idle night sent her scouring through his IG page, so she knew this wasn't his mother.

"Good evening ma," Isoken greeted.

"Good evening my dear, may I help you?" The woman's eyes moved from her face to her hands.

"I'm here to see Tekena." Isoken heard footsteps.

Before the woman could respond, Tekena appeared behind her. The woman looked up at him, rubbed his arm, and retreated inside the house. In uncomfortable silence, they both stared at each other. If she were a lesser woman, she would've melted under his intense, penetrating gaze. Isoken couldn't help but notice the tattoos scattered across his muscular arms. They were put on display because of the grey sleeveless muscle tee he had on over dark blue basketball shorts. His cologne tickled her nostrils sending a now familiar yet unwanted shiver down her spine.

"I know you see me carrying this stuff," Isoken spoke first.

His brow shot up. "And? What do you want?"

"Tekena, I come in peace."

"Peace," he scoffed. "I can't tell." He moved aside for her to enter.

The interior didn't disappoint. The foyer alone was something out of a magazine. The scent of cedar wood and something else she couldn't recognize wafted against her nostrils. The expansive entryway was like a room of its own. The walls, which were a warm white mixed with canary yellow undertones, were adorned with modern and traditional paintings. On each side were two light lemon armchairs with kente covered pillows. In the center of the space was a huge floral arrangement.

Tekena took the bag from her hand. "What's this for?" He locked the door.

"That's my peace offering. I want to make something for you. How are you feeling?"

His eyes danced around in distrust. Without another question, he left her standing there and moved. "Come on."

Tekena walked through the living room and Isoken followed.

"Why haven't you been answering my text and calls?"

"Because I wasn't feeling you."

"How childish. I told you I didn't intentionally make you sick."

"Hmm, that's what your mouth says. But since I don't trust you..." He shrugged.

She wanted to kick him, but what good would that do? They entered his kitchen which would be her mother's dream. The bold cream and black space was a state-of-the-art culinary setup with a massive stove, double door oven, and giant fridge. All in stainless steel. The microwave and other smaller appliances sat to the corner of the granite countertop. The older woman was wiping down the surfaces when they entered.

"Nana Rubi, meet Isoken, Isoken this is Nana Rubi." Tekena set the bag down.

Isoken and the older woman exchanged pleasantries again before she excused herself.

"Okay look. Since day one, we got off to a wrong start. I want to call a truce. We're going to be stuck together for several weeks. For me to do my job effectively, the client and I can't be beefing." She held out her hand for a handshake.

Tekena glanced at her hand before returning his eyes to her. He snickered. "You're full of crap, you know that, right?" He leaned on the island and crossed his arms over his chest. "It takes one to know one. That's exactly the speech I would've given if the situation was reversed. You're scared of what I'll do next."

Isoken shook her head and laughed with him. "Jeez, that speech was so hard to give. I felt the words clog my throat." She placed her hands on her hips. "But really, I didn't try to take you out. I hate cooking but I'm here to make some pepper soup for your childish behind. You gonna let me or not?"

"There she goes." He inclined his head toward the stove. "A'ight do your thing, but you better know how to cook or I'm straight clowning you."

"I hate cooking doesn't mean I don't know how." She walked to the sink, washed her hands, and asked him for the pots. After pointing everything out to her, including how to use his fancy stove, he turned to leave the kitchen.

"Nah playa, where do you think you're going?"

The look he gave her was as though she was speaking a foreign language. "Back to playing my game."

"Nope. Sit down here and watch me. I don't want you saying I did anything to your food. That's why I'm cooking it here and not in my house."

"You already don tried to take me out once, so..."

"Will you be quiet with that.'" She slid the yam tuber toward him with a cutting board. "Here, cut this into cubes."

He slid it back. "Nah, first that thing itches. Second, how are you coming to cook for me but putting me to work?"

Isoken did remember raw yam itched. She'd normally use coconut oil on her hands before cutting. "Okay give it here, but still sit down. We have to talk about the interview."

He sat on the barstool, picked up the remote and turned on the small television that was mounted overhead in the corner. She washed the assorted meat, spiced it, and set the pot on the stove to cook. She made sure they weren't big pieces to lessen the cooking time. She still had to make it home in a decent hour. As she waited for it to boil, she cut into the tuber and began to peel.

"You never answered my question. How are you feeling?"

He shrugged. "After spending an hour in the bathroom, I'm okay but drained."

"I'm sorry. But you forcing me to inhale your nonsense was low."

He lifted his shoulder in a half shrug. "Next time pay attention to what you're giving me to eat."

"I can't stand you."

"Yeah, that's what you say. How was work?"

Isoken looked up from what she was doing and observed him for his true intent. She decided to answer him sincerely. While she cooked, they discussed her day and his trip to see his parents. The woman she had met was his childhood nanny. When he became wealthy, he went back to his hometown in search of her. She had been recently widowed and as was the case in many Nigerian cultures, cruel outdated traditions were mistreating her. He packed her up and returned to Lagos with her. While he traveled the world racing, all she had to do was take care of his compound.

Isoken was taken aback by the side of him she was getting to know. On the other side of his arrogant, demanding and sometimes nonchalant behavior was a well-educated, well-traveled and caring man. He wasn't a *money miss road*. He was kind-hearted, compassionate, and very loving to those closest to him

"Is she the reason your foundation contributes to Naomi's Cause?" Isoken asked.

"Check you out, investigating your boy." Tekena grinned.

Isoken decided to ignore his insinuation. She had checked out his website and was quite impressed. His focus on widows didn't make sense since his mother wasn't one but now, she got the connection.

"Yeah. But not only her. My mom was a widow at one time."

"I'm sorry to hear that. Your biological father?"

Tekena nodded.

This is the reason why he didn't look like the man he called Pops.

"It's cool. I was about six, but I do remember her being treated badly by the so-called daughters of the land."

"I'll never understand the logic behind treating widows that way. It's one thing to lose the love of your life. Then to be treated like you've committed a crime on top of it is heartless. The grief is punishment enough." She forked a piece of meat and took it to him. "Here taste, is it soft enough for you?"

Tekena took the piece of meat, after chewing for a couple of seconds, he nodded. Isoken turned back to the stove and mixed in the remaining ingredients for the pepper soup. Next, she put the pot of yam on to boil. There was silence in the kitchen, so she turned around and saw Tekena was mesmerized by the television. She rolled her eyes when they connected with what had his attention. They were showing highlights of his interview on the evening news.

"Your little girlfriend asked of you when you left." She hated the words the minute they left her mouth. They sounded like she was bothered. And she wasn't...was she?

Tekena looked at her and stroked his beard. "Oh, really now? And why she gotta be my little girlfriend."

"You did good. The ratings were great."

"I see you deflecting. I'mma let you rock." He glanced back up at the television then returned his eyes to her. "I appreciate it though."

"Yeah, you were okay until you started talking about women like you were irritated."

"I was. That's what's wrong with you women. You ask us to be truthful but when we are, then you're mad because it's not what you wanna hear. I ain't checking for a relationship. At least not now..."

"Why? Are you a man scorned?"

"I won't say all that. But women and relationships are a distraction to where I'm trying to go."

"And where is that exactly?"

"To the top of my career. I'm focused on one thing before I retire. The championship."

"And love and commitment will stop that?"

"Why you wanna know? You trying to be my girl?"

Isoken furrowed her brows. "Nope. Nah. No."

"Whatchu mean? I know I can do far more than all those boy toys you keep on deck."

"Tekena, we're not talking about me—"

"We should. Since you been here you've been interrogating me."

"Answer the question. I'll let you ask something."

"Let me? Woman, after I've talked this much, you better answer what I ask you." A beat passed between them before he continued. "Women try to change you in the name of loving you. There was this one lady, she met me on the track, knew I raced cars. She was cool, we were vibing and chilling. Then when we got serious, she began complaining about my job. One day we had a terrible argument, and unfortunately, I also had a race. Not focused, that day, I had my first crash. It was minor but I was done."

Isoken listened attentively. "I can understand her side though. Your job is dangerous Tex. But then again love doesn't try to change you. You want to change because of love. Love is supposed to be selfless. True love is when the other person's happiness is your every waking desire without losing yourself in the process." She walked over to the stove and plated some pieces of the boiled yam into a bowl, before pouring pepper soup over it. She walked it back to him before repeating the process for herself.

"Since you know so much about love, why don't you have a man?"

"Who says I don't?"

"Me, because if you were mine, you wouldn't be in another man's house at this time of day cooking him dinner." His tone challenged her.

"If you must know, because..." She dipped her head in the fridge and came out with two bottles of water. She sat on the other side of him and blessed the meal before they began to eat. "Despite what I said, love is also painful, and I refuse to go through that pain again."

"Again?"

Isoken remained silent. She had never talked about Frank to anyone outside her family members. She didn't know if she wanted to talk about him to Tekena. She was having a surprisingly good time with him and didn't want to bring down the mood.

"Goldie...again?"

"Yeah, my fiancé passed away two weeks before our wedding."

She felt his stare. She lowered her head and tried not to meet it. His hand moved until it settled on top of hers. This was the pity she hated. He squeezed her hands, and she met his eyes.

"I'm so sorry. You wanna talk about it?"

Isoken shook her head. "Thanks, but it's fine. It was six years ago." She stirred her soup and blew on a spoonful before putting it in her mouth. "I guess what I was trying to say is, I've experienced love and how does the saying go...it's better to have loved and lost than not to have loved at all. Relationships shouldn't change you but push you to be a better version of yourself."

Isoken could see he wanted to ask her so many more questions about Frank but refrained. They continued to eat, focusing on lighter topics. Once again, she was so surprised to find out they liked most of the same things. Movies, music, even art. Once they were done eating, Tekena insisted on doing the dishes and cleaning up.

"Where's the restroom?"

"Round the corner, second door on the left. Don't be snooping around my house."

"Boy, I'm not concerned about your shoebox."

Tekena laughed. "You are so funny, but you gonna stop calling me boy. I'm all man, baby. And don't front on my house. I'mma give you a tour in a minute. I saw you admiring my crib."

"Since you notice everything, you should've sensed that milk in your macchiato."

He hiked his brow. "You wanna bring that back up again?"

Isoken laughed, waving him off. "So, we're good? You accept my peace offering?"

"Yes, I guess you all right. Besides, I never play behind my investments."

"Good as long as we agree." She jumped off the stool and followed his directions to the restroom. She admired his décor as she walked through the hallway. Minutes later, she handled her business, washed her hands, and made her way back to the kitchen when she heard Tekena on speaker.

"Hey Ro, what's up?"

"Hey man, please tell me you ain't mad enough to do anything to sis."

Isoken frowned then bugged her eyes remembering she didn't text Itohan when she got to Tekena's. With hurried strides, she made her way to the kitchen.

"To whom? Keni?"

"Yes. I have a pregnant wife who won't sleep until she knows her sister is okay."

Tekena narrowed his eyes at her once she entered the kitchen.

She went to her purse and pulled out her phone. She had ten missed calls from Itohan and five messages.

"Man, I ain't do nothing to this crazy girl."

"Tex, tell my sister I'm going to injure her myself if she had me worrying for nothing." Itohan's voice came through the speakers.

"Come here and dispel whatever you told these folks." He leaned against the sink and folded his arms against his chest. "Making them think I did something to you."

"Hey, y'all...my bad sis."

"Keni—" Itohan began when Osaro cut her off.

"It's your bad all right. You're not about to have my wife worried over you and Tex's issues," he snapped.

Isoken laughed at him. Her sister's pregnancy had turned him into a papazilla. But she was at fault, so she'd let him have it. What surprised her though was when Tekena walked closer to the phone.

"Aye man. Chill out with all that snapping. Sis should've known I won't do anything to her sister." He grinned. "At least not anything she won't like."

Isoken huffed and hit his arm. He had to go spoil his good gesture with reckless talk.

"That's our cue to let y'all go," Osaro said.

"Wait, wait, Keni, what are you still doing over there? Isn't it late?"

"Mind ya business sis. Mind ya business," Tekena teased.

"Tex, you about to let me put my foot in your behind. But he's right babe, mind your business," Osaro said.

Both sisters laughed before Tekena disconnected the call. He then turned and looked at her and shook his head. "I can't believe you. Come on let me show you around before I kick you out. You've overstayed your welcome anyway."

Isoken laughed at him. "Whatever, but I'll let you brag about this shoebox. Let's go."

Back home hours later, freshly showered, Isoken lotioned her body, dressed in her PJs, and wrapped her hair. All with a smile on her face. Tekena insisted on staying on the phone with her during her drive home. He wouldn't hang up until he heard the locks on her door. After accusing her once again of poisoning him but cooking a dinner he termed fantastic, they said good night and disconnected the call. They agreed to be friends.

Isoken settled in her bed and shut her eyes. She performed her normal breathing routine then said her prayers. It had been a good day.

BLINK
your skin is a canvas of bleary eyes
for too long these eyes have said
to each other
don't sleep
stay alert
to blink is to perish
it is night when you whisper with a jagged breath
those words the day shrouds
with sound and light
you must have done something
the blood of His Son does not cover

CHAPTER 15

Days later, Isoken walked into her office and stopped short when she saw two lilac orchids on her desk. A smile crossed her face. She placed her purse on the desk and picked up the card tied to the stem.

Changed my mind. You and I aren't friends. We're our own small gang.

Have a good day

Tex

"This man has rhymes for days," she muttered. She pulled out her phone and sent him a thank you text.

T2: u are welcome friend. See u later.

Isoken moved the vase to the side of her desk. The last few days had gone down surprisingly without them at each other's throats. Every day, they had no less than three media engagements. Radio, television, and cable networks. The day before, they went to Google headquarters to host a live chat. They slipped into a routine of meeting in the morning, fulfilling their daily obligations, then having lunch. Afterwards, she headed back to work to wrap up while he went to his driving school or home. Isoken was glad they were working well together, but at the same time, it opened her eyes every day to another part of him she selfishly wished didn't exist. That way it would've been easier to dislike and keep him at arm's length.

There was an ease to their conversation that she hadn't expected. They teased each other constantly without the other getting offended. At their last meetup, the day before, in true Tekena fashion, he flirted with the newscaster. What made this worse than the first newscaster was she saw him put the lady's number in his phone. It produced an icky feeling in her stomach.

Before she went to bed, Isoken reconsidered becoming friends with him. If she felt bad over him exchanging numbers, she knew it could only go downhill from there. However, she had a feeling he was going to milk this friend thing to death.

She put the rest of her things away and grabbed what she needed for her briefing with Mr. Gambo. As she rushed to the meeting room, she felt a presence by her side. Ben appeared with a smile on his face.

"Good morning." She smiled at him.

"Morning, Keni. You look nice this morning." His eyes roamed her body.

"Err...thanks."

Since she started working at Upward, Ben had been trying to get her to go out with him. Now that he'd been assigned to work on the speedway campaign with her, he had become bolder in his approach. He was a nice guy, but he wasn't her type and she never mixed business with pleasure. The old Isoken would have taken him up on his offer, made him spend his money on her, and called it a day. But she was starting over.

"When are you going to let me take you out?" he asked as they neared the conference room. He opened the door.

"Never. I thought you'd stop asking by now." She walked in, located Lara, and went to sit next to her.

"Hey lady, those interviews are on point. How long did it take to coach him?" Lara asked.

Isoken opened her iPad. "Coach *ke*? Girl, Tex is a natural. You forget he's been doing this stuff for years. He has his own PR team, so I didn't need to do anything."

"Hmm...he's Tex now? I bet there's something more to you guys than you're letting on."

Isoken knew exactly how gossip started and she wasn't in the mood. She smiled and turned to Lara. "He told me to call him Tex. Nothing's going on. He is a client."

"He's cute *sha o. Abeg* leave cute, the man is hawt!" Lara gushed.

Isoken inclined her head. This conversation was getting on her nerves. Lara didn't know how to stop until she got what she was looking for. "You are married, *abi*?"

"And then? That doesn't stop me from looking *o*. It's a good thing you took over the account because if I had to spend time with him—"

"Ladies and gentlemen, good morning." Mr. Gambo's voice interrupted her words.

Isoken sent up silent thanks to God.

"We won't be long this morning. I'll be traveling to the north later today, so I wanted to get a brief rundown of where we stand. We're almost at year end. Mrs. Johnson, why don't you go first."

The room quieted down as Lara gave a recap of her current client and what they had planned before and after the Christmas break. After fielding questions from Mr. Gambo and other interested parties, another team lead, Cheta, went next. Isoken's phone buzzed in her hand. She discreetly looked at the screen. Her lips lifted in a smile when she saw her sister asking, no demanding, she call her. Isoken quickly responded she was in a meeting. When she lifted her eyes, she was met with other pairs staring at her.

She cleared her throat and gave her update. She updated the team on the YouTube Live done at the Google headquarters and the upcoming drive off event that would be announced on the radio later. Mr. Gambo asked some additional questions about the schedule and her plans to keep the momentum going after

Tekena left Lagos. Satisfied with her answers, he moved on to the next team.

After their update was done, Mr. Gambo gave final instructions before dismissing everyone. Isoken and Lara talked for a few minutes before they went to their respective offices. Isoken tossed her notebook on her desk. She pulled out her phone, put in her earbuds and dialed. The phone was answered on the second ring.

"Yes, Mrs. Ikimi, what can I do for you?" Isoken teased. She shoved her iPad into her laptop bag, first checking to see how much time she had to chat before she made her way to the radio station.

"Start talking…"

"About what? Today is the day the Lord has made. I'm well and God is good. I trust He's been good to you—"

"Keni, don't let me hurt you."

"Didn't your husband tell you to mind your business?"

Ben popped his head into her office, signifying he was ready. She nodded at him. "Tell Osa, he has one more time to snap at me."

"He'd had a bad day—"

"And then you had to add your own *wahala*."

"You're the one that said I should check on you…"

"Well, that's true. My bad. So, what's up. I gotta go meet Tex."

"Are you guys good now? Why were you there so late?"

"We're fine and cordial, that's it…"

"That's a start—"

"No, it's not. It's agreeing to work together without animosity. This is Tex we're talking about." Isoken walked out of her office, signaling Ben on the way. "Man *ashawo* Tex. Cocky Tex. Reckless Mouth Tex."

Itohan laughed. "You were the same thing, except cocky before you turned over a new leaf."

Isoken laughed. "Itohan don't let me choke you. And if Osa comes for me, I'm biting him."

"You won't have to. Tex will fight your battles."

"Why are you trying to make this what it's not? Let me say this to you again. I'm not looking for a man. All I want is a secure and stable environment for what I told you I'm going to do. Hold on." Isoken looked up at Ben. "Will the express or the back roads be best at this time.?"

"Back way. Do you want to ride with me?" Ben asked.

"No, I might have to stop somewhere after the interview." She got in her car and tossed her bag on the passenger seat.

"Who was that?"

"My coworker. He keeps hounding me. I mean, he's not bad o. But you know I'm trying to be good." She started the engine, backed out of her parking space, and made her way to her next destination.

"Poor guy. He caught you when you've given up the black book."

"I should probably auction that book. Or donate it to the museum. In remembrance of Keni's Heydays."

"Keni, shut up. Your heydays were only ten weeks ago." Itohan laughed. "Although I'm so glad you've given up that life."

"My lady parts are not."

"They don't count, and they'll be all right."

"Yeah so you say cos you now getting some on the regular."

"You can get some if you open your heart, but I know I'm beating a dead horse."

"Yes, you are, and you should be tired of it by now. But I gotta go. Oh, my new furniture will be delivered this weekend. I'm so happy."

"I'm happy for you. May God grant you the desires of your heart."

"Amen o, my first desire is patience with this pampered celebrity I have to deal with." They both laughed and professed their love for one another before disconnecting the call. The conversation with her sister gave her an idea of how to get Tekena off her mind. Before she put up the black book, she might use it one last time.

———

"I'M TIRED." Tekena dropped down in the chair next to Isoken. Due to Lagos traffic, they'd missed their scheduled slot, so they were waiting for the next show to start. She glanced at his face, trying not to stare at him. He did look tired. When she first saw him earlier, she did everything she could to stay busy to avoid hanging out with him. She took some calls and talked about another project with Ben. At first, Tekena was annoyed, but then thankfully he was called away by Eze, giving her a reprieve.

"Not used to hard work?" she teased.

"Don't play." He leaned his head back in the cushioned seat. "I've been on the go since I landed in this country. Why didn't you space all this stuff out?"

"Because Mr. 'My Time is Short.' It's the holiday season. This is the best time to make you visible, while those visiting from abroad are here. Do you know that at the concert you're hosting, some Black American artists and some other hotshots will be there?"

"I get that, but it doesn't take away from how my body feels."

"Doesn't your season normally run nine months? You should be used to this."

"You right. But then you're forgetting the months of December to February, I get to chill out. But not this time."

"What do you do for relaxation?"

He shrugged. "Watch TV, take walks on the beach, or fish."

"Fish? I never would've thought that."

"That's cos you have me stereotyped. What about you? What do you do to relax?"

Isoken took a deep breath. Poetry used to be her thing. It was one of the things she shared with Frank. Since his death, she'd let it go.

"You're gonna think I'm weird."

"I already think you're weird so…"

Isoken rolled her eyes at him. "Archery—"

"What? The bow and arrow stuff?"

"Yeah, there's a whole club here and everything."

"Get outta here. That's dope. I gotta see you practice sometime." Tekena placed his forearms on his knee. "With your intense personality, I thought you were going to tell me you're a writer."

Isoken smiled. "I don't know what intensity has to do with writing, however, I did use to write poetry…"

"Aha! I knew it. Why did you stop?"

Isoken bent her head. A few days after the funeral was the last time she had written anything.

"Goldie—"

"We're ready for you guys," the lady they were introduced to as the production manager announced. Isoken was glad for the interruption. She stood and straightened her skirt. Tekena stood and placed his hand at the small of her back, ushering her through the double doors to the studio. They shook hands with the hosts of the show.

"Don't think you escaped my question," Tekena whispered in her ear before he walked away to be fitted with his microphone.

Two hours later, they walked out of the studio. As with all his performances, Isoken was pleased. He answered every question straight to the point while hitting the highlights they had discussed. He kept it light, simple, and fun. She was also pleased he could speak Pidgin English, which paid off since sometimes the presenters spoke in the broken vernacular. After the interview, he recorded a commercial for the station.

Walking past his car to hers, she spotted the driver. She glanced up at Tekena and smirked. "I see you got someone else driving you around."

"Since you refused to do it, I had to get someone."

"Lazy."

"Call it what you want. I drive all year round and I'm not up for this Lagos traffic."

"Anyway, this was your last engagement for the week. You have the whole weekend off."

"You wanna come hang out with me?"

"No."

"Why?"

"I thought you said you needed rest?"

"I do but that don't mean I wanna be bored in the process."

Isoken laughed and unlocked her car. "Tekena leave me *o*. I have things to do."

"Like?"

"If I tell you, will you let me go?"

"Depends on how important those things are over keeping me company."

Isoken threw her purse on the passenger seat. She heard Tekena grunt and looked up to see Ben approaching. "Be nice."

"Keni, the scheduling manager said they'd play an encore of the interview during the prime afternoon spot we should've had today."

"Good job, Ben. Thank you so much." Isoken diverted her eyes to Tekena. He raised his brows in a challenge, but she narrowed hers at him.

"'Ppreciate it, man," Tekena said.

"Not a problem. Keni, I'll see you tomorrow."

"No, actually I'm off tomorrow and the next. But I'll attend the Myraas's meeting from home."

Isoken saw disappointment flash across Ben's face and knew Tekena saw it too. "You have a good weekend, and we'll see on Monday."

"Thanks, you too." Ben turned to walk to his car.

She met Tekena's eyes. "I don't wanna hear a word from you."

"Too bad." Tekena turned to look at Ben, then back at her. "They couldn't find you a female partner?"

"Which one are you? My father, big brother or man?"

"Definitely not the first two, the third I haven't decided yet."
He pulled on his beard. "Anyway, back to my question."

"My new furniture is getting delivered tomorrow. That's why
I took the day off. Then I have archery practice in the evening."

Tekena furrowed his brows. "You gonna be at home by yourself with some delivery men?"

"Yes, why?"

He slanted his head toward her. "Not on my watch. What
time are they coming?"

"Eleven and you do know that before I knew you, I did stuff
by myself?"

Tekena turned and started walking to his car. "Keyword...
before. See you tomorrow, Goldie. Text me when you get home."

Isoken pulled in a deep breath and glanced toward Tekena.
He was at his car but hadn't gotten in. He motioned for her to
enter hers. She did and pulled off.

"Father Lord, I cannot like this man. Please, I won't be able to
deal. Help him to mess up so I can go back to hating him. *Abeg.
Laho.*"

Isoken had made a vow of no love. She had come to terms
with it and was content. After all these years, having feelings for
the one man she couldn't have wasn't an option. It couldn't be.

Close your eyes and trust Me.

CHAPTER 16

"You and Keni, is there anything you want to tell me?"

"Nope."

With a white fluffy towel loosely tied around his waist, Tekena rummaged through his closet for something to wear. A hot shower and a full twelve hours of sleep had done him good.

"Man, stop playing," Osaro chuckled at the other end of the line.

Tekena removed a dark green tee and a pair of dark blue jeans from the closet.

"I ain't playing. Truthfully, I don't know. You know me, Ro, that's not where my focus is right now. But I won't deny she's nothing like I'd thought." Tekena dressed quickly. He had an hour to spare before he had to be at Isoken's house.

"They kind of sneak up on you, don't they?"

"Who?"

"Those Adolo sisters."

He drew in a long breath. "You were looking to settle down. I'm not."

"I think she's a good look for you. I know you, and any woman who rolls over for you ain't the one."

Tekena laced up his sneakers, grinning at his friend's comments. That much was indeed true. At first, Isoken was a nut he couldn't crack, so he tried harder. But she matched him at every turn. Their energies were in sync. It was too scary for him to think about, so he didn't.

"Yeah, you right. Her mouth is reckless as heck. Most times, she has me wanting to put her in a headlock. But I remember sis and I contain myself."

"Yeah, please don't put me in an awkward position, but somehow I don't think that will happen."

"How you figure?"

"The way you checked me for snapping on her that day."

"Here you go trying to make something out of nothing."

"If you say so. I'll drop it, but I know you, so I wanna say, don't sabotage the possibilities because of that lie you tell yourself about not being worthy."

Tekena remained silent.

"I've been trying to tell you for years. You're not damaged. God loves you, and most of all, it wasn't your fault."

Osaro was the only person who knew his feelings of inadequacy. He felt unworthy of the things he had accomplished in his life. A teen mistake had robbed an innocent girl of the life she should have had, and he blamed himself for it. What kind of human being was he to allow that to happen to her? For years, he had waited on his punishment, but it never came. Instead, God had allowed him to live a life that others envied.

"I hear you though, but let me ask you a question," Tekena said.

"Yeah, wassup?"

"How do you get over the guilt?"

"Man, you can't. At least not by yourself. I'm not talking about going to church. I'm talking relationship. The only way is if Jesus helps you. The only way He does that is if you ask."

Tekena remained silent.

"Are the nightmares back?"

"Yeah, I had one the day before my last race. I don't know, man. It's like I've lived my whole life waiting on the other shoe to drop. You know for God to say, okay this is the year you pay."

"God doesn't work like that. What kind of movies you been watching?"

"Shut up..."

"Nah, I can't have you out here thinking God is the boogie man. God is love. That's not to say He doesn't get angry, but He's slow to it and He's gracious, merciful. That's the God I serve. You know the devil is the father of lies. He's the one that puts all those thoughts of unworthiness into you. Those are lies. You know that's his job and the sole aim is to keep you from enjoying the abundant life you should."

"Then he's failing because I'm living abundantly."

"No, you're not. You're rich, or even wealthy. You're famous, but you still have this belief that you're not worth any of it. This is me, man. If nobody tells you like it is, you know I will."

Tekena chuckled. "Isoken will too." The minute he said it he regretted it, because he knew what was coming next.

"Aww, snap. She does, huh?" Osaro chuckled.

"Man, leave it alone."

"I will, but that's why I say she's good for you. I don't know the details, but she too has some pain to deal with. Both of you can help each other out."

"Now how can the blind lead the blind?" Tekena picked up his keys.

"We all got some stuff with us. It's by God's grace."

Tekena's phone buzzed and he knew it was probably Isoken. He shook his head reading her message.

Goldie: Gd Morning. Make sure you eat *o*. I'm putting you to work the minute you get here, and I have nothing in the fridge.

This girl.

"Hey, Ro, I gotta go help this girl."

"Who?"

"Isoken. She got some furniture coming."

"Okay, I'mma let you go, but think about what I said."

Tekena picked up his wallet. "I hear you."

"I'm going to send you some verses."

"Good deal."

"Yo Tex..."

"Wassup?"

"Remember the day you came to my house to tell me what went down? Remember Aunty Lizzy prayed for us and showed you how to ask for forgiveness?"

Tekena locked up and got into his car. He remembered it well. It was a night he would never forget. "Yeah?"

"Well, you were forgiven that day. But forgiveness and freedom are two different things. You have to forgive yourself for you to experience freedom. It's been sixteen years too long. My guilt over Ivie almost robbed me of who I know for a fact God meant to be my wife."

"You see you were talking good until you mentioned 'wife'. I keep telling you I'm not trying to marry anyone."

"Man, will you shut up. For me it was my wife, for you it can be anything, as simple as really enjoying the life God gave you. But forgive yourself and turn to Him. I can't call myself your friend and brother if I don't keep singing about accepting Jesus as your Savior, but I can't force you either."

Tekena grunted but didn't speak. If anyone knew what they were talking about, it was Osaro. He wasn't spitting game. He had a similar feeling with the death of his younger sister. His friend had carried the guilt of her passing on his shoulders but was somehow able to let it go. "I know and I appreciate you for it. Send me the stuff and I'll hit you and Malcolm later. Y'all still going to DC?"

"Yeah. If this deal pulls through, I can finally start building our family home in Benin. I want my son to know where he comes from."

"Son? Y'all found out already?"

"Yep!"

"Congrats, man and I hear you. A'ight be easy."

"You too, bro."

Tekena disconnected the call and opened the text thread with Isoken and responded.

Omw. But how you not gonna feed me tho?

Tekena had been up for a couple of hours. He said his routine prayers, exercised in his gym and had breakfast. He wasn't hungry, but her boldness was refreshing. She went totally against the grain. She was very aware of her femininity but wasn't obligated to use it to appease anyone. She did exactly what she wanted to do, without apologies.

Goldie: I said what I said.

Tekena put the phone in the cup holder and started the engine. "Playlist" by M.I ft Nonso spilled through the speakers. As he sped down the highway, he bobbed his head to the beat. The lyrics of the song expressed what his mouth or mind couldn't articulate.

Isoken was growing on him.

TEKENA PARKED his truck behind a large white delivery van outside Isoken's apartment. She'd sent him the address earlier, but he was confused because it wasn't yet eleven, so he knew he wasn't late. Either she gave him the wrong time, or they were early. Her neighborhood was quiet, or rather as quiet as Lagos could be. Her condo was one of four that shared a common gate. Each condo had a perfect little square of well-manicured grass in front of it. He strolled up the gravel lined walkway to her condo with the caramel Frappuccino he'd gotten her from Starbucks.

"Keni," he called out, walking through the open door. He saw two men putting her wrapped sofa in the center of the room. He gave them a head nod. "Keni!"

"Why are you yelling?" she asked, coming from what he assumed to be the kitchen. Her eyes brightened when she noticed what was in his hand. With a smile and hurried strides, she walked up to him. His eyes roamed over her body. She was dressed in grey sweats with a yellow tank top. Her hair was on top of her head in a bun and her face was bare. For a few seconds, he forgot he was upset with her.

"Hey, Tex, welcome. Hope you slept well. Is that for me?" she asked sweetly, batting her eyes.

Tekena raised his hand above her head, putting the beverage out of her reach. "Oh, you wanna be nice to me now?" Isoken wasn't short, but her five feet eight-inch frame couldn't be compared to his six four.

"I'm always nice," she whined.

Tekena chuckled and handed her the drink. "You're so full of it, man."

Isoken took a long sip through the straw. "Gosh, that was good. I've been longing for one since I got up. Thank you."

"You're welcome. We can't all be mean like you. I had to be the bigger person." He inclined his head toward the man screwing on the foot of the plum-colored couch. "They came early. Or you gave me the wrong time?"

Isoken rolled her eyes at him and strode further into the house. "There you go assuming the worst."

Tekena trailed her into the open floor plan space. It wasn't as small as it looked from the outside. Although the living room was disorganized, it smelled good, like grapefruit, mixed with clean laundry and cinnamon. Pieces of African artwork adorned her grey walls.

"Why would I give you the wrong time? They came early."

"Who knows why you do the things you do." He leaned against the wall. "Nice place."

"Thanks." She took another sip of her drink. "Since you're here, there's no need for them to stay *abi*?"

"Yeah, they can bounce." Tekena walked over to the men and asked if there were any other pieces that they had to bring in.

They nodded and minutes later, they came in with her new coffee table and side stools and two standing lamps. Tekena tipped them and they left.

"So, tell me what you want and where." Tekena removed his sneakers. Instead of answering him, she ran to her dining table and came back with her phone.

"Woman, what are you doing?"

"I'm recording this moment. I don't see you nice like this often."

"Goldie, if you don't get your big head over here, I'll leave you to do this stuff yourself."

"The lies you tell, Pinocchio."

"Try me."

Three hours later, all pieces were unwrapped, detachable parts screwed on and her new living room pieces were set and placed where she wanted them. The standing lamps and side tables were in their proper places and the couches had white and black checkered pillows on them. When he was done with the furniture, she vacuumed and started her diffuser. He was kinda right. The essential oil was grapefruit mixed with pine. Tekena plopped down on the couch. Isoken threw the remote to her plasma television to him.

"Here. You wanna watch something while I take a shower?"

He nodded, leaned back, and closed his eyes.

"Tekena," she called his name softly.

Tekena opened his eyes and turned his head to look at her.

"I appreciate you helping me out. I would've been here all day if it weren't for you."

"You welcome."

"I also ordered us something to eat and it should be here soon."

"Oh, you're feeding me?"

"I guess I can feed the celebrity since you did some manual labor."

"How kind. But what you need to be doing is shopping. I peeped your kitchen. You ain't got nothing."

"Will you take me?"

"Yeah sure, I might as well complete my day's work."

Isoken laughed and climbed the stairs while he looked for something to watch. In truth, he wasn't ready to be out of her presence. He enjoyed every minute he spent with her. Even if most of it consisted of them playfully arguing about sports, world affairs, or the good and evil of reality shows.

***

THE SHRILL RING of the doorbell cut through Isoken's wayward thoughts and set her feet in motion. She darted from her bedroom knowing it was the food delivery. If she didn't hurry, Tekena would end up paying for the food. He had exceeded her expectations and feeding him was the least she could do. She was happy with their newfound friendship. It was exhausting having to always be on her toes with him. She would be lying to herself if she pretended the intense chemistry between them didn't exist. Not only was she aware of it when he was close to her, but Tekena had also begun to creep into her dreams. Since they were both clear about a relationship being the furthest thing from their minds, she felt safe.

"I'll get it. Don't you dare get up." Isoken pointed at him and scurried to the door.

Tekena didn't so much as flinch, which she found strange, but ignored. She opened the door, but there was no one on the other side.

"I thought I heard the doorbell?" She closed the door and moved over to him. His head was still leaned against the headrest.

He turned to her. "You did. The food is on the dining table."

Isoken folded her arms across her chest. "But I just heard the bell."

"What you probably heard was them bringing the silverware they forgot."

"Ugh…"

"What? You thought I was going to let you answer the door yourself?"

"I told you, I've been taking care of myself."

"And you'll continue to do that when I'm gone. Stop sulking and serve the food. I left it in the bag, or I can do that too."

Isoken stomped away. He was insufferable. Sweet, sexy, but still insufferable. She took the food to the kitchen and placed the big, grilled, peppered fish on a platter. Then she plated the sides of rice and fried potato slices on another plate. She walked into the living room and set it on the coffee table. Tekena pushed it out a little further and sat on the floor. She looked at the television and saw he was watching *The Punisher*. They said grace and began to eat.

"You're giving me the silent treatment?" Tekena asked.

"You're so infuriating sometimes."

"Since it's only sometimes, I'll take it." He shrugged and put a piece of fish in his mouth.

She pointed to the television. "You like *The Punisher*? I tried to watch it, but I couldn't."

"Why? The blood?"

"Not only that. The hero was so burdened with grief. It felt too real." An enemy trying to get revenge on the main character killed his whole family and he walked around with the grief and thirst for payback. If the show had been out when Frank first died, there was a fairly good chance she would have binged watched it.

"Your fiancé?"

Isoken nodded.

"I'm here if you wanna talk. I'm a good listener."

Isoken studied him for a few moments, then began telling him about Frank. From how they met to her wanting to run in the opposite direction when she found out his profession. She shared fond memories of both of them, his proposal, their wedding preparation, and his death.

"His death changed my life. It changed the way I view it. It even changed my relationship with God."

"I'm so sorry, Goldie..."

Isoken wiped the corners of her eyes. Tears she didn't want to shed gathered. "You know the thing about grief, after a while, people expect for it to just disappear. God forbid they were used to you being the life of the party. People expect you to be able to get over it and resume the role you played in their happiness. I love my family very much, but their expectation of when I should feel better was and sometimes continues to be exhausting." She made air quotes for the word feel. "The first chance I got, I ran, and I didn't stop running until I couldn't anymore."

"With the job?"

"Yes," she whispered.

"That means you haven't grieved properly?"

Isoken shrugged. "I think I have. I mean, I've been in denial, angry, confused..."

"Is he why you don't date?"

"I do date. But not with intention."

"Yeah, I heard about your six-date rule." He smirked at her. "Why six?"

"Because the sixth date is when I knew I was in love with Frank."

"So, you wanna grow old alone with cats?"

"You all in my business, what about you? What was that lady's name and is she the last time you were serious about someone?"

"Cynthia and yes. She was the only woman apart from my mom and Nana Rubi I've loved."

"What? You've actually told someone you loved them?"

"Are you gonna listen or keep interrupting me?"

"My bad, continue."

"There's nothing else to add really. We were good until we

weren't. I met her during my first year on the circuit. Eight months in, the change started. Suddenly, when I called her after my away races to talk about it, she hadn't watched. Which was cool, since my mom doesn't always watch them either—"

"Why?" Isoken saw sadness wash across his face.

"That's a story for another day."

"Well, it's her loss, because look at you now." Isoken nudged him with her shoulder, trying to lighten the mood.

Tekena smiled at her, but what he was about to say was cut off by his ringing phone. Isoken watched him pull the phone out of his pocket and a crease appeared on his forehead as he stared at the screen.

Tekena sprung to his feet. "Hey Andreas, you good?" He paused. "Oh, hey Elle, what's going on? Is he okay?" He paced.

Isoken stood and cleared their plates to give him privacy. In the kitchen, she put the leftovers in Tupperware containers and stored them in the refrigerator. She busied herself by washing the dishes. All she could decipher from the questions he asked was that the call had something to do with his teammate. When she returned to the living room. Tekena was off the phone and seated on the couch. He rested his elbows on his thighs and cupped his bowed head with both hands.

With hesitant strides, Isoken moved closer to him. She knelt before him and lifted her hands to his wrists. He allowed her to pry his hands from his face but kept his head down.

"Tex, what's wrong?"

His eyes met hers. They were dull and empty. He bit down on his lips, she assumed in an attempt to control his emotion. His downcast expression shattered her heart into a million pieces. Isoken idly caressed the back of his hand with her thumb.

"My teammate and fri—"

"The one that had the accident?"

"Yeah." He took in a breath. "He had a seizure. He's never had one before."

"Oh no. Is he going to be okay?"

"They have to do a lot of tests to make sure he doesn't have some...permanent brain damage." His voice trembled. "I talked to him yesterday. He said he's been having bad headaches lately and now this."

"Tex, I'm so sorry." Isoken pulled him into a hug. She didn't know what else to do with this Tekena. The one who exposed her to his vulnerability.

Minutes passed and they remained in each other's embrace. The moment transcended from her providing him comfort, to them finding a home in each other's arms. A calming, intoxicating sensation took over as Tekena ran his palm up and down her back. Every muscle in her body disobeyed her mental command to move. His beard tickled the crook of her neck, sending shock waves down her spine. Everything about this moment was so wrong but felt so right. With willpower she didn't know she had, Isoken pulled away.

Tekena locked his arms around her waist. She remained in place and rested her hands on his arms. Their eyes remained locked, charging the atmosphere with an electric current that threatened to take them under. Tekena pulled her closer, his smoldering gaze rested on her lips.

"Tex...what are you doing?" Her voice was barely above a whisper.

He traced her bottom lip with the pad of his thumb, his eyes never leaving hers. "I'm trying to see something." His voice had lowered many octaves.

"What?"

"This..."

At that moment, the back-and-forth banter, the arguments, and the immense chemistry between them combined in the moment and erupted when Tekena's lips came crashing down against hers. He cupped her face and invaded her mouth with his tongue performing a slow sensual sweep of the premises. Every nerve ending in her body sparked to life. She had been kissed many times, but nothing compared to the euphoric web she found herself caught in. The thought of her floating with no bearing twisted her gut in fear.

Not again.

Her brain kicked into gear giving her the strength she needed to pull back. She bolted to her feet, wrapped her arms around her body and moved back. Tekena studied her for a few seconds, then he stood and sauntered over to her.

"What's wrong?" He caressed her cheek.

She moved. "That was a mistake. It should never have happened."

Tekena put his hands in his pockets and stared at her. Confusion was written all over his face. He let out a frustrated breath.

"I can't do this with you." Isoken rushed to clarify.

"I'm confused. You enjoyed it as much as I did, so what's the problem?"

"The problem is that you're... you." She pointed an accusatory finger at him and raised her voice in frustration.

He folded his arms across his chest. "What does that mean?"

"I can't have anything to do with you."

"But those other men running around you are cool?" He looked at her as though she was a sour taste. His intense gaze rattled her.

This conversation was going left quickly, and she didn't want that. "It's not that?"

"Then what is it?"

"Tex, you're not good for me." That wasn't what she'd intended to say. She meant it, but not in the way he probably took it. Before she could gather the right words, his expression turned stoic. The damage had been done. In silence, Tekena walked to the counter, and picked up his keys.

Sighing, she squeezed her fingers together. "No wait...I didn't mean it the way it sounds."

"Nah, you good. You said exactly what you meant. See you around." He walked to the door and without a second glance, walked out.

Several minutes later, Isoken lay on the bed beating herself up. She should've handled what happened better. Kissing him confirmed every fear she had about getting too close to him. However, it was only a kiss and she regretted acting like an inexperienced teenager. Chemistry she could control. She had done it for years, so why did she freak out?

They had become friends and worked well together, and she didn't want things to be awkward. She now knew the real him and wasn't ready to lose his friendship. She had to fix this. Decision made, she said her prayers, pulled up the covers and went to sleep.

CHAPTER 17

Contrary to Tekena's initial thought, seventy-two hours wasn't enough time to rid him of the gnawing feeling in his gut. And unfortunately, his... *Nah it can't be.*

He'd done everything in his capacity to rid himself of the strange feeling he had regarding Isoken's actions the other night. Once he left her house, her rejection filled him with rage. He had no one to blame but himself. He'd allowed himself to lose focus. That was all over with now. He was determined to redirect the course of their relationship. Women didn't fit into his agenda and he'd do well to remember that. Especially when it came to someone who thought so low of him that she proclaimed him to be bad for her.

"I'm so excited. I get to see you drive today."

Aduke's comment shook him from his thoughts. He glanced over at her in his passenger's seat before returning his eyes to the road.

The night he left Isoken's, he ran into her at the gas station. Over the last two days, to distract himself from Isoken, they'd been texting back and forth. She was cool. But if she wasn't talking about the glitz of his life, she was fishing for the "real" on his love life. Those questions always brought his mind back to Isoken, although truth be told, she never left.

His communication with Isoken had been strictly via email. He'd arrived at his scheduled appearances and left immediately after. Ben had been the one representing Upward Solutions. Normally he would raise a stink about her unprofessionalism, but he also needed the reprieve from her presence. Pretty soon, however, he knew that they'd have to see each other.

His eyes darted to the timer on his dash. In about twenty minutes to be exact. They were on their way to the Velocity Drive Off event at his driving school. It was one of the biggest events of his promo schedule and he knew there was no way Isoken wouldn't be there.

"Nah baby girl. I can't drive in that capacity due to contractual stipulations. But I'll do a little something."

"Aww, what a shame. Well, I'm glad you invited me," she said.

During one of their conversations, she inquired about the drive off. Somehow, the conversation ended with her inviting herself. Tekena didn't put up much of a fight then, but now he wished he had. Giving her a faint smile, he turned on the radio and "Nobody" by DJ Neptune spilled through the speakers. With the music in the background, he mentally prepared for the day ahead.

Tekena parked in his private parking spot and climbed out. As he and Aduke approached the building, Afrobeats blared from the outdoor speakers. On the way to the private elevator to his office, Tekena paused to look out the front. He was pleased with the setup. The track had been re-marked with white paint. The DJ booth was to the side and the various vendors were ready to go with food, merchandise, drinks. Some months ago, he had five stock cars shipped down to Lagos. Two of them had been decorated for the day's event.

He'd come to learn that if for nothing else, he could count on Isoken to do her job with dedication and excellence.

"This is so nice. I never knew something like this existed in Lagos."

Tekena hiked his brows in surprise. For a minute, he forgot she was with him. "Really? That means I need to step up my advertising. You gonna hook me up?" He waggled his brows at her and she giggled.

These women and the giggles.

He turned back toward the elevator and she followed, slightly brushing her shoulder against him. She'd been doing a lot of that since he picked her up earlier. He didn't want to snap at her, but she seemed to take that as a license to continue.

"Well, come by and see me, then we can talk." She pulled her bottom lip between her teeth.

Tekena smirked and held the door for her to get on. They rode to the second floor in semi silence. He walked up to his receptionist who gave him a quick update on other matters that needed his attention. As they were talking, Eze walked up to him.

"Hey man, I tried to call you earlier." Eze's eyes darted to Aduke then returned to him.

Tekena felt his back pocket. "My bad, I think I left my phone in the car."

"Ms. Korode, nice to see you again." Eze stretched out his hand to Aduke.

"Please call me Aduke and it's nice to see you too." She looked around the lobby. "I was telling Tex, you guys have a nice set up here. I'm glad he invited me."

Eze nodded and smiled. His eyes met Tekena's and quickly returned to Aduke. "Thank you."

The nervousness of his voice reflected the curiosity and confusion in his eyes. If Aduke caught it, there was no indication because she beamed back at Eze, then went back to admiring the décor, the awards showcase, and the paintings on the wall.

Eze pulled Tekena to a safe distance. "Tex, are you crazy? You know Isoken is here."

"And?" He folded his arms across his chest. "I'm not married to either one of them. Nor do I owe them an explanation."

"What happened? Or never mind, the less I know the better." He waved him off.

"Stop being dramatic."

"Look man, we've been planning this event for a long time. Don't cloud it with your drama. You keep that overseas remember?"

Tekena laughed. "You watch too much reality TV. Speaking of, has she arrived?"

"Why do you care?"

"Man, stop playing. This is business."

"Yeah, she's been here. Supervising the setup. I think she's out on the track."

Tekena grunted and signaled to Aduke to join them. She strolled over, her smile still in place.

"Okay cool, I'mma head up to my office before everything starts." Tekena turned to Aduke. "You wanna stay down here or come up with me?"

"I'll go with you," she gushed.

Tekena's eyes met Eze who shook his head. "Good deal, lemme go look for Isoken and see if she needs *my* assistance." Eze gave him the peace sign and chuckled.

Tekena narrowed his eyes at him, but all that got him was a shrug. Why did he even care? He needed to focus.

ISOKEN HANDED OVER THE last batch of t-shirts to the vendor that would be selling them. She had noticed Tekena's car on her way back from the parking lot. She must have missed him when she went to her trunk. Her heart knocked against her ribs. She had a legitimate reason for not seeing him in the last three days. But this event she couldn't miss. So as awkward as she knew it would be, she had to get them back on the same page. To her surprise, she really did miss him.

Isoken walked into the building and spotted Eze. "Hey Eze, I saw Tex's car. Is he here?"

"Erm yeah…"

"Where is he? I need to talk to him. I'm surprised he didn't come look for me."

Isoken followed Eze's gaze to the elevator before they returned to her. His eyes shifted and he rubbed the back of his neck. His vibe was off to her. As though he was uncomfortable. She quickly dismissed the thought. What did he have to be uncomfortable about? They had less than thirty minutes before show time and she needed to see Tekena before everyone started to vie for his attention.

"Is he in his office?"

"Erm, yes. I can help you with whatever you need."

She smiled. Over the last few weeks, she had gotten to peg him as a nice guy.

"Aww, thanks. But I think we're done with the setup. I just brought in that last batch of t-shirts and Ben is helping with the raffle machine."

"No problem, Keni. Thank you. Everything looks great."

She told him she'd see him later and headed to the elevators. Moments later, she was outside Tekena's office. She lifted her hand to knock but was halted by the laughter coming from the other side of the door. *He's not alone.*

"So, you were serious when you said you were single?"

"As a dollar bill."

"What will it take to change your mind?"

Isoken knocked once. Not waiting for an answer, she entered.

Tekena looked up from the laptop in front of him. Their eyes locked on each other. In his eyes, she saw surprise, which quickly turned into defiance. This was a bad idea. He was behind his desk while the newscaster chick was perched on the side of it drinking a Coca Cola.

"Hello, Isoken," the newscaster said.

Isoken tried to remember her name but failed. "Hi," she responded, her eyes not leaving Tekena's.

Tekena stood. "Hey Isoken, you need something?" His tone was dismissive.

"I hope I'm not in the way of anything?" The newscaster lady put her drink on the table and stood.

"Errm...I wanted to—"

"Nah, you're not, baby girl. Isoken is working the event. She probably needs me to okay something." Tekena drew the woman closer to him and placed a kiss on her temple, a gesture the woman relished.

Whatever Isoken wanted to say was blocked by the clog in her throat. The words refused to flow. The sinister look on his face told her he was indeed aware of his actions. What pained her the most was he seemed so unaffected by the hurt he inflicted.

Why is he so mean? When did I relinquish so much power to him? Enough that he can even hurt me.

The woman's giggle snapped Isoken's spine back into place. She straightened her back, took in a lungful of air, and cleared her face of any expression.

"No, I didn't need anything. I only wanted to make sure Mr. Tamuno was ready to give the opening address."

"Yeah. I'm good. We'll be down soon."

Isoken nodded and headed toward the door. A sharp shot of anger pulsed through her veins and if she didn't get away from him, there was no telling what she might do. One thing for certain, she'd never let her guard down with him again.

Later that evening, Isoken took off her sneakers and slipped her feet into her open-toed slides. She wiggled her toes, giving them the room they needed to breathe. She threw her sneakers into her backpack and walked over to the DJ booth. The event was a huge success. It kept her on her toes and gave little time to worry or think about Tekena. Soon after leaving his office, he walked out with his new attachment in tow. The Sports Commissioner opened the event and Tekena gave his address soon after. Then the real fun began.

There was a raffle drawing where the winner won a ride around the track with Tekena. There were biking races and plenty of other games for adults and kids. The food and music flowed endlessly. Isoken got a lot of people to sign up for the grand opening updates by SMS. The press – television, radio, and major newspapers – were all on deck to cover the event. Thankfully, all day, she had no reason to engage with Tekena alone. She wanted to keep it that way. All she had left to do was pay the DJ his balance and head home.

"*Oga*, you did a great job today *o*. Thank you very much," Isoken handed him a brown envelope.

He took the envelope. "*No wahala*. Me too I had fun. Who knew there was something like this in *Naija*?"

"Well hopefully, after today a lot more people will know the sport and come visit the speedway at Ibeju-Lekki."

"I'll spread the word."

"Good, now let's settle so I can get home. I know you're tired too." Isoken waited as he counted the money. She thanked him again and left. She was almost at her car when she saw Eze approaching. Isoken groaned. She had no more energy to be lively or smile. All she wanted was a hot shower, some Lauryn Hill, and her bed.

"Hey Keni, good job today. To see what you had on paper come to life was a sight to behold."

"Thanks, but all I did was supervise. I'm glad it was a success."

"The workers can only be as good as their leader."

Isoken chuckled at the saying he had backward. "The cleaning crew will be here bright and early tomorrow to break down the tents and clear the area."

"Okay, I'll tell security to be expecting them."

Isoken unlocked her car and tossed her backpack in the back. "You have a good evening, Eze. I'll see you soon. Well, after Christmas. Since we have that concert on New Year's Eve."

"Yeah, that's right. With all that's going on, it's hard to imagine Christmas is in five days."

"Yep, well goodnight." This was the longest she'd spoken to Eze. Any other time, Tekena would bamboozle him out of the way. She looked over and saw his car. She didn't want to run into him. So, without giving Eze the room to keep her talking, she got in her car and left.

When she got home, Isoken did exactly what she had envisioned. Even with the hot shower and food, sleep refused to come. This restlessness was familiar and the reason she kept her heart guarded. It was almost midnight and instead of enjoying a trip to la-la land, she was sitting crisscross applesauce in the middle of her bed eating ice cream. Thinking about a man who had shown her he didn't care about her.

She turned on the television and flipped through her cable channels. She came across the show, *Snapped*. A smile crossed her face remembering it used to be her sister's favorite show. With the way she was feeling, she regretted teasing her sister about the show. She saw now why she needed it. It was therapeutic.

Isoken was halfway through one episode when her phone buzzed. Setting her bowl to the side, she reached under her pillow. The two simple words she saw stopped her heart and made her see red at the same time.

T2: I'm sorry

Isoken deleted the message and returned the phone to its position. His apology did nothing for her. The only thing it did was fuel her rage and melt her ice cream. Isoken stumbled out of bed to her kitchen. She rinsed out her bowl and returned to her bedroom. Her physical exhaustion finally caught up with her. The chorus of "Take A Bow" by Rihanna popped into her head as sleep took over, ending the turmoil going on in her mind. She'd have to deal with Tekena another day. She rubbed her stomach, reminding herself of what was really important to her.

Christmas came and went with Isoken still not talking to Tekena. The last few days had been torturous, to say the least. He would kick his own behind if he could. He had texted, called, and gone by her house. All to no avail. She was gone like smoke in the wind. The only place he hadn't tried was her office. For one, they were on a break for the holidays and two, he didn't want to give the impression that something was wrong with their working relationship. If he had to do it all over again, he would've had a conversation with her. He hadn't expected things to go the way they did at the drive off.

The minute she walked out of his office, he realized he'd blown it. He tried to fix it, but she wouldn't give him the chance. She had ignored him the whole event. To make matters worse, Eze and Ben swarmed around her like moths to a flame. Eze, he knew wouldn't try anything, but Ben not so much. The jealousy that raged through him had him clinging to Aduke more.

He'd wanted to get a reaction and distraction from Isoken. That backfired. Now Aduke thought they were more than they really were and had been blowing up his phone ever since. Not able to take it anymore, he had a conversation with her, apologizing for giving her the wrong impression. He flew home

Christmas Eve to spend the holiday with his parents. Now it was two days after Christmas and his flight from Port Harcourt had landed in Lagos.

Seated in the back of his car service, Tekena was en route to Isoken's house before she eluded him again. It was now a full week since she had disappeared, and he was determined to get her to talk to him. Tekena had finally broken down and asked Osaro where she was. She'd left Lagos to Benin the day after the drive off but had landed back in Lagos last night. It was barely seven, so he knew she would still be home.

Sometime later, Tekena knocked on her door with an urgency he couldn't explain but was warranted. He put his hands in his pockets and leaned his head on her door. He rang the doorbell and soon he heard the locks disengage. He straightened up and waited for the door to open. When it did and her face came into view, he let out a breath he didn't know he was holding. The words he wanted to say remained trapped as his eyes roamed over her body. Her hair was wrapped in a silk scarf with the end of the large plait hanging on her shoulder. The yellow silk pajama set she had on contrasted perfectly against her skin.

Thank God she put on a robe.

He must've taken too long to speak because her voice broke him away from his thoughts.

"What are you doing here, Tekena?" Her voice was still groggy from sleep. "Didn't you go home?"

"I did..."

"Okay..." She folded her arms across her chest and raised her eyebrows. "Do you know what time it is?"

There she is.

"I wanted to...no I needed to talk to you."

"Why? Did I forget some work I was supposed to get done for you?"

Tekena raised his hand to his beard and tugged on it. This was going to be more difficult than he thought. "May I come in?"

"No. What do you want?"

"Come on Goldie, I texted you."

"I know."

"I called. Many times."

"*Ehn*? Do you want an award?"

"Please let me in so we can talk."

"Mr. Tamuno, I don't want to—"

"Knock it off Keni, I'm trying to apologize."

"For what exactly? You're good."

"Look I didn't come here to fight—"

"Glad we got that cleared up because I don't have the energy to engage you. But what's not gonna happen is you coming here, before normal people are up, and demand I accept an apology I didn't ask for. You showed me my place and I'm occupying it with pleasure." She placed her hands on her hips.

Tekena narrowed his eyes at her. He should've known that coming to plead with her nicely wasn't going to work. She wasn't listening to him and he was running out of time. Her next move would be to slam the door in his face, and he might not be able to get her to open it again. If they didn't mend the crack in their relationship now, it would only grow wider. After the last couple of days, her friendship wasn't something he was willing to let go of.

Before she uttered another word, Tekena picked her up and threw her over his shoulder. He entered her house and used his leg to slam the door shut.

"Tekena, what's wrong with you? Put me down."

He ignored the light blows she gave him on his back and walked to the kitchen. He placed her on the counter and stood between her legs. He stared at her. Her beauty set off emotions and reactions he wasn't used to. He took in a breath then exhaled.

"What I did was wrong. I didn't do anything with her. I don't have an excuse, but to say I was a jerk—"

"Are..."

"Huh?"

"You *are* a jerk."

"Can you let me get this out? Please."

Isoken folded her arms across her chest and rolled her eyes at him like a disgruntled child. He'd take it as long as she let him talk.

"Thank you. Like I was saying I was a jerk and I'm sorry. I don't handle rejection very well."

She shrugged. "From what I could tell, you were very well received."

"Give me a break, Isoken. I'm talking about you. You!" He pushed away from her.

A few beats passed between them. They kept their eyes locked, but neither of them spoke.

Isoken sighed and rubbed her hand against her forehead. "Tekena what do you want me to say?"

"Say you forgive me. You don't only work with me, but you're also my friend. I don't want to mess that up. Please tell me I haven't."

"You hurt me." Her voice was low.

The pain in her tone felt like a broken shard piercing his skin. He walked back over to her. "I know and I'm so sorry. I'll make it up to you. Give me a chance. Losing you can't happen."

"You haven't lost me. We lost our way I guess, but we'll be okay."

"Thank you." Tekena kissed her forehead. He helped her down and moved back.

"Don't thank me yet. You will be making this up to me." She poked his chest with her index finger. "And the next time you decide to get in your feelings and hurt me...I'll put an arrow in you."

"I won't have it any other way." He fanned his hand in front of his nose. She frowned at him. "Now go brush your teeth. That breath is bumping."

Isoken cupped her mouth and blew in her hand. Tekena laughed at the evil look she gave him.

"This is why I can't stand you. You play too much."

"Whatever you say, Goldie, but go get acquainted with your toothbrush real quick."

Isoken waved him off and called him a couple of names under her breath as she made her way up the stairs.

"Get yourself together and come take a ride with me. I'm buying breakfast."

"Leave me alone," she hollered at him.

"Didn't we just establish that can't happen? Hurry up, I'm starving."

ISOKEN SNAPPED the lid on the plastic container and put the left-over fried rice in the refrigerator. "Capable God" by Judikay played in the background as she tidied up her house. Her mind pondered the verse from Mathew 14:31, ***Jesus immediately reached out his hand and took hold of him, saying to him, "O you of little faith, why did you doubt?"*** The ladies from her Bible study had just left. They discussed doubt and its underlying cause. Man's preference. The reason we often find ourselves doubting God's presence was that we expected His presence to accommodate our preference. When that doesn't happen, we doubt His ability. She thought about all the times she had done that over the years. The ringing of her phone interrupted her thoughts.

She picked her phone up from the couch. She smiled when she saw the caller. Tekena had been busy with Eze while she was pulled away to contribute briefly to another project. So they barely talked the day before.

"Hello?"

"Hey you? How was Bible study?"

"You remembered?"

"I remember everything you tell me. So how was it?"

Isoken was glad their minor hiccup was behind them. After barging into her house, he had taken her to breakfast, then they drove to the Speedway to see the progress. It was on the outskirts of Lagos, so it took them about an hour. She teased him about really being sorry because he didn't ask her to drive once and she knew how he hated driving. They ended the day with an early dinner then a trip to Nike's art gallery.

For the next few minutes, Isoken gave him a recap. He asked a few questions before changing the subject to their upcoming itinerary. Isoken turned off the lights downstairs and headed to her bedroom. She yawned.

"I see you tired. I'mma let you go. But before that I got a favor to ask you."

Isoken plopped down on her bed. "Should I be scared?"

Tekena chuckled, a sound she had come to love. "No, bighead."

"Hmmm, I'll be the judge of that. What do you want?"

"I have this event I gotta go to in a couple of days and I want you to go with me."

Isoken sat up. Hanging out with Tekena and going out together for an event were two completely different things. "Black tie?"

"Yeah."

"Why me?"

"Whatchu mean, why you? You're my friend and I don't wanna go alone."

"So, you mean to tell me that as long as you've lived in Lagos, you don't have any women on standby?"

"I do have women on standby. If you tell me no, I'll call one of them."

Isoken rolled her eyes as though he could see her. She hated how brutally honest he could be at times. But she loved that he always kept it straight with her.

"Look, these things are always so boring. At least with you, my friend. I wouldn't go completely out of my mind." He took a breath. "What do you say?"

"What time does it start?"

"Seven thirty."

"I know you said black tie, any particular dress color?"

"No. Just put on something sexy." Isoken grunted and he chuckled. "I'll pick you up at seven."

"Okay."

"A'ight get your beauty sleep, beautiful, and I'll talk to you in the morning."

The minute he disconnected the call, panic set in. She had just agreed to be seen with Tekena in a capacity that didn't involve her job. What was she going to wear? She already had a standing appointment for her hair and nails for the next day. But where would she find a dress at the last minute? Somehow, something old in her closet wouldn't do. The thought lingered on her mind throughout her shower, prayers and until she closed her eyes for the night.

CHAPTER 19

Two days later, with her make-up done, Isoken stood in front of the mirror for a final check. She ran her hands down the cool satin, noting with satisfaction how gently it flowed over her curves. From the moment she saw the olive-green dress on the store mannequin, she'd wanted it. Lucky for her, her seamstress was able to fit it for her, adjusting the dress to her exact measurements. With her hair in an updo and soft tresses falling to each side of her face, she smiled at her image. Her doubt that she may not be able to pull off a sequin-adorned bodice was unfounded. The dress was made for her.

Isoken leaned into the mirror and touched her lips up with a nude lip gloss when her doorbell rang. When she reached the door, she took in a deep breath and opened it. Her breath hitched as her heart went into overdrive at the sight before her. Tekena had on a tuxedo. The burgundy double-breasted jacket completed the Monte Carlo look with a white shirt and black pants underneath. He finished his look with a black bow tie and pocket square. He looked like he fell out of heaven and onto the cover of a magazine.

Isoken followed his gaze as he lazily perused her body, sending shivers down her spine. When his eyes lifted to hers, she smiled back at him.

"Oh wow!" he whispered. "Beautiful is too small a word." He lifted his hand to caress her jaw before cupping her neck. "Simply amazing."

The warm woodsy scent of his cologne floated up her nostrils. "You...you clean up pretty nice yourself." She cleared her throat. She needed to get a grip. *I'm doing a favor for a friend.* Isoken reminded herself of a fact she struggled to keep close to her mind all day.

"You ready?" He opened his hands.

She nodded, giving him her keys. "Ready."

"Then let's do this." He ushered her out and locked the door behind them. Settling her in the passenger seat, he caressed her cheek with the back of his hand. "I'm going to be the envy of every man there tonight."

Several minutes later with his hand rested on her back, Tekena ushered Isoken into the prestigious Bolderna hotel. Isoken was grateful for the little time she had in the fresh air. The tension in the car, their chemistry and his cologne all conspired to drive her insane.

Isoken's eyes bugged as they entered the ballroom. Crystal chandeliers spiraled from the arching lavender ceiling, illuminating the shimmering wall and floors that were accented by large windows draped in expensive looking fabric. The bar was in the corner of the room that opened to an outdoor patio area. The melody of "Doyin" by Mr. Eazi & Simi blared from the speakers. Tekena introduced her to a few people as they made their way to their seats. After making sure she was seated, he walked over to the bar to get them something to drink.

"Here's to an enjoyable evening with gorgeous company," Tekena toasted when he returned.

Isoken smiled before they clicked their glasses together. She took a sip of her raspberry fizz and they talked while waiting for Eze.

"You're gonna be okay by yourself, right?" Tekena glanced at his phone briefly before returning his eyes to her. "Eze is parking now."

Isoken leaned back and furrowed her brows. "Yes, I'll be fine. This is my home all year round, remember? Besides, I know this is work for you."

Tekena was about to respond when Eze walked up.

"Hey, you two." Eze smiled at them.

"Wassup, man," Tekena absently responded to a text on his phone.

"Hey, Eze."

"You look lovely, Isoken." He stretched his hand. She took it and he lifted it to his mouth.

"Man, get your mouth off her. You don't see me sitting here?" Tekena growled.

"Thank you. You look handsome yourself." Isoken narrowed her eyes at Tekena. He lifted his brows in challenge, and she nudged his shoulder. "Leave him alone."

Eze chuckled. "Calm down, fighter. Let's go. Our attention is needed over there." He pointed to a group of people on the other side of the room.

Tekena turned to her. "I'll be right back."

Isoken nodded and both men turned to leave when Tekena halted and retraced his steps. He lowered his head to whisper in her ear. "I'm not in the mood to fight tonight. Behave yourself. Any man that comes close to you, send them on their way."

"Tekena, it would be in your best interest to walk away now." She shook her head and lifted her glass.

He kissed her cheek. "I'm gone. But please don't test me."

After sitting for a couple of minutes, Isoken got up to mingle. Her eyes often found Tekena's. From across the room, their gazes locked and held for a few seconds before he winked and returned to his conversation. Several new connections and tons of small talk later, Isoken made her way from the bathroom. She turned the corner and walked into Tekena.

"Don't disappear on me like that again," he said, lifting himself from the wall he was leaned on.

She shrugged. "You were busy. Didn't want to distract you."

He walked closer to her with his hands in his pocket. "You're my best kind of distraction." A grin formed at his lips. "Come on, the schmoozing is over. Let's get something to eat and enjoy the rest of the party."

Hand in hand, they walked back into the main ballroom. As they filled their plates with delicacies from the buffet, Tekena filled her in on the outcome of his talk with the potential sponsors. Soon after, they were seated at their table and engaged in a light conversation.

"King" by Fireboy started to pump through the speakers and some made their way to the dance floor. Isoken forked some fruit from Tekena's plate, earning her a smirk.

"Always eating off my plate."

Isoken closed her eyes and savored the juicy fruit. Tekena wiped the corner of her mouth with the pad of his thumb. Putting the extra juice in his mouth, he stood.

"Dance with me."

In the middle of the floor, he swung her around gently and her arm effortlessly went around his neck while the other rested on his chest. Tekena hooked one arm around her waist and clasped his other hand over hers. As they swayed to the rhythm, Isoken struggled to regulate her breathing and quiet the neurons firing bullets to her nerve endings.

"I hope you're having a good time," Tekena whispered against her hair.

"What have you done to the real Tekena?" Isoken wasn't used to the man who stood before her, sweet and gentle.

He let out a light chuckle. "It's me, baby. You thought you had me figured out, huh? I'm multi-talented."

"I'm beginning to see that. And I am having a great time."

"So...does that mean I'm completely out of the doghouse?"

Her head jerked back in surprise. "What? You were never

really there…"

"A week woman, you didn't speak to me for a freaking week." He dipped her playfully. Then whispered in her ear. "I almost went crazy."

"We thank God you didn't." She giggled and Tekena smiled. They'd fallen back into step, but they or rather she, deliberately avoided talking about what went wrong. From the look on his face, he was now ready to.

"I need to ask you something."

"Go ahead."

"I know you said I'm not good enough for you, but in the years since your fiancé's death, nobody has been?"

Isoken stopped moving and frowned up at him. "I never said you weren't good enough for me. I said you are bad for me."

"Same difference."

"No, it's not."

"Explain."

"I enjoyed kissing you. I—"

Before she could get the next words out of her mouth, Tekena practically dragged her off the dance floor. He muttered under his breath. Stunned, Isoken let him lead her to the patio.

"Will you slow down? *Your craze don dey start again?*"

He glanced at her over his shoulder and kept moving, although he slowed down some. A few minutes later, they were in a corner away from other guests. The Lagos skyline provided a beautiful backdrop. One she couldn't fully admire since Tekena seemed to have something more important on his mind. Before she could ask him anything, Tekena bent down and covered her lips with his. Isoken snaked her arms around his neck. He pulled her close, their bodies meshed. He caressed her nape sending her brain into a frenzy. Their mutual need for air pulled them apart. The smoldering stare he gave her sent shivers up her arm.

"What was that about?" she asked once she caught her breath.

"You had me going crazy for days. Kicking myself for coming on to you and wondering why I wasn't good enough for you.

Only for you to turn around and say you enjoyed it?" He put his hands in his pockets, let out an exaggerated breath. "You're going to be the death of me."

Isoken chuckled. "No. Your imagination and ego are going to be the death of you."

His brows lifted and she shook her head. "You brushed me off remember? Before that, I was trying to explain that you didn't do anything wrong. But you and I can't happen." Isoken rubbed her hand across her arm to abate the evening chill.

Tekena removed his jacket and draped it over her shoulders. "So, I'm clear...why not?"

"It has nothing to do with you as a person—"

"Spit it out, Goldie." Tekena's brows moved together, showing his growing impatience.

"Because I can't get involved with another man who has a death wish."

"So your resistance is because of what I do?"

"Yes, but I don't want you to change. I want you to be all that you can be. And achieve all your heart's desires. I can't risk involvement while you do it. What we have now is good."

Tekena smiled down at her.

"Why are you smiling?"

"No reason." He walked into her personal space. "Good to know I have an effect on the no nonsense Isoken Adolo."

She rolled her eyes. "There goes that ego of yours again."

"Call it what you want. I'm glad I'm not out here by myself. The attraction between us can't be denied."

"True, but that doesn't change the fact that we can't act on it." She folded her arms across her bosom. She studied him and watched a grin creep across his face. "Tex...I'm serious. In about six weeks, you'll head back, and we'll be good."

"Well, luckily for the both of us, I don't want a relationship either." He focused his gaze on her lips before connecting with her eyes. "But nothing says we can't be kissing friends."

"None of that either."

He raised his hands in surrender, but every cell in her body told her that he wasn't going to make this easy for her. Her phone buzzed and she removed it from her clutch. Looking at the message, she snickered.

"Who's that?"

"Someone wishing me a happy belated birthday."

"You had a birthday? When was it?"

"Two days before Christmas."

"Why didn't you tell me?"

"I wasn't speaking to you...duh. And it never came up before then."

"You're so petty. Now I feel terrible."

"As you should. Don't you think we should go back in? Won't they be looking for you?" She glanced back at the door.

"Come away with me next weekend," Tekena blurted out.

"To where? We have a tight schedule; we can't be gallivanting."

He grabbed her hand. "I know and there's nothing on it for next weekend." His eyes pleaded with her. "We have the concert for New Year's Day in two days and another photoshoot, but after that we're good. You've worked me to death woman. I need rest."

"You had a week of rest."

"You weren't speaking to me. Trust me I wasn't resting."

"Aww, I feel special..."

"Don't let it get to your head. Now, what do you say? I want to make up for missing your birthday."

"You haven't told me to where and are you going for business or—"

"It's a business trip, but I'll move some things around so we can have playtime."

"Okay, where?"

"Morocco, well it's actually Tweede Kans Cove."

"Never heard of it."

"Me either. Eze got me a meeting with the guy that's

supposed to be a heavyweight," he said. "His sister is getting married that weekend, so will you please be my plus one?"

Isoken took out her phone, opened a browser and put in the keywords Tweedes, Morocco and wedding. After buffing for a few seconds, an entertainment blog came up. She quickly browsed the article.

"What! Of course, I'll go with you. Thank you." She danced at the spot. She didn't know the DuBois-Arazis, but the groom was the producer of the 891 Crew. That meant her crush, Niyi DaSilva would be there. Since she missed the chance to see him at her sister's photo shoot, this was her chance. God's always faithful.

"Okay, now you got me looking at you funny. Why what's up?"

"Niyi DaSilva is going to be there and—"

"Who's that?"

"If you let me finish. Anyway, this article says the Dubois-Arazis are filthy rich. The oldest daughter is marrying the producer of the 891 Crew."

"Yeah, Eze said she was marrying a singer, but why does that make you happy?"

"I'm sure his best friend will be there—"

"Okay, you not going. That's dead. I'm standing right here and you're crushing over someone else." Tekena turned and began walking toward the door.

Isoken followed him. He was shaking his head and she was doing everything she could to stifle her laughter. "Come on, friends do nice things for friends."

"I ain't that kinda friend, baby. Now drop it; you're not going." Tekena held the door open for her. A couple more dances and they were back at their table. Tekena refused to talk about the trip again. Isoken found it cute but knew she would be on that plane.

Yes Lord, You always come through!

CHAPTER 20

"Aye man, do I need to buy you your own iPad?"

Two days later, arriving backstage at the Grand stadium, Tekena located Isoken. His mood soured when he saw Ben hanging over her shoulder. Isoken turned and gave him her signature stare. The one that was supposed to scare him but was as sexy as looks came. Tekena stood on the other side of her and gave Ben a head nod which sent him on his way.

"You know I'm not afraid of you."

"That was unprofessional. Stop doing that," she whispered tersely.

"We passed professional even before we started working together. So don't give me that."

"Whatever...stop acting like a jealous boyfriend. That's how rumors start. You know you are big time. Or should I say bigger time in *Naija* now."

Tekena groaned. Coming home used to be his refuge, unlike Europe where he moved around under the radar. He had known he'd have to promote the motorway. What he didn't expect was how good Isoken was at her job. Now especially on the Island, he didn't go unnoticed. That wasn't going to change his behavior toward Isoken though.

He shrugged and shoved his hands in his pockets. "If he can't defend himself, then he doesn't need to be standing next to you."

"Tex, stop."

"Goldie, no." He mocked her voice then looked around. "So, what we got?"

Isoken gave him a pointed look then called over the promoter and the host of the event. The event was sponsored by the government and he was tagged as the guest celebrity host. For the next couple of minutes, they both explained his role in the night's celebration. She reiterated how he should incorporate the opening of the speedway. They had promo reels on standby which would play between acts. They wrapped up and left. The next words Tekena wanted to say were interrupted when someone yelled out Isoken's name.

"Keni! Keni!"

They turned in the direction of the unwelcomed howl. Isoken squinted her eyes and tugged Tekena's arm sending his nerves on high alert. Tekena saw a man making hurried strides their way.

"I need a favor," she whispered.

The panicked look on her face annoyed him. "You know him? Did he put his hands on you?" Tekena tightened his fists.

She placed her hand on her hip. "What? No."

"Then what? You better hurry up. He's getting closer."

"I kinda stood him up a while ago. And I'm not ready for any drama. So, act like we're together."

Before he could respond, the man was in their presence. Tekena sized up the man that stood before them. He glanced at Isoken. He didn't get how this man was someone she'd given the time of day.

"Hey Keni, I thought that was you,"

Tekena watched in irritation as the guy literally undressed her with his eyes. His annoyance caused him to swing into action. Tekena stood behind Isoken and pulled her closer. Their bodies almost flushed with her back against his chest. The peachy vanilla scent of the perfume she had on drifted up his nose. They'd established that friendship was all that could exist between them. That however didn't mean he couldn't have some fun.

"Hey Akin, what are you doing here?"

"I came with my uncle. He's the manager of one of the performers tonight." Akin's eyes roamed her body once more before he said. "You look really beautiful tonight."

Tekena had heard enough. *Am I invisible?* He cleared his throat and Isoken let out a light chuckle laced with nervous energy.

"Akin, meet Tekena. Tex, this is Akin." She made the introductions.

Tekena watched as the man's expression changed from surprise to annoyance before settling on his version of a blank stare. He stretched his hand out for a handshake which Tekena ignored. Instead, he acknowledged him with a head nod. "Hey, what's up."

Isoken elbowed his stomach lightly, but he ignored her. Dude lost the respect of a handshake when he openly lusted over her while he was standing right there. Akin got the message and put his hand down.

"Keni, can I talk to you in private please."

"Erm—"

"Aye man, don't you see me standing here?" Tekena scoffed.

"Tex..."

"Yes, baby?" Tekena leaned down a little placing his chin in the crook of her neck. He used his teeth to graze her skin softly, then blew on the spot before brushing his lips against her skin. He was sure it was against her will, but her body melted into his and her breath hitched. A satisfied grin spread across his face as he lifted his head. She turned to him, he saw the fire in her eyes, and mixed in there was desire.

"Since when do you allow anyone to talk for you? The Keni I knew wasn't a pushover."

"Look dude, she ain't going with you. And she's not a pushover, but respectful of her man." Tekena knew he was going to get chewed out once this was over, but he was enjoying himself too much to stop.

"Babe, I can speak for myself," Isoken said with clenched teeth. "Akin, this isn't a good time. The show is about to start."

"Nah baby, you are giving the man false hope for the future. Don't do that..." Tekena shook his head playfully. "Don't play with the man's feelings like that."

She narrowed her eyes at him. He puckered his lips and gave her an air kiss. She turned to speak when Akin blurted out.

"You know what it's fine. I knew you weren't wife material anyway."

Tekena moved to Isoken's side. "Hold up, you were trying to marry this dude?"

"If the two of you don't shut up, I will smack you both." Isoken turned to Akin. "I went out on two dates with you...two. Don't come here acting like it was more than that. If you were looking for a wife, too bad because that was never happening." She then turned to Tekena. "And you, don't play me." She turned and walked off leaving both of them standing there.

Tekena felt bad for the dude because despite giving him a hard time, he could see he liked her. He didn't feel bad enough to apologize though.

"Man, go on, here you come messing up my happy home." He turned and saw Isoken with nerd Ben again. *How am I fighting off men left and right for this woman? I don't even have this much drama.*

"I'm coming to the rescue, honey," he hollered. He raised his hand for emphasis jogging toward her.

TEKENA TOOK the microphone and walked on stage the final time that evening. The show was thrilling from start to finish. He not only enjoyed himself but got to meet a lot of new people.

"As they say, all things must come to an end. I wanna thank each one of you for coming out tonight."

The thunderous sound of the audience's applause and cheers was deafening. Tekena waited for it to die down before he invited them to check out the website for the remaining events of the year. Minutes later, he walked off the stage and was met by Ben. Isoken was mad at him going overboard so she avoided him when she could. All night she gave him dry responses and one-word answers. He found it amusing, but to send Ben to him was annoying.

"Where's Isoken?" Tekena asked.

"She wasn't feeling well, so she went to the car." He handed Tekena a paper.

Tekena took it but didn't bother looking at it. "Is she still in the car?"

"Yes, but I'll let her know the show is over so she can go home."

"Don't." Tekena frowned and moved in the direction of the parking lot. He was stopped by Eze who wanted to introduce him to some people.

"*Abeg* either stall or set up the meeting for another time. I gotta go." Tekena jogged out of the arena. When he arrived earlier, he parked in the space she had reserved next to her car, so he knew exactly where she was. He walked up to her car. His heart rate quickened when he saw her chair reclined. She rubbed on her stomach with one hand and clenched her phone with the other.

Tekena instantly felt anger rise within him. She was sick and out here by herself because she was too stubborn to tell him. He'd seen her in discomfort earlier, but she brushed him off when he inquired. He thought she was still mad, but she was ill and didn't want him to know. He knocked on the window lightly, careful not to scare her. She turned on her interior light, then frowned when she recognized him.

"Goldie, open this door with your hard head."

She lowered the window. "Is it over?"

"Yes. Why didn't you tell me you were sick?"

"Tekena, don't start with me. How was I supposed to tell you in the middle of an event? Besides, you can't do anything for me."

"I don't wanna hear nothing about no event. Open the door."

She did as he asked. He squatted next to her. "What's wrong with you and why can't I help you?"

She opened her mouth to talk, but a long groan escaped instead. Her face contorted with pain.

"Baby, what's wrong" He lifted his hand to brush the hair that had fallen in her face. She looked at him and he saw a tear. He'd never seen this level of vulnerability in her. She worked extra hard at keeping her wall up. Her teary eyes were like a vice to his heart.

"I have cramps and it hurts really bad," she whispered.

Relief washed over him. At least it was something he could handle. He hadn't been around a lot of women during their monthly cycle, but he remembered his mom used to have them bad.

"Have you taken any medicine?"

"No, I wasn't expecting it. So, I don't have any with me."

"At home?" He continued to brush her hair lightly.

She nodded.

"Okay, hang on." Tekena stood, brought out his phone from his pocket and dialed. "Aye Eze, I need a favor." After giving him instructions, Tekena placed the phone in his pocket and squatted next to her again. "You need anything from this car tonight?"

She looked at him puzzled. "No, I'm going to go home."

It was clear she didn't understand his question, but when she grunted again, he didn't have time to explain. "Come on." He bent down to lift her.

She crinkled her forehead. "Where are you taking me?"

He lifted her bridal style. "Relax, I'm taking you home. Don't fight me, you'll lose."

To his surprise, she didn't say another word. He carried her to his car and placed her in it. Isoken groaned and curled her body in a fetal position. He reclined the seat and fastened her seat belt. Returning to her car, he retrieved her items and locked it. Placing them in his back seat, he climbed in. Her groan pierced his heart. He gently removed her hair from her face before starting the engine.

Tekena arrived at Isoken's house and hurried to get her out of the car. He wanted to pick her up, but she insisted on walking. He helped her into the house, turned on the lights and guided her to the couch.

"If you want to go shower, I'll fix you one of those sandwiches you like," Tekena said.

Isoken nodded, took her shoes and purse from him and made her way up the stairs while he headed to the kitchen. He put on the water for the citrus tea she loved. Next, he made some sardine sandwiches. Minutes later, he carried the food to the living room as she descended the stairs. He placed the food and beverage on the side table then looked at her. His words were caught in his throat by her beauty. She was freshly showered, and he could smell the scents of mango and strawberry.

"Why are you staring at me like that?" Her tone was low.

Her question brought him out of his daze. He wasn't going to answer though. Instead, he asked, "How are you feeling?"

"Tired."

"Come, sit down and eat."

She walked closer and gave him a faint smile. "My favorite. Thanks, Tex."

Tekena watched as she took dejected steps to the couch. "You're welcome, but what's wrong? You seem sad."

Isoken waved him off. "It's nothing." She picked up one of the sandwiches. "These are really good. Are you trying to make up for going overboard earlier?"

"When?"

"When I told you to do me a simple favor and you turned it into a fiasco."

"I have no idea what you're talking about. You asked for a

favor and I delivered. "For that you owe me. Me taking care of you...that's completely on the house."

He motioned to what she had in her hand.

"What's this?"

"My heating pad and my meds."

"Okay give me the pad let me get it ready. And get you some water. Eat and drink your tea before it gets cold." He walked toward the kitchen.

"Yes, doctor."

Soon after, he returned, giving her the pad which she placed on her stomach. He set the water down. She finished eating, drank the medicine and lay down. Tekena covered her with a blanket and took the empty plate to the kitchen. By the time he finished washing up, she was asleep. Not wanting to wake her, he picked her up and carried her up the stairs. He placed her under the covers she'd already thrown back. Tekena covered her and brushed his lips lightly against her forehead. Turning to leave, his eye caught a pamphlet on the nightstand. His curiosity heightened when he saw babies on it. Against his better judgment, he picked it up and flipped through.

Fertility clinic?

Was she trying to have a baby?

Was she adopting one?

Was she being a surrogate for a family?

All these questions ran through his head in quick succession, causing his chest to tighten. The most important question however was...why?

CHAPTER 21

"Talk about traveling in style."

Isoken walked to the back of the jet with Tekena following. Eze had stopped at the cockpit to give the crew some instructions. She settled into a seat and closed her eyes. It had been a stressful week. After the concert, she was no longer in the mood for Morocco. Even Niyi couldn't get her excited.

Worse than that, she couldn't stand another concerned look from Tekena. He'd been so sweet and attentive the last few days, but she hated feeling weak. She was the strong one. The person everyone brought their problems to. This was only a setback; she'd try again. She mentally dismissed the disappointment that threatened to swallow her whole.

"You want something to eat or drink?"

Isoken opened her eyes and turned her head to Tekena. Dressed in a simple, black striped jogging suit, he settled in beside her. Everything about him screamed to her fluttering heart. She desperately needed his arms around her, but she couldn't go there.

"We just had breakfast. I'm fine. I promise."

He searched her eyes. "You've been saying that for the past couple of days. But I don't believe it."

"Well, I can't help you there."

He observed her for a few more minutes. She winked causing him to smile and let her off the hook. Soon after, with Eze and his lady friend on the other end of the jet, the pilot announced their intention to take off. Isoken buckled herself in and braced for the flight. While Tekena worked on his iPad, Isoken put on her earphones and listened to music. She rubbed her stomach wondering what went wrong.

A few hours later, Isoken's tired eyes adjusted to the darkened space. Tekena's head was slightly leaned against hers while hers was on his shoulder. She didn't want to wake him but the pressure on her bladder trumped her good gesture. She stirred a little, causing him to wake up.

"You okay?" His raspy voice tickled her skin.

Without speaking, she nodded and pointed to the back. After handling her business, she freshened up a little and returned to her seat. Tekena had two glasses of juice for them. Smiling at him, she shook her head, ridding it of her funk. She was determined to get it together. This trip was big for him and she didn't want to put a downer on it. He opened his mouth to speak and Isoken put her index finger to his lips.

"Please don't ask if I'm fine. I am. I've been in a bad mood and I'm sorry."

He took her hand. "You wanna talk about it?"

She shook her head. "No. I'm okay. I promise." She looked at the screen on his open iPad. He had his driving school website up. He followed her gaze and was about to turn the device off.

"No, if you have to work, it's cool."

"Nah, I was only responding to an email. I'm done."

Isoken took a sip of her juice. "I don't think you ever told me how you got into racing. Or the school for that matter."

Tekena glanced at his device again. She couldn't place the emotions she saw travel across his face. He returned his eyes to her, his expression blank.

"It's not a rosy story. It's not the typical 'I was four years old and I knew' story."

Isoken laughed. "I know right? It's always four, five, or six."

Tekena chuckled. "That generic story always bothered me. Why can't seven or eight get some love?"

They enjoyed a laugh, something she hadn't afforded herself in recent days. "Okay don't change the subject. Tell me."

Tekena turned his full body to her. "Let's make a deal. If I tell you, you have to promise to answer a question for me."

Her forehead crinkled. "Okay..."

His eyes bored into her. "I'm serious, Goldie."

Isoken studied him. His tone was solemn. In a matter of seconds, a playful Tekena gave way to a subdued one. They'd come a long way. She even trusted him but wasn't sure she was ready to bare her soul completely to him. Especially now that she was feeling vulnerable. But if she wanted to take, she had to learn to give.

"Deal."

He hung his head for a few seconds, then lifted it. His eyes were sad. Over the next couple of minutes, he told her the detailed story of his dad's death and how his mother's remarriage so soon after affected him. As he spoke, so many things began to make sense. She'd always wondered why he seemed closer to Nana Rubi than his mom. She knew he loved his mother, but she always felt something was off. Isoken's heart bled for him and the instability of being carted from place to place at such a young age.

At least for her, when her parents were preoccupied, she had her siblings. He had no one until Osaro. It was no longer a mystery why he didn't want a relationship until his career was over. Despite the excuse of love trying to change him, she could feel his underlying need to be present in the life of any family he created. Currently, his traveling all around the world wouldn't cut it.

"In Florida, I tried to stay detached. There was no need to get to know anyone. But unlike before, we stayed longer. I allowed myself to grab what I'd always longed for. Stability and friendship. For a couple of years, everything was good. When I turned fifteen, my parents decided it was time to leave. This time, Spain. I couldn't take it anymore and that night I ran away. That changed my life."

Tekena paused. The anguish on his face stalled his words. Isoken reached out and grabbed his hand. She squeezed it but remained silent. She could tell he hadn't purged the demons that plagued him and wanted to give him space to do that. People often tried to shoo away her pain and she didn't want to be that type of person for him.

"Roaming the streets, I met some people. At the time I didn't know they were a gang. I should've gone to Osaro's, but his uncle was sick, and he had a lot going on. For two weeks, I was a runaway, hanging out with these new kids. They introduced me to drag racing. It was illegal, but at that point I didn't care. The thrill and adrenaline took my pain away. I wanted to belong somewhere, and they provided that, but at a cost. As part of the initiation, they took me to a party..." His voice shook. "By the time I figured out what they wanted me to do, it was too late."

"What did they want you to do?" she whispered. Her heart raced, scared of his response.

Tekena removed his hand from her grasp and put both palms over his face. Isoken resisted wrapping her arms around him and telling him he didn't have to talk about it. He needed to.

"It still gives me nightmares sometimes. They wanted me to rob a local corner store. But that was only a distraction from what they really wanted to do. They needed the commotion to be able to lure the attendant's sister to their hideout. Apparently, she was a church girl who'd brushed off the leader of this gang. It wasn't until later that evening, I found out their intent." I panicked and ran as fast as I could." He shook his head. "I should've run to the police station, instead I ran to Osaro's. I entered through the window as we did sometimes and begged him not to say anything. At least until morning.

The next morning, Aunty Lizzy took me to my parents. When I told them the story, they took me to the police station to give a report. I ended up being held for three months in a detention center. The girl had been sexually abused and hospitalized. I blamed myself for not doing things differently. When I got out, I went to look for her. I wanted to apologize."

"Did you find her?"

"Yeah man, but she wasn't the same bubbly chick I knew from school. I damaged her and that has haunted me ever since."

"How were you not deported?"

"I'm a citizen. My parents had me in the US, and when I was three months old, we went back to Nigeria." He took in a deep breath, then exhaled. "For years, I blamed and punished myself. After that incident, I no longer cared about my own wellbeing. I was reckless and drag racing and street fights became my drug. Osaro was the one who helped me keep it together. Despite his own problems, dude would track me down and drag me home." Tekena chuckled.

"My parents stayed an extra year in Florida, realizing moving me around was detrimental. Aunty Lizzy stepped in and they came to some agreement that I could move in with them. When Osaro got caught in some mess and Aunty Lizzy shipped him back to Nigeria. I had to step up and take his place for his family. I got myself together, but racing was still my thing. So my stepdad got me a trainer. I needed to do it the legal way. The rest, they say, is history." He picked up his glass and drank.

"I'm speechless. How's your relationship with your mom?"

"Oh, we're straight. She blames herself for my racing. Says I fell into it because I needed attention." He shrugged. "She's forever in my business so all is well."

"God turned your mess around."

Tekena remained silent for a minute. "I sometimes wonder why He bothers."

She could relate to the sentiment, but it had cost her years of intimacy with God. She was trying to repair it, but some days, she still struggled. "What? Why wouldn't He? You're His child and He loves you."

"After all I've done, I find it hard to be close to God when I see others doing the Christian thing so much better."

"Why? Because of a teenage mistake?"

He tilted his head while his brows met in disbelief. "What? How dare you belittle the ordeal? My recklessness allowed someone who served and worshipped Him to be tainted. Violated. For years, I followed her on all social media platforms to make sure her life was going well. When I got money, I hired a P. I. Not to report her everyday life to me but let me know if she was ever in need. Nothing...nothing has helped ease my conscience."

Tekena stood and walked to the back of the plane, into the bedroom. A part of her wanted to give him space. But she couldn't. This was tearing at him. It had been sixteen years. Isoken followed him. She knocked and opened the door. Tekena was lying on the bed with his hands behind his head, staring up at the ceiling. Isoken toed off her shoes and joined him. Sitting with her legs underneath her, she caressed his cheek. He didn't look at her, but she felt his tension melt at her touch.

"Tex, I'm sorry. I'm not belittling your demons. What I was trying to say is that it was a mistake, driven by your own pain. Trust me, I know about pain. But I also know that with Jesus, we can thrive through. You know me; I'm far from perfect, but I don't have to be to tell you what I know works. Besides, who says those doing the 'Christian thing' are better? We're all trying to do the best we can by His grace. His grace and our faith – the only things that save us."

Tekena turned his head to her. "I feel so unworthy of all He does for me."

"You are worthy. The blood of Jesus made sure of it. You have to accept it, but you have to forgive yourself first."

"Now you sound like Ro." He turned to her; the sparkle in his eyes was back.

"Well, my brother-in-law is smart. If he could break my sister down, he gotta have some sense," Isoken teased.

Tekena gave a dry laugh. "I wanna try, but it's hard. Habits and all."

"That's 'cause you're trying to do it by yourself. God wants your heart first, then He'll help you change your habits. He's looking for a willing heart, not a perfect one."

Tekena gazed at her then reached over and drew her to him. She laid her head on his chest. The silence between them was palpable. It was so easy for her to give him advice, but she struggled taking it for herself. Her relationship with God was much better. However, if she was being honest, a small part of her hadn't submitted completely. Logically, she knew that stood against the faith God wanted. But...she needed a cushion in case those gut punches resurfaced. And for a few days, she thought one did. Thought, because God was still working on her.

"I can't believe I told you that. The only people who know are my parents, Aunty Lizzy and Ro." The vibrations from his chest brought her from her thoughts.

"Not even Malcolm?"

"No."

Isoken smiled. "Well, I'd like to think it's because you trust me." She looked at him and sighed. "Don't be mad. I won't bring her up anymore, but I hope you've called off your P.I. That's stalkerish."

Tekena laughed. The sound was like music to her ears. "Yes. She's married with kids and seems happy."

"And when you pray, ask God to take control. That's all you can do."

Tekena massaged the nape of her neck. "So, it's your turn to trust me."

"Okay, what do you want to know?"

"Are you trying to have a baby?"

TEKENA FELT her tense under his touch. She tried to get up, but he tightened his hold. He wasn't letting her run; neither was he ready for her warmth to leave him. He continued massaging her nape, giving her the time that she needed to speak. He knew she wasn't expecting that question, but it had been bothering him for days. After taking her home that night, he made it his duty to check on her every day. She wasn't the same, distant even. Every time he asked what was wrong, she gave him a fake smile and changed the subject. He wanted to fix what was wrong, but couldn't if he didn't know what it was. So many scenarios played through his mind. Did she get rejected as a surrogate? Hadn't they found her a donor? Was it her job? A client? Her mood was driving him crazy and he needed answers.

"I'm guessing you saw the pamphlets in my room. The short answer to your question... yes." She tried to get up. This time he let her, but only because he wanted eye contact. He sat up and pulled her in front of him. This conversation was far from over.

"Give me the long answer."

"I need food for this conversation."

"You're stalling, but we got time. We don't land for another two hours."

Tekena picked up the phone to place an order with the crew. While they waited, he allowed her to divert the conversation to lighter topics. He also didn't want to be interrupted by the hostess when she arrived with the food.

They placed the food between them, shared grace and ate for a few moments before Isoken started talking.

"I had a dream for my life. The fairytale, white picket fence and all. For a while, I was on track." She leaned into him like she was about to tell a secret. "I even saved myself."

Tekena choked on his food. His eyes bugged. "You saying your first time would've been on your wedding night?"

"Yep." She took another bite of her sandwich.

He sensed she was trying to brush it off. To ease the tension and make her comfortable, he reached for her hand. "I think it's sexy."

Isoken gave him an incredulous look. "Really?"

He shook his head. "Yeah. Couldn't be me, but it's sexy."

She rolled her eyes at him and chuckled.

Mission accomplished.

"Anyway, I already told you how I became an air hostess. So for six years, I enjoyed the escape it provided. I was never in one place long enough to feel. I traveled the world and enjoyed my share of casual flings. Until last September..."

Tekena was glad she skipped over the flings. "What happened?"

"My runway ran out of space. I was hit with another detour. But this path wasn't new. I was back to where I'd started. In addition to what happened with my job, I had a health scare."

"You okay?" He touched her arm.

"Yeah, I'm fine. Let's say it birthed my new celibacy commitment."

He chuckled. "Oh no, Goldie don't tell me somebody gave you something?"

"No, can we move on?"

"Yes, my bad. Continue."

"That, seeing my sister with her new family and my brother headed towards his own family, gave me cause for pause. Before all this happened, I knew God well. Jesus and I were tight. I should've known that if He allowed an interruption in my life, like Frank dying, there was a bigger purpose. But who wants to dwell on that when your heart has been shattered into a million pieces? Because who does that to a child He loves? Instead of running to God, I ran away.

"I now find myself back where I started with nothing to show for it. All my dreams have been reactivated with being still. I want to publish a book of poetry, I want my own agency one day, but most of all, I want a baby. So if I can't have the happily ever after,

I can still have a baby." Tears he wasn't expecting streamed down her cheeks. She hung her head.

Tekena moved the food to the side table and gathered her in his arms. He sat her in his lap and allowed her cry. "Talk to me, baby. What's wrong?"

"The cycle I had was confirmation the insemination didn't work."

Tekena caressed her back as she sobbed. "Are you going to try again?"

This solved the puzzle of her mood but caused his mind to go into overdrive. He wanted to be there for her, but his heart thumped in anticipation of her answer. She was trying to have another man's baby. One she didn't know, but another man's all the same.

She lifted off him and wiped the corner of her eyes. "I must look like a mess."

He caressed her cheek. "My beautiful mess."

She shook her head, turning her lips up in a small smile. "Yes. The first time was the day after the drive off. By the end of this month, I'll have another procedure scheduled." She took in a breath. "Tex, no one knows but my sister. Not even my parents."

"And your secret is safe with me. I do have a question though."

"Shoot."

"A minute ago, you acted like your relationship with God is back to where it's supposed to be."

Isoken frowned. "Act? Why do you think I'm acting?"

"Well maybe not acting, but it seems like you're trusting Him with a little, but not all of you. Why are you ruling out your white picket fence? The fairytale. Settling for less."

She wrapped her arms around her body. "I don't want the fence anymore."

"You have too much zest and passion for life for that to be true—"

"Well, it is, so keep your judgments."

"I'm not judging. You can talk to me about my past mistakes, but I can't talk to you about this? All I'm saying is, you seem to be willing to trust Him with everything but your heart."

"No, I'm protecting my heart."

"You think He can't protect it? You've sentenced yourself to a loveless existence."

"I'll have the love of my child." She moved away from him. "And you're one to talk Mr. 'I don't do love'."

He ignored the aggression in her tone. "No, I said I don't have time for love and commitment now."

"You've heard the saying that procrastination is the arrogance of believing you have another day." She raised her brow at him.

He brushed his hand over his face. "It's not the same thing, Isoken, and you know it."

She scoffed. "Yes, it is. You're doing what you know is best for you considering your circumstances. I'm doing the same."

"The reason behind it is different. You're doing it out of fear."

Isoken scooted off the bed. "How hypocritical of you. You're not into love and commitment because one woman tried to change you, making all women a distraction. Any way you slice and dice it, it's rooted in fear." She opened the door and walked out.

Instead of going after her, Tekena moved to lean his back against the wall. They were so alike, so he knew she needed space. Alone, he pondered their situations and concluded she was right. He had no room to judge her. They were two people who'd let their pasts hold them hostage. Did they even have the courage to want freedom?

CHAPTER 22

Mustafa DuBois-Arazi crossed his ankle over his knee. "Recently, we had the soft opening of Grand Amour in Ghana. As part of our promotion, sponsorship in a major Nigerian event with an international star will benefit us, considering the proximity of both countries. I now feel more comfortable with the answers provided to the questions I and my siblings had when we went over the proposal."

Tekena and Eze had been in a meeting with the herculean Arabian for the last hour. Eze hadn't been exaggerating when he spoke of the beauty of this place or the family's wealth. Mustafa was a man of little words. It was as though he didn't believe in wasting them. He nodded a lot, grunted and was straight to the point. He and his siblings owned the Grand Amour Resorts. During their conversation, Tekena found out that their grandparents had sponsored some French Formula One drivers in the fifties. When the circuit stopped racing in Morocco, they withdrew their sponsorship, but were still big fans of the sport, which trickled down to their grandsons.

Tekena rested his forearms over his knees and leaned forward. "Good deal. I appreciate it. It'll be worth your while. I might be back in Italy then, but Eze here would be in contact. If you need me to sit in on any meetings, I'll make myself available."

Mustafa closed the folder before him. "Sounds like a plan."

The three of them stood and shook hands.

"Thank you again for meeting with us. We'll check out the resort and see you tomorrow at your sister's wedding," Tekena said.

Mustafa put his hand in his pockets. "We're taking my future in-law out tonight. Unless you have other plans, both of you are invited. My brother arrives from Botswana later today and he'd be thrilled to see you."

Tekena looked at Eze who nodded. He knew he couldn't make a commitment without finding out what Isoken wanted to do first. It sometimes scared him how close they were. "Let me get back to you on that. I'm here with my friend, and she might have plans for us. If I don't make it, we'll definitely be at the wedding tomorrow."

"Okay, that's fine. I'm sure my sisters won't mind including her in their plans. I'll leave the information at the front desk."

Tekena nodded and Mustafa led them to the door. As they walked out of the building, Eze received a phone call that allowed Tekena some minutes with his thoughts.

Those thoughts traveled back to two days ago and the time he and Isoken shared in Marrakech. Once he found out he missed her birthday, he worked with Eze to set up something for them for when they arrived in Morocco. The day after they arrived, they took a 4X4 ATV tour of the area, enjoying the camels, local cuisine, art, and every type of tea that existed. They ended the day with a candlelight dinner in a tent in the desert, gazing at the stars.

Long gone was the tension after their conversation on the plane. In his opinion, it brought a deeper trust between them. All evening, they laughed, argued, and laughed some more. It took every ounce of control he had not to ravish her lips. Her guard was down, and she was filled with genuine joy and appreciation. When he thought about all the pain, she'd been through, he wanted to be the one to keep a smile on her face permanently. He told her she didn't have to be strong with him.

The odds were stacked against them. But for the first time in his career, he toyed with the "what if." With two more years on his contract, he didn't know if he had the energy to go up against her. Because with her, the fight wouldn't be an easy one.

HOURS LATER, on Isoken's insistence, Tekena was out with Eze, honoring Mustafa's invitation. He didn't like leaving her alone, so they had lunch together, then she went to the spa. He felt his lips curl up in a smile when he remembered asking her what she'd do after the spa. She told him to mind the business that pays him. He threatened to blow up her phone in five-minute intervals if she didn't answer him.

She gave him a list of movies she would watch in her villa. Satisfied, he let her be. Over the last several weeks, he'd found out that despite her boldness and strength, she was an introvert. Almost anti-social. If it wasn't her sister or Ajoke, she wasn't game for making new friends.

That night, the men played pool with music in the background and an endless supply of food and drinks. He had been introduced to the groom, Kojo Sarbah. He was accompanied by his personal pastor who would be officiating the ceremony, Pastor Mensah Afortey. They were both Ghanaian. Tekena also met members of the 891 Crew including the Niyi guy Isoken seemed to like. He didn't get it, but she knew to keep that under lock and key when he was around. Omar, Mustafa's brother, was the last to arrive. He and Tekena clicked immediately. On the other hand, Mustafa hadn't really said much all evening.

"So you're trying to tell me that no matter how much you prepare, you're never a hundred precent ready?" Eze's question brought Tekena's attention back to the group.

"No, you can't be ready. How are you ready for something you've never done?" Pastor Mensah asked.

"Yeah, but my brother-in-law here has been married before," Omar blurted out. "He better be ready."

The men laughed. Everyone except Kojo.

"O, I'm gonna let you slide off the strength of your sister who's my life. Once she becomes a Sarbah tomorrow, I'm messing you up." Kojo pointed a finger at him and bit off a piece of lamb from his skewer.

In the few minutes he'd known them, Tekena picked up on the back and forth between both men. Omar got under Kojo's skin. Kojo responded with playful threats of bodily harm.

"This is the second marriage for both of them. That notwithstanding, this is a new union. They should apply good things from the previous marriages, but they haven't been married to each other, so there is room to grow," Pastor Mensah responded.

Eze picked up his glass. "I'm not ready for the thought of that."

"Me either," Omar chimed in.

Both men clicked their glasses together in agreement.

"You'll think that until that one you can't do without comes along," Kojo said.

"Man, you don't count. Let you tell it, my sister has been your wife since you were eighteen, even though both of you couldn't get it together then," Omar said.

"The more reason to listen when I talk," Kojo said.

"Let's hear from the man of God. How did you know your wife was the one?" Niyi asked.

"I didn't at first, but as time went on, I knew I couldn't live without her. The odds were stacked against us. But I knew that days are not promised anyone. Even as a pastor, I messed up and when I turned around, she was gone. Those were the most excruciating four months of my life."

"Four months. She punished you good." Omar laughed.

The pastor shrugged. "Whatever it was, the journey has been more than worth it. We're building a life and legacy."

"What about you Tekena? Any special someone?" Omar asked.

Tekena's eyes darted to Eze, who was staring at him with a smirk on his face. "Nah, not really. My sole focus is the track. I can't afford to be tied to any woman. Not now." It was the truth his head agreed with, but when it came to Isoken, his heart sang a different tune. Since their kiss, he kept reminding himself his heart didn't count.

"You don't sound sure," Mustafa said. "Complicated?"

Oh, now you wanna offer input.

"Yeah, you can say that." Tekena took a sip of his drink, deciding to keep it short.

"What's stopping you from uncomplicating it?" Pastor Mensah asked.

Tekena shifted in his seat. He'd known these men for less than twenty-four hours. He didn't want to share things with them that he hadn't even shared with Ro. He mustn't have answered quick enough because Kojo spoke next.

"I don't know your situation, but I'll tell you from experience, if you got someone, uncomplicate it and lock her down, or let it go. At the very least, tell her how you feel. Don't take anything for granted. My mistake caused me eighteen years apart. Life seldom turns out the way you envision it."

Pastor Mensah nodded. "True. On one hand, procrastination is arrogance, but then according to Romans 8:28, all things work together for your good. Learn to pick up on the clues God throws your way. He is always on point with His providence."

"Don't let somebody else slide in there," Niyi said.

That response could have come from anyone and Tekena wouldn't have minded, but it came from him. He was about to respond when the waitress walked in with a fresh batch of *briouats*.

The guys immediately began refilling their plates and talking about sports while Tekena was left with his thoughts. He regretted coming out. He should've stayed indoors with Isoken and watched movies. They were nice men, but now the thoughts he had settled were running wild. Just when he'd gotten to a place of acceptance with Isoken, he was now left to deal with thoughts that angered and confused him and quickened his heartbeat.

CHAPTER 23

Isoken stood sandwiched between Tekena and Eze as the melody for the bride's entrance song began to play. Her eyes met Tekena's briefly and he lifted a hand to move the hair covering her eye. She gave him a faint smile and he grabbed her hand again and squeezed. Isoken loved his touch against her skin, but she was unraveling under it. She mentally counted down the number of weeks left for them to be in such close proximity. Five. Five more weeks. She would miss him terribly, but she needed a reset.

He'd been acting weird all morning and she had yet to figure out why. At first, she thought it was him being sensitive to the effect a wedding might have on her considering her past. She reminded him that they were at her sister's wedding together then he relaxed a little.

A violin cover of Ed Sheeran's "Perfect" continued to play as everyone's eyes remained glued on Yasmine Dubois-Arazi as she walked down the aisle escorted by her older brother. A little flower girl and ring bearer had preceded them. Tekena told her they were the couple's kids from their previous marriages. Also, at the altar was the maid of honor and bride's sister, Selma. And Isoken's man in her head, Niyi Da Silva, stood next to the groom.

Isoken was sure the bride's dress was custom made. Its simplicity was enhanced by the details of the rhinestones and diamonds in it. Her hair was in an updo with loose tendrils falling to the side of her face. She didn't have on a veil, but a tiara. The woman was gorgeous and despite the intimate crowd, she was laser focused on her groom. Along with what Isoken read on the internet, Tekena had told her the little he knew of the couple's story. It was a beautiful thing. Some people were lucky. To have a second chance like that after so many years was rare.

Isoken turned her head toward the altar and noticed Niyi hand the groom a handkerchief which he used to wipe the side of his eye. Isoken lifted her gaze to the sky and asked for forgiveness for lusting after the best man. He oozed confidence, swag, and was so sexy with it. When she saw him earlier at breakfast with Tekena, she almost passed out. Once again, Tekena threatened to rescind his invitation to the wedding. A smile plastered across her face at the brotherhood between Kojo and Niyi. As though on cue, she felt Tekena's lips against her ear.

"You love when I show out."

Isoken reeled in the smile that had her face hurting. She glanced at him and rolled her eyes. "There's nothing to show out for."

"Not now you two. Please," Eze whispered.

Isoken shook her head. He already blocked her from talking to the guy at breakfast, now he didn't want her admiring God's work. She tried to remove her hand from his grasp. He secured his grip and caressed the back of her hand with his thumb. His way of soothing her. Isoken decided not to even fight him and concentrate on the expression of love before them.

The bride's brother handed her over to the groom and the pastor officiating the ceremony asked them to be seated. She'd been introduced to him and his wife before the ceremony. The minute Isoken heard the name Ayanti Effiong-Afortey, she knew it sounded familiar and Google was indeed her friend. Setting a house on fire, gusty move. Ayanti was her kinda chick.

Refocusing on the couple of the hour, Isoken watched as the bride and groom gazed lovingly into each other's eyes and exchanged vows they'd written. Their families beamed with pride as the two of them declared their love for one another. In the moments that followed, Isoken felt her stomach tighten and her heart began to beat with an irregular rhythm. The surge of feelings for the man who sat beside her fed off the deep words of undying love the couple uttered. In that moment, it felt like the attraction to Tekena had deepened to something more. In a panic, she retrieved her hand from his. He glanced at her, and she rubbed her other arm silently, giving him a reason, she needed her hand back. He refocused on the ceremony.

She'd always been attracted to him, but now her heart was signaling something deeper. Tekena had somehow, found his way in and set up camp. She felt the control she had slipping. Isoken took in deep breath to regulate her breathing. She was determined to maintain control. There were no other options, especially not with him.

"For God so loved the world that He gave His only begotten Son. To die that we may be saved. That is the ultimate second chance love story. Man got a do-over through the blood of Jesus Christ. Yasmine and Kojo, not everyone gets another chance to get it right. However, don't negate what you've been through as it has led you back to this moment. Even as Christ walked the earth, many things had to happen to get Him to the Cross." Pastor Mensah's voice was a welcomed jolt from the rabbit hole of emotion Isoken was headed down.

"Now, with the power vested in me I pronounce you man and wife. Kojo, you may—"

The crowd erupted in laughter and applause as the groom cupped his new wife's face and went on a scavenger hunt in her mouth.

"Ladies and gentlemen, it's my honor to introduce to you, Mr. and Mrs. Sarbah."

The couple disconnected for air and the kids ran to meet

them. The crowd rose to their feet, still clapping. Isoken looked up at Tekena. He had a faint smile on his face. She couldn't read him. Her thoughts were interrupted as the couple danced back down the aisle. The ceremony was intimate and so beautiful. Isoken couldn't wait to eat and dance the night away. Tekena recaptured her hand and led her back to the resort where the real fun awaited.

"COME ON, cry baby. I'll introduce you." Tekena huffed, taking her hand.

The reception had been going on for a few hours. They'd danced, ate and Tekena introduced her to important people. If she thought he was a big shot at the gala in Lagos, she was completely blown away here. He gave her the gist about the DuBois-Arazi men being fans, so she assumed they told their friends about him. There was still one person he refused to introduce her to.

Isoken could've walked up to Niyi if she wanted to, but she was here with Tekena and it was disrespectful. With both their statuses in the public eye, she didn't want to be in pictures with Niyi that could potentially be taken out of context. She was plotting how she would accidentally run into him at breakfast the next day, but that plan was now out the window since Tekena grabbed her hand.

Her eyes bugged and she placed her free hand across her chest. "For real? Thank you. I knew you had some good in you." She handed him her phone. "Will you please take us a picture?"

Tekena halted his steps. "I wanna see only ten teeth. If I see thirty-two, I'm deleting the picture."

"Stop being a baby. Complete the Lord's work you've started. At least this way, I can rub it in Itoh's face that you were the one who introduced me to him when she failed." She wiggled her brows at him.

"I know you think you're finessing me. The only reason I'm doing this is I'm not ready to hear you whine all the way home. So, let's get this over with."

Seconds later, they were at the other end of the hall, where Niyi stood with the other members of the 891 Crew. He and the groom were huddled together as the other members got behind the instruments. It was Isoken's guess that the groom was about to serenade his new bride. Their first dance to "Rest of My Life" by Bruno Mars was simply magical. Isoken could only imagine what he was going to do now. On their approach, the men stopped their conversation and smiled at them.

Tekena dapped the men one after the other. "Nice ceremony, man. Congrats again."

"Thank you. Thank you." Kojo's eyes went from Tekena to her and back to Tekena. He then turned and looked at Niyi and they both gave a subtle nod.

Tekena cleared his throat. "I don't wanna hold you long, but this is my friend, Isoken Adolo. She's a big fan and will kill me if I don't make an introduction."

His generalization of her admiration didn't go unnoticed, but it was all good. She simpered at the men before her.

"It's nice to meet you, Isoken. I'm Kojo and thank you for your support." He held out his hand and she shook it in a brief handshake.

"Hi, I'm Niyi. It's always an honor to meet a fan. We don't take the support for granted." He held out his hand and she placed hers in it. Her breath caught and she thanked God for His handiwork. Niyi then went a step further and lifted her hand against his lips and pecked it.

Tekena cleared his throat. "Easy, playboy."

That solicited a chuckle from the other men. Isoken was convinced there was an inside joke somewhere. She couldn't stress over that now. She needed to decide if she'd be washing her hand later or not.

Isoken bumped her shoulder against Tekena. "Pay him no

attention. Can I have a picture?" Now that she had been introduced, she had no problem asking for what she wanted.

Niyi moved closer to her. "Of course. Why don't we take one with the group and then individually?"

Isoken heard Tekena growl and she narrowed her eyes at him. She knew he'd have a lot to say later and she'd deal with it then. For the next several minutes, Tekena served as her personal photographer as she swapped band members and positions. For someone who had a lot to say, he made sure the lighting was good and the pictures were perfect for her. Tekena was a walking contradiction and that, in truth, was one of the things she really liked about him.

After the mini photo session, Isoken thanked them and faced Tekena. He handed her the phone. She busied herself going through the pictures but heard Tekena in the background thanking the men for their time. She looked up and saw the end part of a handshake. Tekena sauntered toward her and placed his hand on the small of her back. She knew that was his play of dominance and she let him have it. As they turned to leave, Niyi called out.

"Aye, man…"

They both turned. Isoken's eyes darted between both men, surveying them.

"If you don't, I will." Niyi smirked.

Kojo lifted his fist to his mouth, stifling a chuckle. Isoken looked up at Tekena. He took her hand, threw out a, "I'd like to see you try," and they continued on their way.

"What was that about?"

"It's nothing," came his curt reply.

Isoken shrugged her shoulder. She dismissed the interaction. Nothing could deflate her mood. She finally got to meet Niyi DaSilva.

———

IT WAS PROBABLY a little after midnight; she wasn't sure. Time seemed to be of little relevance after the day she'd had. It was wonderful. The waves knocking against the sea, the stars in the sky and moonlight reflecting perfectly in the night, convinced her more than ever of the magnificence of God.

"What are you thinking about?"

Tekena's voice tore through her thoughts. Her hand was in one of his as his other held their shoes. They were still in their formal wear and decided to walk the beach before retiring for the night. After the groom serenaded the bride, they thanked everyone for coming and dashed away in a tinted-window, black SUV. When they left, some attendees dispersed, but others stayed to continue the festivities. She and Tekena didn't seem to want the evening to end, so they decided to take a walk.

"The whole day." She leaned her head against his arm. "Thank you for inviting me. I have met a lot of important people over the years, but this was amazing."

"It's nothing. I enjoyed seeing you let loose. I'm glad you came with me."

They continued to walk in comfortable silence. In between their pauses, they talked and laughed about anything that came to mind.

"I'm going to miss you when you leave," Isoken confessed. "You leave second week of February, right?"

Tekena groaned. "You had to dampen the mood."

Isoken let out a chuckle that lacked humor. She knew she should welcome the separation, but that did nothing for the ache in her stomach.

"I can feel you thinking. For the record, I'll miss you too." He drew her to a halt. He placed his hand on her nape and caressed her neck with his thumb. He held her gaze and she lost the ability to breathe without effort. Her heart thundered against her chest and Isoken knew she should move away, but her feet remained planted.

"How am I gonna survive without the woman who gets on

my nerves, makes me laugh, checks me, and give sage advice all in a matter of minutes. And looks sexy doing it too, might I add."

"Aww, that's so sweet." She leaned her forehead to his chest, then made baby noises that always irritated him.

"Aye, cut it out."

"And we're back." She laughed and he joined in. The mushy stuff wasn't them. They continued their stroll, and she remembered his mood earlier. "Is that what was wrong with you today?"

"Whatchu mean?"

"I don't know; you were broodish..."

"Nah, I'm good."

With the way he dismissed her, Isoken was certain there was more to it than he let on. She was about to question him further when he spoke.

"How's the baby thing coming?"

Isoken stopped walking, also bringing him to a halt. "That was random."

His eyes remained on her, but he didn't respond.

"Nothing new from what I told you on the plane. My next try is the end of the month."

"You sure about this?"

"Yeah, I've given it a lot of thought. Why? What's going on?"

"I wanna make sure you're ready."

Isoken frowned up at him. Something was definitely up. "Is anyone a hundred percent sure of anything? But this is something I want and I'm going to give it my all."

"Then let's go half on it."

Isoken's eyes stung from how wide they stretched. Tekena's mouth was moving, but nothing registered. The only thing she felt were the knots forming in her stomach.

CHAPTER 24

"Isoken...Isoken...Isoken!"

Tekena snapped his fingers to bring her out of her trance. An intense fear creeped up his spine. It was as though she hadn't taken a breath since the words left his mouth. He had carried those words with him all night and all day. Now her shocked expression had him second guessing the relief he had at getting the words out. Tekena grabbed her shoulders and she blinked.

She shut her eyes tightly before opening them again to gawk at him. "What...what... did you say?" She rubbed her arm.

She was already wearing his jacket, but he grabbed the lapels and secured it closer around her. Draping his arm around her shoulder, he walked them further ashore, away from the water. He leaned her against a boulder, dropped their shoes in the sand and stood with his hands in his pockets.

"I said, let's go half on a baby. I want to be your baby's father."

"Why?" Her voice was low, shaky, and layered with disbelief.

"Why? You don't think I'll make a good candidate? He tried to diffuse the tension with humor. Her blank stare caused him to roll his shoulders back and adjust his stance. "Look, I've been doing a lot of thinking—"

"About my baby?"

"Not about—"

She shook her head as if ridding herself of the fog which she seemed to be stuck in. "I don't understand. I mean, you don't want a relationship."

"And neither do you. But I'm not asking for one."

"Yeah, right. Says the man who acts out when he sees me with someone else."

"And I offer no apologies. But this isn't that, besides, you've already rejected me once. I get the message." He folded his arms across his chest. He needed to rein in his frustration before he ruined everything.

"Oh, enough with that." She raised her hands. "I didn't reject you. I told you, I'm protecting me."

"Same difference."

"Then why are—"

"Woman, will you let me speak!" His tone was higher than he intended, but that seemed to be the only way to get her to focus on what he was trying to say.

Her brows met in a sexy crease and she placed her hands on her hips in defiance.

"Look, I've been doing a lot of thinking since our conversation on the plane. We both have our reasons for sticking to our convictions. But being here, conversations about missed opportunities and second chances made me look at the future differently. It isn't something I have control over. I wish I did, but I don't. Neither can I redo my yesterday. The only thing I have is today. Time is fragile and the slightest possibility of not getting my tomorrow because I didn't seize today terrifies me.

God has been so good to me. I've had several scrapes in my career and He's kept me through them all. Until I talked to you, I didn't realize how I've been taking that for granted. I have two more years of racing and I can't predict what will happen, but I don't want to leave this earth without someone I can pass on a legacy to."

Tekena's ear rang with the pounding of his heart as he waited for her response. What he didn't expect was for her to shove him in his chest. Her unexpected reaction had him stumbling back.

"Get away from me." Isoken tried to move past him.

He blocked her path, caging her in. "No. Talk to me!"

"No? You're standing there telling me you're planning on dying and in the same breath, you want me to have a child with you." A tear rolled down her cheek.

Tekena thumbed it away and pulled her closer. It wouldn't be Isoken if she didn't fight him. However, her strength was nothing compared to his and he succeeded in wrapping his arms around her. He rubbed her back to calm down her sobs. This wasn't how he expected this to go.

When he returned to his room the previous night, sleep eluded him. He came to the realization that there wasn't any scenario where he would be comfortable with Isoken being with someone else. He no longer wanted to be only a friend, but he also knew that with her unresolved grief and his phobias, the timing was off. But then he concluded that he wasn't okay with her carrying another man's baby. His talk about legacy was true, but the number one reason was that he wanted to be tied to her now. Leaving room for him to plead his case for more in the future. There was no question about their chemistry or care for the other, but he also knew fear was a powerful thing. If he talked about anything more now, he was sure she'd run.

"Goldie, baby, I know for a fact you got two degrees. Nowhere in my speech did I say I'm planning to die."

As expected, she chuckled lightly and lifted her head. "Shut up. You get on my nerves."

Tekena planted a kiss on her forehead. "You okay?"

She wiped her eyes and nodded.

He took in a deep breath. Deciding it was better to rip the band aid off, he continued, "No one plans to, but we never know what will happen and all I want is to have a part of me here in case..."

"If anything happens to you, my child won't know you."

"Huh? You were going to have an unknown donor. Dude wouldn't know the child either. At least you know me." His head was spinning with her logic, but he needed to stay focused on the goal.

She shifted her weight from one leg to the other. "Why me?"

"Why not you? You're smart, witty, compassionate, beautiful...should I go on?"

"Yes, I need to be convinced..."

"And crazy." He made a circular motion with his finger near his temple. He cradled her face in his hands. "But for real, although there are some good insemination stories, I've also read horror stories."

"Read? You researched it?"

"Heck yeah, I had to come prepared." He tucked her hair behind her ear. "I've heard of doctors using their own sperm. Names of recipients being leaked on accident. How you know this donor doesn't have children all over the world? His other kids might track yours down and ask for an organ or some stuff."

Isoken laughed and folded her arms. "Now you're exaggerating."

"I'm not kidding. Some of them might be crazy. One day you wake up and the child is standing over you like Chucky. Goldie, you don't want those problems."

"And you are sane?" Her raised brow challenged him.

"In the grand scheme of things, yes. Let's face it, we both got screws loose. We don't lose them at the same time, so it works."

Isoken softened her expression, giving him an opening to hit her with his closer. "Look at our genes; the kid will be good looking, super smart and have a pretty good financial cushion as a bonus."

"Tex, I do not need your money for anything." She pressed her lips together in defiance.

He stroked his beard and narrowed his eyes. He counted down from five in his head. "I didn't say you needed it. I said it'll be a bonus. Why are you focused on putting words in my mouth?"

Isoken remained quiet. Tekena's attempt to read her expression fell short and it bothered him. "Goldie?"

"It's a lot Tex. I'll..." She wrung her hands.

Something was off. She suddenly changed from being his sparring partner to someone in distress. He shoved his hands in his pockets. Anything to keep them from shaking. She was about to reject him, and he didn't know if his heart could take it. His ego took a hit as each second passed by. The night she'd rejected him flashed through his mind.

Anger rose in his stomach and before he could think, he spoke, "Wow, so it's this hard for you to decide to have a baby with me. But you're cool with a total stranger."

Isoken crinkled her nose and her hands went to her hips. Her stare was intense. He regretted his words, but not enough to take them back. He wanted to know what was wrong with him in her eyes.

"Are you kidding me? You want to know? Because of this." She wagged her finger between them. "I know you! I care for you... a LOT. My unknown donor is exactly that. Unknown!" She yelled and walked away.

For what seemed like eternity, Tekena remained frozen in place. He never thought he'd hear her admit her feelings. He smiled inwardly but dared not let it show. He turned to catch up with her when she abruptly stopped and walked toward him.

She poked him in the chest. "I'm not gonna feel bad because you can't handle me not immediately jumping on your idea." She turned and continued her hurried steps.

Her abruptness jerked him into action. He jogged, reached out and grabbed her arm. She struggled at first, but then relaxed. He pulled her close and bent his head to rest his forehead against hers. He whispered. "I'm sorry. I'm sorry."

A beat passed between them. Each took in the others breath, then her arms snaked around his waist. "I was about to say I'll think about it."

"And that's all I can ask for." He trailed kisses from her forehead to her nose until he got to her lips. He covered them with his. Their connection started off as a delicate brush against her soft lips. He inhaled her breath and felt the warmth emanating from between them. The sound of her moan drove him to a maddening frenzy. He pulled her closer. Her hands went to his hair as their tongues battled like wrestlers trying to pin the other down. The need for air and the fact that any minute now, they'd both be laid out on the beach tore them apart.

He cupped her face and they locked eyes as they tried to get their breathing under control. The waves splashed, breaking them out of their trance.

He let out an exaggerated breath. "Come on, let me get you back to your room. I have a brief breakfast meeting with Mustafa in the morning, then I'll come get you so we can leave for the air strip." He took her hand, interlocked their fingers as they made their way back to the resort.

"Cool..."

"You want me to have breakfast sent to your villa, or you'll order something?"

"You can order fo..."

He turned to see what stopped her speech. She had her index finger under her chin in contemplation. "Or maybe I can go to the restaurant and see if I run into Niyi before we leave?" She winked.

Tekena narrowed his eyes at her. "Keep testing me. When he comes up missing, don't say I didn't warn you."

"Oh, you wouldn't do that to the love of my life..." She snatched her hand from his grasp and took off running.

Tekena followed. Catching up to her, he dragged her down into the sand. Straddling her, he captured her hands above her head with one hand and tickled her with the other. Her laughter and plea for mercy was like balm to his soul.

"He's your what now? I didn't hear you the first time."

Isoken's laughter filled the air. "It was a slip of tongue. Please. Get off me. See now my dress is soggy from this wet ground."

He brushed his lips against hers. "That's what I thought." He stood, pulled her up and dusted off the excess sand from her legs.

"I'm now wet," she whined. "And my hair."

"Next time don't write a check you can't cash." He bent down in front of her. "Get on cry baby."

Isoken climbed on his back and started humming the melody to "So Into You" by Fabulous ft Deborah Cox. As he rapped the second verse by Fabulous, Tekena realized how happy Isoken made him. She stimulated all parts of him: mind, body, and soul. Never would he have thought that when he boarded a plane to Nigeria weeks ago, he'd be working with her. He knew there was a possibility that having a baby with her could complicate things between them. However, he wasn't going to entertain that thought. He was focused on doing everything within his power to maintain their bond.

For the first time in a long time, Tekena accepted the possibility that he deserved something good. The shame of his past always had him shying away from fully accepting the grace and mercy of God.

Isoken was his good thing.

He also knew that there was a possibility he would be the one to sabotage them. Her words and Osaro's had been playing in his head on a loop. He couldn't overcome by his own strength. Before this trip, he had been willing to put whatever he felt for her on the back burner until he finished out his contract since his career was such a big deal. That was no longer a viable option for him. If he were to have any chance of keeping this feisty, beautiful, and compassionate woman in his life, he needed to get it together.

He had to be a dependable rock in her corner. To help her conquer her fears, strengthen, and encourage her when she felt weak. He loved how strong she was, but he wanted her to know with him, she didn't have to be strong all the time. As it stood, there was no way he could give her what he didn't have.

A solid foundation in his faith.

THE NEXT MORNING, Tekena sat alone at a table in the back of the resort's restaurant. He looked at his watch to ensure he was on schedule. The meeting with Mustafa was over and went better than he expected. While Eze explored the gift shop with his lady friend, Tekena waited on Omar. He walked by minutes earlier and overheard Tekena ordering Isoken additional pastries for the road. Omar offered to prepare a special to-go basket for her instead. Taking a sip of his orange juice, Tekena pulled out his phone and typed a message.

Hope you enjoyed your breakfast? Be ready in forty-five minutes.

Seconds later, three dots appeared indicating she was responding. Before her response could come through, Tekena felt a presence next to him. He stood when he noticed it was Pastor Mensah.

"Good morning, Mr. Tamuno." He held out his hand.

Tekena chuckled and shook his hand. "Pastor, we've played pool together, you've given me relationship advice, we even danced to Michael Jackson's "PYT" on the same dance floor. I'm quite sure you can call me Tekena."

Pastor Mensah laughed. "Fair enough."

"Are you leaving today?"

"No, my wife and I took the week off to explore Tweedes." The pastor's eyes moved to the carry-on case by Tekena's side. "I guess you're leaving."

"Yep, I have to get my friend back and tidy up a few more things before I head back to Europe."

"Good deal. If you don't mind, let me pray for you."

Tekena quickly bent his head slightly. Maybe God had heard his prayer last night. He had wanted to call Osaro when he got back to his room to talk about this sudden push he felt toward God but didn't. Not because he didn't trust his boy, but Osaro knew everything about him, so, he sometimes was biased and brushed off his concerns too quickly.

The pastor prayed God's guidance and protection over him in this upcoming season and beyond. Then ended it in Jesus name with an amen.

"Amen."

"Here." Pastor Mensah pulled out a card from his denim shirt and handed it to him.

Tekena took the card, flicking it over, he glanced over its details. Calvary Is The Way Church, with locations in Atlanta and Accra. On the back of the card were the words, "Acknowledge. Believe. Declare." Each word had some Bible verses listed under it. Tekena returned his eyes to the man that stood before him.

"Any time you need to talk, or whatever. Give me a call."

Tekena flipped the card between his fingers and nodded. "Cool. Thank you."

"As men, we sometime shy away from talking about our faith. Coming to the realization that we are not as in control as we think we are, can be daunting. Despite the strength society ascribes to us, we need God to survive this life." A beat passed. "We can't do anything without Him."

Tekena swallowed the words he wanted to say. Instead, he put the card in his wallet and said, "I'll take you up on that, because I got a lot of making up to do with God."

Pastor Mensah chuckled. "No, you don't. That's what Jesus did on the Cross. All you need to do is acknowledge you're a sinner, believe that Jesus died and resurrected for your sins and declare that He is Lord." The pastor shrugged. "Then you ask Him to help you live right. It's that simple."

The words Isoken spoke to him on the plane came back to his mind. *In Jesus you are worthy.*

"God's relationship with man is not transactional."

Tekena rubbed the back of his neck, suddenly becoming uncomfortable with the conversation.

Pride comes before a fall.

The words his mother always said popped up in his mind. He wondered why. Maybe it's because he talked to her earlier. He didn't dwell on it, instead he asked, "How do I do that?"

Tekena thought it was only Osaro and Malcolm's eyes that lit up when he asked a question about God. But here before his eyes was a man whose face transformed as if he'd won the lottery.

"Do you acknowledge that you're a sinner and have come short of God's glory?"

That was a definite yes. He knew that he was in no way doing what he should be doing. "Yes."

"Do you believe that Jesus Christ died and rose for your sins?"

Why He did that while people were still doing whatever they liked was never something Tekena could wrap his mind around. "I don't know why He did. But yes, I believe."

"The why is simple. He loves us."

Tekena remained silent.

"Last question. Do you declare that Jesus Christ is Lord and invite Him to be your Savior?"

"Yes. Yes, I do. I must admit I'm anxious about how I remain in check."

Pastor Mensah patted him on his shoulder. "That, my friend, isn't for you to figure out. On the back of that card are some verses to cement what we just did. Read them and ask the Holy Spirit to help you. He will. Repeat after me. Dear Lord Jesus, I know that I am a sinner, and I ask for Your forgiveness. I believe You died for my sins and rose from the dead. I turn from my sins and invite You to come into my heart and life. I want to trust and follow You as my Lord and Savior. Amen."

Tekena repeated the prayer and opened his eyes as Omar reached them. He placed what he was carrying in his hand on the table and stood to the side of the pastor.

"Hey, my friend. I'm sorry for the delay." He then turned and smiled at Pastor Mensah and they exchanged greetings.

"No problem man, I appreciate it."

Pastor Mensah looked at his watch. "I need to be on my way. My wife is probably wondering why her breakfast is taking so long."

Omar wore a puzzled look. "Why didn't she order room service?"

"Because she's spoiled, and I take sole responsibility for that." Pastor Mensah smiled, then looked at Tekena. "It's done. Use the card and remember my offer. Have a safe trip back." He walked away after shaking both their hands.

Tekena dapped Omar and walked through the double doors leading to the villas. It was time to gather the troops and head home. He couldn't wait to tell Isoken what happened with the pastor. As he walked down the path, he pulled out the card wondering what the verses were. He'd have to wait to satisfy his curiosity. In the past several years he'd gone on many fantastic trips around the world. However, this trip to Tweede Kans Cove would for now go down as the most memorable trip of his life.

CHAPTER 25

When Isoken splurged on her elliptical bike, the investment was for the sole aim of producing a taut body, lowering the risk of disease and stress relief. Currently, she wasn't getting the return on her investment in the stress relief department. It'd been two days since she'd been back from Tweedes and her daily hour regimen had yet to provide any relief.

She was still wrapping her head around Tekena's offer. She would've never thought she'd be in this place with him. Her plan to get far away from him was failing miserably. Leave it to Tekena to complicate things by throwing in the possibility of their lives being permanently entwined, not by marriage, but a kid.

"Lord, please guide me. Help me to make this decision. Is he the right person?"

She'd thought seeing him the morning after his request would've been awkward. It was anything but. They picked back up like it never happened. There was no tension between them, and for that, she was grateful. When they landed, he dropped her off then offered to give her space to think. She hadn't seen him since then, but his texts in the morning, midday and night arrived as usual. Isoken was glad he kept his word and didn't broach the topic. Problem was, she didn't have that much time left. If he was going to be her donor, he had to go with her to her next appointment before her procedure. She had already picked a donor but could always change her mind. There was prep work to be done so she had to decide fast.

Although he had laid out a good case, she wasn't sure her heart could take "Tekena the race car driver" occupying such a huge role in her life. Whether he was having a tantrum, being a sweet gentleman or trying to bend her, he was now an important person to her. She was already in too deep with him for her own sanity. Who was she kidding? Although she really didn't want to, whether she had a baby with him or not, she'd always worry about him.

Logically, his argument made sense. She'd have peace of mind with someone she knew as opposed to a total stranger. Isoken stopped the bike, climbed down, and picked up her towel. She left her spare bedroom, wiping the sweat from her body. There had to be a way they could both get what they wanted. At least what she wanted.

To share a baby but maintain her independence from him.

She climbed up the stairs to take a shower, her mind searching for the perfect solution. She wished she could call her sister, but lately Itohan was super emotional with her pregnancy. She saw every move Isoken made with Tekena through the eyes of Cupid and rainbows. Her decision to go to Morocco with Tekena had her sister planning an imaginary wedding. Isoken shook her head as she tossed her clothes for the day on her bed. She didn't have to go into the office, but she had several projects and contracts to work on later. Shedding her clothes, she stepped into the shower. The warm water hit her skin as an idea struck.

It was perfect.

Isoken quickly washed her body, smiling to herself as the details of her plan came together in her head. It was brilliant and she hoped Tekena would be on board.

ON THE OTHER side of town, Tekena was out on a morning jog around his estate. His decision to give Isoken some space was messing with his mind. He wanted her to make an independent decision, but at the same time it was time he had to be away from her. Time was something he didn't have the luxury of with his stay in Lagos coming to an end.

He spent most of his time between his driving school and delving deeper into his new relationship with Jesus. He'd talked to Osaro who was happy for him as expected. Osaro gave him Bible verses on love.

Tekena was still for being Isoken's child's father, but he now knew more than before, it wasn't something he could pressure her into. He wanted her to make the decision for herself but prayed to God that she made it in favor of him. If for nothing else, he knew that unlike his childhood, his child would have a stable home environment since Isoken was no longer an air hostess.

"How did David go from withering beneath the weight of sin induced guilt, to classifying himself as righteous, to being called the man after God's own heart?" The words from his Bible plan came through his ear buds.

After telling Isoken about his encounter with the good pastor, he also told her about his concerns about not feeling any different inwardly. Several times on the plane, that voice in his head that constantly reminded him of mistakes, made an appearance. Isoken suggested a Bible plan on the plane and this was his first day of study.

"After you've sinned, the little judge inside of you tells you it's wrong. The problem arises when the enemy jumps on that voice and allows it to play continuously in your mind. Suddenly like Adam, you're hiding behind fig leaves. The Father already knows, and He's calling you with open arms. Some of us are constantly revisiting mistakes we made in our marriages, in college, in our finances, but I have good news for you. You're worthy of a new beginning. Stop allowing the enemy to hijack your new beginning.

"Today, I'll leave you with Hebrews 9:14, *How much more shall the blood of Christ, who through the eternal Spirit offered himself without spot to God, purge your conscience from dead works to serve the living God?*"

Tekena removed the buds from his ear and muttered, "Holy Spirit, remind me repeatedly that the blood of Jesus has indeed set me free. Amen."

Making a turn, he headed back home when his phone buzzed in his pocket.

Goldie: GM, breakfast? Your place or mine?

Tekena smiled and typed his response.

Good morning beautiful. Give me two hours, and I'm all yours.

Goldie: See you soon

Two hours later, Tekena cruised the Lekki-Ekpe Express way toward Isoken's home as "Your Love" by Limoblaze ft DJ Horphuray played from his speakers. His heart raced in anticipation of her decision. In record time, he made it to her house and rang the bell. A few seconds later, he was greeted with a smile that he credited for lighting up his world. His eyes roamed over her simple white v neck tee and blue jeans.

She reached to take the bag of assorted juices he brought with him. "How thoughtful of you. Come on, food is almost ready."

"You look beautiful."

She stopped, glanced back at him, and simpered before she continued on her way. "Thank you."

They arrived at her dining table and his stomach growled at the spread. He couldn't wait to dig in. Tekena pulled out her chair, and after she sat, he took his. Isoken said grace and they began to eat while discussing the appointments they had for the remainder of his stay in Nigeria. He wanted to get right to it and ask for her decision but decided to let her control the pace.

Several excruciating minutes later, with breakfast done, they moved into the living room. Tekena sat and she did the same, but opposite him, her legs bouncing up and down. His antennas went on alert. She was acting strange.

"What's up, Goldie?"

Isoken stood and walked to him. If he didn't know better, he would think she was nervous. But she couldn't be, not with him. She handed him her iPad which she had been tapping on.

"Here."

Tekena glanced at the device but didn't take it from her. "What's this?"

"Will you take this thing. What do you think I'll do?"

He took the device from her and laughed. "This is you we're talking about. You can do anything."

She shook her head but chuckled. "I thought about what you said." She tapped her fingernails against her palm. "I might regret this, but it's a great idea."

Tekena smirked and cupped his ear. "Say it again. You think something I said is a great idea."

She rolled her eyes at him. "Don't make me take it back. I drew up an agreement."

"What agreement? You need money or something?" He looked down at the device, curious to see what she was talking about.

"Really? I'm about to rethink this arrangement."

Tekena chuckled. The screen had timed out, so he handed it to her for her password. Instead of taking it she waved him off. "Adolo, the number 3, then the asterisk sign."

He put in the password. His eyes scanned the top of the screen and let out a loud cackle when he read it.

Half on A Baby Contract

Tekena looked up at her. He could tell she was trying hard not to laugh, but he saw the humor in her eyes. "You really had to name it this?"

"Sure did. I don't want you having any ideas on what this is."

Tekena grunted and started reading the document. She had a

list of rules both of them had to agree to. The first was no feelings. She had the word feelings in caps. If this was when he initially got to Lagos, he would've agreed wholeheartedly. But he knew now they were way past that. He knew it, and she did too. If she wanted to act like they hadn't crossed that line, he'd humor her for now.

He continued to read. The second rule was no multiples. He lifted his eyes toward her. "What do you mean by no multiples?"

"That means while I'm pregnant, you can't have multiple women at your disposal. I don't want to wake up to a new flavor of the week all thirty whatever weeks of the pregnancy."

Tekena furrowed his brow. "First of all, you know that's not me anymore, I'm trying to do better. Second, if we're not to have any feelings, why does it matter?"

She sighed. "You might be trying to do better, but your multiple women haven't gotten that memo. And it matters, that's all you need to know."

Tekena moved his head back at her tone. It held more aggression than necessary. Far different from when they were enjoying breakfast together. "Aye, watch it now. You do know you don't run nothing."

"It's my body—"

"And my soldiers, so now what?"

She let out an exaggerated breath to which he chuckled. Her strong will was sexy.

"This rule better go for you too. Since I've been in Lag, you've had more men lust over you than I care to count."

Isoken laughed. "You're exaggerating."

"You say that now, but don't abide by this rule and watch what I do," he warned.

He knew that for his warning, she'd try to poke him. But she'd be in for a surprise since she probably hadn't learned not to poke the bear.

Tekena continued to read. The next rule was they had to be tested, and he agreed. The next one was that they'd each give the other advance notice before popping up or coming over. Then no calling or texting obsessively. He needed clarification on this because after more than three missed calls, he was pulling up.

"How long is this advance notice?"

"Well considering you'll be abroad; I say two weeks."

He shook his head. "That ain't gonna work. You got twenty-four hours."

"Tex, you do know I have a life."

"In my opinion, number three and four are connected. The only way I'm pulling up is if I call you and I don't get an answer."

"I'm not answerable to you."

"You got it twisted, baby. You may not be answerable to me, but while you're carrying our cargo, I'm responsible for your well-being. Don't ask me to give up that responsibility because it's not happening." Tekena's stare gave her no room for an argument. At least not one that he'd give a second thought.

"Fine!"

Tekena looked at her with wide eyes. "Wow, no counter argument from you?"

"I'm not unreasonable."

"What? You're the stubbornest woman I've ever met."

"You must think you're a piece of cake."

"Whatever, let me read this thing so I can go. You're about to make me backslide so soon." Through his peripheral, he saw her cross her arms over her chest in defiance, causing him to chuckle.

"I'm sorry." Her voice came across in a low whisper.

Tekena looked up at her and nodded. He turned his attention back to the device. The next rule was if they saw each other outside with anyone else, they couldn't have an attitude. He wasn't sure about that, but he'd agree for now. There were three lines that were blank.

"What are these blank lines for?"

She shrugged. "In case you want to add something. But I think I got it covered."

"You would think that. I do have some things to add." He

placed the iPad on the coffee table. "Number one, we won't tell anyone we're doing this. And I mean no one. Nobody will know who my baby mama is neither will anyone know who your baby daddy is."

"I won't be your baby mama but the mother of your child, and fine, I don't want to be publicly attached to you anyway."

Tekena detected hurt in her voice and against his will, his chest constricted. He didn't mean to hurt her, but he knew how these things went. Once the word got out, folks would be expecting wedding bells and that would put pressure on their already dicey situation. Her safety and his clear mind were his utmost priority.

"Come on, Goldie. I don't want people in our business."

"Yeah, whatever. What else you got?"

"If at any time you get into a relationship, it can't be with someone I know—"

"What? How am I supposed to know who you know?"

"Better call me or get to Googling."

"You only want me to run my nonexistent future man by you first?" She smirked

"What you said doesn't even make sense, but as long as you get the picture."

She waved him off. Through her pout and balled up face, he saw her displeasure. She could be upset all she wanted as long as she understood the rule was nonnegotiable.

"Don't try me Isoken. Please don't play with me."

"Oh, I'm Isoken now?"

"That should let you know how serious I am." Tekena locked eyes with her. "You have to keep me in the know of all appointments. That way I can move stuff around to FaceTime with you." He picked up the iPad and handed it back to her. "If you're good, type my own rules in."

She took it from him and typed for a few minutes. Soon after, she looked at him with a smile that always twisted his insides. "All done."

He squinted his eyes at her. She was too cheery. "Bring that here let me read it again. You might have added something extra."

Isoken laughed and handed it to him and walked into the kitchen. She had already signed the document. Tekena read it again and although his head was telling him this was the right thing to do, he couldn't escape the nagging feeling that both of them would end up driving each other insane before the nine months was over. He signed his name on the document. They hadn't talked about money, but they didn't need too. He was automatically vetoing her spending her money on anything.

Tekena smiled as she reentered the room with two malt drinks.

"Let's seal the deal with a toast and a prayer." She handed him his drink.

He took it with hesitation. *A prayer?*

"Okay...to our legacy." He stood and raised his bottle, and she did the same. They clinked bottles and took a sip of their drinks.

"Now let's pray."

Without waiting for him, she closed her eyes and clasped her hands together. "Father, You know the traits we... well I, don't want, please eliminate them. Amen."

Tekena glared at her and she winked at him.

"What?" She picked up the iPad and looked over the document. "I'll send this to your email so you can have a copy."

Tekena placed his drink on the table, hooked his fingers in the belt loop of her jeans and drew her to him. "You love to rattle me, don't you?" He grazed her bare shoulder with his teeth. He loved watching her come undone under his touch. "You love testing how far you can push me." He blew on the spot. Lifting her arms around his neck, he pulled her closer.

"Don't pout. You know you can't do without the spice I add to your world." She tugged his earlobe.

Tekena kissed her neck and teased her lips with a kiss before releasing her. "I wish I didn't, but I gotta go."

She stepped back and cleared her throat. She had no idea what she did to him. But then this was Isoken, so maybe she did. For both of their sakes and souls, he needed to go. In silence, she walked him to the door.

All fun and games aside, the seriousness of what they were about to do wasn't lost on him. He prayed to God that no matter what, the well-being of their child would always come first.

CHAPTER 26

Days passed. Excruciating days. Seventeen since her IUI. Twelve since Tekena left Nigeria.

Isoken looked at the phone calendar. February had rolled into March. Her gaze shifted to the -pregnancy tests laid out on the bathroom vanity. Her insides squirmed as she ran her sweaty hands over her bathrobe. Her missed period was a sign she couldn't afford to depend on. Her cycles hadn't always been the most consistent.

She wanted to call Tekena so he could be on the phone with her, but she remembered she currently wasn't talking to him. He'd been driving her crazy for the last three days and she threatened to block him. He didn't take that threat kindly and proceeded to check her. In the end, he begrudgingly agreed not to ask about the test for the next three days. Her grace period had expired and by the time he woke up, she wanted to have an answer for him.

Something in the pit of her stomach already confirmed what she knew was true. She was about to be tied to Tekena and his shenanigans for the next eighteen years.

No matter how mad he made her, she didn't think it was possible to miss another human being that much until he left for

New York. From the time they'd signed the agreement to the day of the actual procedure, they had visited the clinic three times to get him ready. The speed with which his lawyers had non-disclosures drawn up, signed and money disbursed gave her whiplash.

After the IUI, he'd taken her to his house where he had a bedroom set up for her with all her favorite things. He knew the presence of his Nana would make her feel uncomfortable, so he gave her the whole weekend off. That meant he did everything because he refused for her to be on her feet. As usual, he was over the top. Her explanation that her needing to lie down or put her legs up was a wives' tale fell on deaf ears. He'd carried her from the clinic, into his house, up the stairs and catered to her every need. Snacks, games, movies – he even bought her writing supplies in case she felt like penning a poem. The only time he gave her space was when she took a shower or slept. Isoken loved and appreciated every minute of it, but it scared her because against her will, they grew closer, something she didn't think was possible. Trepidation crept up her spine as she lifted the cup to pee.

Forty-five minutes later, Isoken drummed her fingernails on her phone as she waited for the doctor to walk in. After three anxious minutes crept by, two tests came back positive but before she got her hopes up, she needed to be sure. Causing her to set an emergency appointment. Her buzzing phone startled her. Frowning, she sent Tekena to voicemail for the umpteenth time. Didn't he sleep? She was sure that with the six-hour time difference, she'd be ready by the time he called. Despite his desperation and her anxiety, she couldn't share with him what she didn't know for certain.

The door opened and Isoken made a futile attempt to decipher the doctor's expression. For a moment, she couldn't until his lips turned up in a smile. She let out a heavy breath. He leaned against the desk and handed her the paper. At the bottom was the word...Pregnant.

"Congratulations. I need you to schedule an appointment with your Ob-Gyn to start your prenatal—"

Her phone buzzed, interrupting them.

Tekena.

Isoken sent him to voicemail again. She loved "Can't Find The Words" by Karina but was now regretting assigning it as Tekena's ringtone. She had texted him earlier that she would call him soon. Instead of waiting, he called her immediately. Now, he wasn't even texting, so she knew he was angry.

"I'm sorry. Please continue."

"To start your prenatal care."

Isoken stood and shook the hand he extended. "Thank you so much for everything."

"My pleasure. I wish you the best."

Isoken nodded and walked out, her heart overflowing with joy. She was about to be somebody's mother. With quick steps, she moved towards her car to return Tekena's call.

He answered on half a ring. "Isoken Marie Adolo. I am about to fly to Lagos just to kick y—"

"You'll really do that to your child's mother?"

"I'm supposed to be headed to the track for practice...wait. Run that back. What did you say?"

Isoken smiled. Disconnected the call and FaceTimed him. He answered immediately.

"Don't play with me. Are you for real?" A sexy grin took over his face.

Isoken nodded and turned the camera around to face the paper she held in her hand. She focused on the word pregnant for a few seconds. She turned the camera back around and he was doing the *zanku* dance step.

"What! My soldiers are potent. Man, one time and issa goal. I wonder if I can make this a side hustle?" He continued to dance.

Isoken sucked her teeth. "And I'll cut off the supply."

Tekena stopped dancing. "That sounds painful. Why you bothered? You don't own it."

"Ha. Ha. Try me first and find out."

"Territorial already. I don't know if that's a good sign, Ms.

Independent. You're acting like you love me or something." He winked at her and laughed.

The truth of his words stung. "Tekena, leave me alone. You're spoiling a good moment."

"Yeah, you right. My bad. Congratulations, baby. I need to get back." He let out an exaggerated breath. "Now I can concentrate. I'll call you later so we can celebrate."

"Okay, I work from home today, but I'm back in the office tomorrow."

"Don't work too hard."

Isoken rolled her eyes. "Ugh. Please don't start. I'll talk to you later."

Tekena blew her a kiss. He'd started doing that every time they ended their phone conversations. As she always did, she lifted her hand and caught the air kiss and placed her hand on her cheek. Tossing her phone on the passenger seat, she squealed. It was real. She was going to be a mom. The next person on her call list was her sister. She'd do that later. For now, she wanted to bask in the moment.

Father, thank you!

***

THURSDAY AFTERNOON, weeks later, the melody of "No Air" by Jordan Sparks ft Chris Brown played through the speakers as Isoken swayed around her kitchen. She picked up the kettle of boiled water and poured it over the rice noodles she'd bought earlier. She set it to the side and poured olive oil in her pan for her stir fry.

Air.

That's exactly what seemed to be missing from her life nowadays. She wished she didn't miss Tekena so much. She wished she didn't see his face in every man that spoke to her. She wished she didn't spend half the day dreaming about him. She wished she hadn't committed to memory the minute down to the second he would call her every day. She wished she didn't burst out humming the melodies to his favorite songs during the most random times of the day. She wished she didn't anxiously count down the days until she would see him again.

She wished.

She wished.

She wished.

What was happening with her now was exactly what she tried her hardest to avoid from the moment Tekena opened Osaro's door that fateful Thanksgiving Day. The only thing that made the hollowness and longing she felt bearable was the life that was growing within her. She rubbed her stomach. At eight weeks, she didn't have a bump yet, but anticipated the day she would. Sometimes she attributed her yearning for Tekena to the fact that he was her baby's father. This wasn't part of her grand plan. This mushy stuff was her sister and Ajoke's thing.

Not her.

At least not anymore.

She sounded pathetic, even to herself.

Isoken poured the peppers, onions and mixed vegetables into the hot pot and stirred them together. Her eyes traveled to her phone. It was a little past five p.m. Tekena was late. Since the day she found out they were expecting, he called her by this time every weekday.

Isoken smiled remembering that day. As promised, Tekena called her later that evening. Even after all those hours, he was still in disbelief. His joy overflowed through the phone. They both were ecstatic. She almost forgot it was Tekena until he warned her to re-read their contract so they wouldn't have any problems.

The next morning, she was greeted with flowers at work, by lunch time, her favorite eatery had food delivered, and to top it off, a fruit basket awaited her at closing. All courtesy of "T3's Pops." He'd already pronounced their kid a boy and a junior. She didn't see any harm in letting him humor himself, so she let him have it. Whatever it was they were doing was nice and steady. The one thing that still hung over them was his career.

Isoken prayed for him constantly, but never watched a race. To keep her sanity and against everything she believed in, she pretended that part of his life didn't exist. She felt awful when he asked about her day and what was going on in her life and she couldn't return the gesture. He listened to her details, asked questions, and gave suggestions or advice when she needed it. The one time she had the courage to ask and he informed her of a race coming up the following day, Isoken found herself holding her breath for what seemed like the whole day. It wasn't until he called her after the race that the log stuck in her chest disappeared.

That was the first and last time she asked. She was sure he noticed it as well. She didn't ask for these feelings. All she had wanted to do was have a baby and mind her business in her own corner of the world. Instead, God had allowed Tekena to bamboozle his way into her life. Why did it have to be *that* marketing agency? Why did it have to be during the period that she needed a job to provide a stable environment for her child? If he were never put in her path, she would've gotten an unknown donor and continued with her life. She knew she made a choice, but she wouldn't have if she wasn't presented with the option.

She sighed, put the drained noodles in her stir fry mix and twirled absently. As her mind rattled over the whys of her heart condition, the verse from Sunday service came to mind – Matthew 10:29, ***Are not two sparrows sold for a cent? And yet not one of them will fall to the ground apart from the Father.***

Her pastor had titled the message, "Providence." She quickly plated her food and headed to the living room with her phone. She opened her church's app and clicked on the message. She wanted to hear the exact way he delivered it. Hitting play, she set the phone beside her and started to eat.

"God is not a passive participant in this world. He sees, has seen and He acts accordingly. Naomi's sons and husbands had to die for her to go back home. She had to be headed back home for Ruth to follow her. Boaz had to marry Ruth for Obed. Why? Because his son, Jesse would eventually produce David. David had to take food to his brothers, and that indirectly caused him to slay Goliath. That eventually changed David's life.

"Where do your Goliaths reside? Are you avoiding them or facing them head on? By all calculations, David could have run away. I mean look at his size compared to the giant. But his focus was on the God that resided in Him and not his fear or what he saw with his eyes.

God's providence is not only His foreknowledge, but His active sustenance and control of the world. You see—"

The ringtone she looked forward to all evening blasted through her device. Setting her almost empty plate to the side, Isoken picked up the phone. She answered Tekena's video call, but her brows immediately knit together when she saw his face. It didn't carry the usual smile or tiredness it normally did. Instead, he was frowning, well more like panicking.

"What's wrong?"

"Hey, I'm good baby, but I need a favor."

"Anything. What do you need?" There wasn't a question in her heart that he really needed her. He normally would be hounding her about resting.

"Nana Rubi. She wasn't feeling well this morning and went to the hospital, but I can't get in touch with her. I have called and called. I hit Eze up to stop by, but I forgot he went out of town. Please, I need you to call her. Maybe it's my connection, but I got you so..."

As Tekena kept rambling, Isoken was headed up the stairs to change. She knew how important the woman was to him. He talked about her more than his own mother. If it would help him calm down so he could have his head in his race, she was on it. Her heart skipped a beat at what might happen if he was distracted.

"Calm down. Your house isn't too far from here. I'll drive

down. Give me a minute to change." She placed the phone on her dresser as she pulled on a pair of jeans.

"Nah, I don't want you driving at night."

"It's not night. It's only a little after five."

"Nah, hold on. I'll order you a car service."

Isoken picked up the phone and looked at him. "Tekena, will you stop. I drove myself to work this morning and back. I'm not an invalid. But if it makes you feel better, I'll Uber."

"Thank you. But be careful, I can't be worried about both of you."

"And you won't. The minute I get to your house, I'll call you." Isoken picked up a light sweater and headed back down the stairs.

She should've known he would be this overbearing and put a rule against getting on her nerves in the contract. But now wasn't the time to argue with him. She had a more important mission at hand. She needed to go check on Nana Rubi.

CHAPTER 27

Isoken had done a complete 180.

Well, not actually a 180. More like a ninety and Tekena couldn't for the life of him figure out why. One minute, he was telling her to go check on Nana Rubi who praise God was okay, to three weeks of him being treated like a necessary evil.

Tekena sat up against his headboard and rubbed his hands over his eyes. He hadn't been getting much sleep because of the puzzle that was Isoken. He replayed the events of that night in his head for what seemed to be the millionth time.

That night, Nana Rubi had taken a sleeping pill and switched off her phone. Isoken's knocks woke her up. They went from that, to her acting different. He'd inquired on many occasions if she was feeling well. She assured him she was, but he wasn't sure. The one thing he was sure of was that his baby was healthy. As she'd always done, when she had appointments, they were scheduled when he could attend via video call. He asked his questions as usual and was satisfied. Instead of them talking after, she always had something to do.

A baby.

It still blew his mind. Now he knew what Osaro felt. The only problem was he couldn't share his good news with his friend. And now his girl was pulling away from him.

Yes, his girl.

That's what she was even if she didn't want to admit it. She was the only woman he wanted to be with. When her guard wasn't up, she said things that let him know he wasn't in this alone. He knew his career scared her, but racing was in his blood. They tried talking about it once and she had shut the conversation down. He gave up and let it go. As long as there wasn't another man sniffing behind her and she was carrying his child, he'd let her call them anything she wanted to...for now. The recent emotional distance between them was something he couldn't bear. It had to end soon. He was tired of the dry responses and unfulfilled promises to return his call.

Tekena stroked his beard and picked up his phone. He went to his calendar to view the day's schedule. Training, press junkets for a new sponsor, and a business meeting. The meeting was a last-minute thing Amara wanted him to attend. The person he was meeting with had specifically flown into Germany to meet with him. Somewhere in between, he had to eat and call Isoken. He would've called her now, but knew she had meetings with some clients.

He was already guilty of an unknown offence; he didn't want to get her angrier at him. He'd wait until later. He really wanted to get to the bottom of whatever was bothering her. The opening of the speedway was in a couple of days and he would be in Lagos then, but he didn't want to waste time arguing when he got there.

For now, Tekena did what he found himself enjoying as the weeks and months rolled by – spend time with God.

A FEW HOURS LATER, Tekena finished an interview and headed to the car that was waiting to take him to the prestigious Wirtshaus Güldener Engel for his business meeting. His security detail got in the front of the tinted car service while Tekena climbed in the back. He pulled out his phone while his detail chatted with the driver. Tekena looked up and his eyes met the driver's through the rearview mirror.

"*Schönen Tag.*" The driver greeted in the native language.

"*Hallo.*"

Over the years, Tekena had learned simple phrases in the countries he visited most to make it easier for him to navigate the terrain. Putting his earbuds in, he dialed Isoken. For the second time. He let out a sigh of relief when she answered on the third ring.

"Hey."

Tekena shifted his position, her voice bringing him the calm he needed. "Hey yourself. How are you? Everything good?"

"Yeah, I'm fine." Her tone was distant, and her attention seemed divided.

"I tried to reach you earlier." Tekena struggled to reign in his temper.

"Yeah, I saw that. I was pulled into another meeting," she stated matter-of-factly.

Her indifference stung. "And you didn't bother to text me back?"

Before her switch, she'd text him while in her meeting to tell him what was going on. It had been five hours since he called her and not a word.

"You do know we're not in a relationship, right?"

He counted to ten in his head before he answered. "And what does that have to do with anything? I always call and check on you and the baby."

"But instead of checking up on the baby, you're having a fit because I didn't call you back."

"Keni, what's wrong?"

She let out a big sigh. "Tekena, nothing is wrong. I've been busy. You know I have a job and am answerable to somebody for a paycheck?"

"Don't give me that. You've always had this job and we've been fine until some weeks ago. Are you going to tell me what's going on?"

"Nothing is going on. I needed some space to think." Her tone was resigned.

"Think about what?"

"You... this thing we're doing,"

"Huh? I'm thousands of miles away. How much more space do you need? And according to you we're only friends, so I don't get the problem." Tekena closed his eyes, praying she contradicted his friendship tag. An eternity passed before she spoke.

"Don't mind me. Maybe it's hormones. Your baby is making me emotional." She giggled.

The sound crawled up his spine, its usual comforting warmth replaced by superficial iciness. She'd gotten away with it for weeks, but he was done letting her slide.

"Goldie, look—"

"*Wir sind hier,*" the driver announced their arrival.

Tekena looked up, they were currently in the valet line and he had to get out. "Okay,

eine Sekunde." Asking the driver for a second, he returned his attention to Isoken. "I gotta go. I have a meeting now, then a race later tonight. Promise me you'll answer when I call later. We need to talk, and I don't want to wait till I see you next week."

After what seemed like forever, she responded. "Okay. I promise."

"Take care of yourself and of course, my baby. I'll call you later."

Isoken chuckled and this time, the nostalgic feeling returned. He disconnected the call and put on his sunshades. He thanked the driver and climbed out of the car.

Minutes later, Tekena was being escorted to his waiting party. When the man saw his approach, he stood and extended his hand. "Mr. Tamuno—"

"Please call me Tekena."

They exchanged a firm handshake and took their seats. Tekena and the representative from Zeidu fashions engaged in small talk, acquainting themselves with one another. By the grace of God, he'd gotten to a place where he could decline certain endorsement offers if he didn't like them. Apparently, Amara had already met with them and thought their offer for Tekena to model their loungewear was a good one. Tekena couldn't make that meeting and since Amara knew he always liked to be involved in his projects, she set this up. If it were a good fit, Amara would conclude the negotiations with his lawyer.

The man pulled out the proposal and they went through it. According to the document in front of him. Zeidu was a successful East African owned fashion brand that currently wanted to break into the West African market. With the new speedway, he was the latest craze and they wanted to get in on the wave. Tekena flipped through the document as the man talked. He was already with a European clothing brand, but it would be good to do something for an African company.

"So, you also have an underwear line?" Tekena flipped through the pages.

"Yes, we do." He pulled out another folder from his briefcase. "In fact, that campaign is wrapping up and we're seeing wonderful results." He pushed the new folder towards Tekena.

The waiter arrived with their meals, interrupting the next question Tekena had. For the next several minutes, they moved business to the side and ate.

"As I was saying, the campaign we just concluded was success-ful. We plan to use the same agency for this campaign once you agree. It's the same one you used for the speedway so I'm sure you can attest to their effectiveness."

"Y'all been clocking me?" Tekena smirked. "But I didn't hire them. The state did but I agree they are good." His mind wandered to Isoken. He needed to wrap this up so he could call her before the race.

"Agreed. We had our wrap up gala yesterday. I couldn't attend because Mrs. Dike told me you were in Germany and this was the only time I could get on your calendar."

Tekena understood. His schedule was tedious during the season. Sometimes, he couldn't remember the city he was in. The only free time he got was the two to three weeks between Prixes and they weren't always free for him.

"In there, you'll see some pictures." Robert's voice interrupted his thoughts as he slid his iPad across the table.

Between bites, Tekena swiped through the photos. He smiled seeing familiar faces like Mr. Gambo and Lara. He wondered where Isoken was until he came across an image that quelled his curiosity and sent his rage soaring. He dropped his fork with an unintentional clang against the plate. His teeth clenched as he squinted his eyes to get a better look.

"Who is that?"

"Oh, that's Yadi. The face of the underwear brand. He's a British Nigerian model who…"

Robert's words faded out as nothing he was saying was important to Tekena in this moment. What was important was why this model and his baby's mother were looking like they were a couple. The unanswered questions had his eyes cross and back teeth hurting. He couldn't even appreciate how stunning Isoken looked. Why was this clown's hand around her like there was something more between them? He decided to act as if he didn't know who she was.

"Is that his girl?" Tekena pointed to Isoken.

"I don't know. She oversaw our campaign. I don't know if they started something or not. But if they did, I wouldn't be surprised. He's a pretty boy and she is gorgeous."

Tekena's effort to refocus on the conversation at hand was futile. Isoken flooded his mind. He knew how she'd been with him during his campaign. He knew how attractive she was to any man. He also knew that she was him or used to be him in a skirt. Use and dump. They'd both given up that lifestyle but with the way she was behaving toward him he couldn't help but wonder.

So many scenarios played through his head. He couldn't afford that, not before his race in a couple of hours.

Minutes later, the meeting officially concluded. Truthfully, it wrapped when he saw Isoken in pretty boys' arms. The car service came to a stop in front of him and he got back in. Immediately, he pulled out his phone to call Isoken. As the phone rang, his chest tightened. He hoped she wasn't out with that the Yadi dude. It was past her working hours and she knew he was going to call her back. After two failed attempts, he tossed the device to the side and rested his head back on the headrest. This was the reason why he'd avoided anything serious for years. When he loved, he loved hard and couldn't play all these games. He had a plan, and, in this moment, he regretted going against it. Since she didn't want to talk to him over the phone. She was going to have to do it in person.

Tekena picked up his phone and dialed his assistant.

"Yes Boss."

"Hey B, I need you to change my flight for me..."

TEKENA NARROWED his eyes to measure the distance to his target. Did he want to go over or around the tables? Which would get his hands around the pretty boy's neck quicker? Every time she laughed, he wanted to stab something. Tekena sat in the corner of the bar of Xovar Lounge nursing a drink and observing the woman who was carrying his baby. She laughed without a care at what he was sure were dry jokes. He was jetlagged and ready to punch something.

His initial plan was to head to New York from Germany, wind down for a few days before boarding a flight to Lagos. Those photos blew those plans to smithereens. Despite that gut punch, nothing compared to seeing her, now in person. He'd landed a couple of hours ago and went straight to her office. Good old stalker Ben had told him she went out to lunch with dude. He knew Ben was probably salty that another person had come in and commandeered her time but that was a personal problem for him to deal with. All Tekena needed was information on the restaurant which he got. Tekena finished his drink and decided it was time to make his presence known.

"I reckon you don't like carrots *ehe...*"

Tekena could hear the guy ask in his fake British accent. He grabbed a chair from the nearby table and dragged it until he positioned it backwards between Isoken and her lunch date. Tekena straddled the chair and sat. He could feel Isoken's eyes on him, but he'd get to her in time. Now it was her date that needed his attention.

"You reckon correct mate. She's also allergic to seafood. Hates orange juice but loves oranges. She doesn't wear white and her day hasn't started without a caramel Frappuccino. She's a huge fan of horror movies but can also sing all the sappy songs of every Disney movie. She's afraid of heights but has no problem flying around the world. Her favorite flower is a lilac orchid, hates roses. She loves the beach but hates swimming. And while she's a beauty to behold, she's a grouch before ten a.m. but a night owl. She loves animals especially dogs but cries when she sees a cat. She's like Xena the Warrior Princess with a bow and arrow. But you know what? All that information is irrelevant to you. You wanna know why? Because she's all me."

Tekena lifted Isoken's glass of lemon water, took a sip, and stood. She and her date still hadn't said a word. She probably out of shock, he, Tekena could care less. He bent to kiss her cheek and whispered in her ear. "Get rid of him."

Tekena walked out of the restaurant without taking a backward glance. He knew Isoken better than she knew herself, so she was going to come at him with fire. But he was ready and this time he wasn't allowing her to shut down or push him away.

SWEET MIST
sincerity, I believe is the opening of the heart
now that we've arrived here
in this season of refreshing
drenched by the mist of sweet love
watch me pour the contents of mine all over you

CHAPTER 28

Isoken had driven past Your Health Is Wealth Drug store for the third time in the last couple of hours. Before tonight, she didn't even know the drugstore existed. She could now credit the knowledge to the force that is Tekena Tamuno.

"Isoken, when did you turn into a fugitive?" She muttered to herself. She made a turn into the parking lot to reverse her car. She'd roamed enough, it was time to head home.

She placed a hand on her small bump. "Hopefully, your daddy has gone home, and we'll deal with him tomorrow."

Before that night when she'd gone to check on Nana Rubi, everything was wonderful between them. She even allowed herself to dream a little of what they could be together. Isoken had stayed a few hours with the older woman, who prepared another meal for her. Everything was good until Nana Rubi decided it was Tekena story time.

Isoken knew the older woman was proud of him, but she didn't seem to notice Isoken's discomfort when the stories veered into his near-death experiences. She already missed him with a physical ache. In those moments, the painful realization that, that ache could become permanent if anything happened to him slapped her in the face. The unexpected gut-wrenching feeling tightened her heart. She would never regret her baby, but for a split second, she regretted their arrangement. Really regretted it.

That night as she rode home in the back of the Uber, her heart rate quickened, she started to sweat, as her ears rang. She hadn't had anything close to a panic attack in years and she was all alone. Isoken remembered the Uber driver asking her numerous times if he should take her to the hospital. She'd declined, but when she got home, she let go and the tears flowed. Sadness, anger, and frustration were the emotions that took over in rapid succession. It was only a matter of time before something happened between them. Something that could mess up his concentration. Multiple scenarios played in her head. No matter how hard she tried, she couldn't shake the paranoia. She had tried denying that part of his world because it made her feel weak and disgusted with herself.

She woke up the next morning with a new resolve. To pull away. There was no way she could give him her full self. It was better to retrace her steps now than to risk devastation for both of them somewhere down the line. Now he was here in Lagos, days ahead of schedule. It was time to have the conversation she was dreading.

In under an hour, she was back home. At a little past seven in the evening, she sighed in relief when she didn't see Tekena's car. Isoken got in, powered off her phone, showered, brushed her teeth, and put on a pair of pjs. As she was about to climb into her bed, she remembered her nighttime snack and water. Every night, she found herself hungry at two a.m. She was fixing a sandwich when her doorbell rang. She knew exactly who it was. She also knew him giving her space until morning was too good to be true.

Isoken put her hand on the doorknob and closed her eyes to calm her breathing. Opening the door, she came face to face with Tekena. After all this time the anger was still in his eyes. His glare roamed her body and his eyes softened at her bump. He reached out and palmed her stomach with both hands. He closed his eyes taking in the feeling. She watched his lips move as though he was communicating with their child. Then it was as though a switch turned on in his head because his eyes quickly hardened. She stepped aside and he entered.

I really had to pick the crazy man as my baby's father.

Isoken took her time closing the door, locking it, and walked back to her living room. Tekena was pacing the length of the space with his hands in the pocket of his navy khaki shorts. The black tee shirt he wore showed exactly how much he had been working out since he left. She really wanted to hug him, he looked so good. Her fantasy was cut short when his sharp voice cut through the air.

"How is it you can't survive without a man in your face all the time?"

His words sliced her. "What did you just say to me?"

"You heard me. Is he the reason you've been evasive? Are you planning to have his baby next?" He let out a harsh breath.

Isoken's eyes bugged and her mouth flew ajar. Fury shook her body at his audacity. "How dare you!"

"I dared and you haven't answered any of my questions."

"Yes, without a man I'm hopeless." She flung her hands in the air. "What was the other question. Oh yes, he's the reason I haven't had time for you."

"Don't play with me Isoken," he roared.

"Who says I'm playing. The minute I drop this precious cargo. He's next in line." She taunted.

"Stop it!"

She wasn't done yet. "In fact, I need to update the contract because you seem to be confused on the terms. I can't have him doing the same thing." She needed to hurt him the same way he hurt her.

Tekena's face contorted into something she didn't recognize. He walked up to her. She knew he'd never hurt her, so she wasn't worried and stood her ground.

"You mean this contract?" He pulled a paper from his pocket, tore it up, and let the shreds fall on the floor.

"Are you insane?"

"No, but you're getting me there."

"How Tekena? Because I went out for lunch with someone else?"

"No, because you're playing games that I'm not beat for."

For the next several moments, they stared at each other, neither of them backing down. Tension filled the atmosphere. She blinked as Tekena grabbed her face and crushed her lips with his. It didn't take much for her to open her mouth and let him in. In a frenzy, they devoured each other. She didn't realize how much she needed him until she didn't have him.

Didn't have him.

He could be taken away from her.

Isoken pushed against his chest and backed up. "I can't do this Tex..."

"Can't do what exactly?"

"This..." Not meeting his eyes, she pointed her index fingered toward him and her.

"Not an option. Try again." His voice was feral and low.

Isoken looked up at him. She walked over to her couch and plopped down. She closed her eyes and placed her hands over her face. She opened them when she felt Tekena kneel in front of her. His arms snaked around her body caging her in. "Talk to me. What happened?"

Isoken shook her head.

"Goldie, I can't play this game with you. Talk to me."

His plea shattered her resolve and the tears she'd held onto since the day she saw Nana Rubi last, flowed. Tekena stood, scooped her up, took her place on the sofa with her in his lap. He held her tightly as she cried. She buried her face in his chest as she once again released the wave of emotions that she'd tried so hard to deny. He rubbed her back softly, whispering in her ear. "Whatever it is, it's going to be okay. Goldie, I need you to talk to me. Please. I can't take your tears. Tell me what I can do to fix it."

Isoken lifted her head and narrated her encounter with his

Nana, the panic attack on the drive home and the thoughts that have tortured her ever since. How she had a nightmare about him and Frank waving at her as they went into heaven.

"You're telling me I made it to heaven?" Tekena kissed her forehead. "I'm glad 'cause I've been trying so hard to live right."

"Tekena, I'm not playing."

"I know you're not, baby. I'm trying to lighten the mood." He thumbed away a tear from her face. "What can I do to alleviate your fears? You want me to quit? I will."

Isoken didn't know how serious he was, but she'd never want him to do that. "No! Don't you dare. I can't ask you to give up something that you were born to do. I see the fire in your eyes. I know how much you love it. I feel so bad I can't be excited and talk about it with you. I'm so scared that something might happen to you that I pretend that part of your life doesn't exist. That's unfair when it's a huge part of who you are."

"I'll never force you to talk about my races. But I still have another year in my contract. So, what are you proposing?"

"Maybe if we can go back to—"

"Can't do that. That's dead." He watched her for a challenge, but she had none. "I used to think I wasn't worthy of God's love. I used to be so ashamed to accept His blessings. Always waiting for the other shoe to drop. I mean, no way can He love me after what I've done. You, you made me want to be a better man. I went to Him because of you, but when I got to Him, I knew I needed to stay. I can't imagine any future without you and my child with me. I know that as a child of God, I deserve good things and my best thing is you."

Tekena rubbed her stomach and kissed it then looked back at her. There was something deep and intense in his eyes. He brushed his lips lightly against hers.

"How are you here?" In all the frenzy, she didn't ask him.

"My girl was acting like she didn't know who I was, so I had to remind her," he shrugged.

"I'm your girl now?"

"You were my girl the moment my sperm met your egg. I just let you think otherwise."

"You're so nasty. Must you say it like that?"

"Wasn't that what happened?"

She was about to respond when her stomach growled.

He tapped her lap. "Get up, let me make your sandwich and tea."

Isoken smiled as he stood up and set her down on the couch. "You noticed?" Every evening when she talked to him, she would be making her nighttime snack.

"I notice everything..." He walked into the kitchen. "Go up and I'll bring it to you."

Isoken knew that they had a lot to talk about, but she was glad that she finally told him how she was feeling. She wasn't sure what was going to happen next. Whatever it was, she prayed her heart could take it.

Several minutes later, Tekena knocked on her bedroom door. Once she invited him in, he entered with her sandwich in a zip lock and peppermint tea. He set the food on her nightstand and walked up to her bed. He drew the covers over her and kissed her forehead.

Resting his forehead against hers, he whispered, "Everything is going to work itself out. I love you, Isoken." He took in a breath and exhaled. "I'm deeply in love with you."

Isoken's words were stuck in her throat at his declaration. He didn't seem affected by her lack of a response. She knew she loved him too but wondered why she couldn't voice it.

He kissed her stomach. "I'll lock up."

Before she could utter another word, he turned and walked away.

The chime indicating the arming of her house alarm set her into motion. She felt for her phone under her pillow. With shaky fingers, she located his number and dialed.

He picked up on the second ring.

"I love you too." The words poured from her lips, satisfying her soul.

"I know, baby. Get some rest. I'll see you in the morning."

"Good night."

They disconnected the call and Isoken picked up her teacup. The erratic beat of her heart morphed into a calm symphony. She had arrived here, drenched in the mist of a love she'd tried her best to deny. Her fears hadn't been eliminated, but Tekena's reassurance fueled her desire for a working heart. She didn't know what the future held, but she was going to do better at trusting the One Who did.

CHAPTER 29

Ten hours. It was the longest Tekena had slept in the past several weeks. The first picture she had sent him with her bump took his breath away. Seeing her, however, was a whole other experience. Things weren't completely resolved between them, but now more than ever, he was happy he changed his plans and arrived in Nigeria ahead of schedule. His mission for the next couple of days before the opening ceremony was to work on his relationship with Isoken. No longer was the status quo an option. He had let her control their pacing all this time, but if pushing him away was part of her game plan, he was taking over. He had to get her past her fears.

Chugging down the remainder of his lukewarm morning roast, he decided that a change of scenery might do them good. Walking back to his bedroom, he sent a text to Eze.

Hey man, I need a charter flight.

When?

ASAP. No matter how much.

OK. Give me a few mins.

Tekena nodded in satisfaction then opened another thread.

Good morning baby. Hope you had a good night?

Tekena didn't have to wait long before her response came.

Hey, good morning. Your baby gave me a hard time earlier, but I'm good.

His brows knit together at the thought of her being in discomfort. He was about to dial her number when Eze's text came through. Pleased with the update, instead of calling Isoken, he sent her a text.

Hey, pack a bag. I'll be there in 45 mins.
Where are we going?

Tekena smirked. It wouldn't be her if she didn't question him.

Goldie, 45 mins or I'm putting you in the car in whatever state I find you.

Tekena didn't wait for her response. Instead, he made a few more calls to get things ready for them, then headed to the shower.

A few hours later, they were airborne and Isoken lay asleep with her feet in his lap. His foot rub knocked her out. Shame and fear had both of them shackled for so long that they had forgotten who they were without those demons.

As he watched her sleep, he became firmer in his resolve not to let her slip through his fingers. He knew they were bonded by the life she carried and while that had been the way in which he wanted to keep her in his life, it was no longer enough. He needed all of her, mind, body, and soul. He still saw the skepticism in her eyes, but he saw the love as well and for the next couple of days, that was what he intended to build upon. No phones, only the two of them enjoying nature and discussing their future. They had to figure out how to get this thing right.

TEKENA STOOD when he saw Isoken approach. The glow from where the sun hit her skin captured him in a trance. Her ensemble was simple and chic. The off-the-shoulder yellow top popped against her rich skin, while the capri jeans sent his gaze to her well-manicured feet she now had clad in yellow sandals.

They had arrived at the luxurious Zaina Lodge in Ghana a while ago. After they checked into their tented chalets, he made sure she had something to eat while he booked her a full spa treatment. They were going to take the safari tour, but he wanted her well rested first. She looked worn out when he saw her at the restaurant the previous day, but his anger wouldn't let him address it. After her massage, she had come to his room with the intent to watch movies, but she ended up falling asleep on his bed.

Tekena pulled out a chair for her. "You look amazing."

They were having an early dinner on his private balcony by the pool, overlooking the seemingly endless savannah.

"Thank you. So do you."

"Rested?"

"Yes, I didn't know how much I needed it." She took a sip of her water. "I still can't believe you put all this together so fast."

Tekena took his seat. "I wanted us to get away. Besides, you've done such a great job that I can't move as incognito as I'd like to."

"True. I'm so good at what I do." She brushed her shoulders and winked at him.

Tekena chuckled. "That you are."

The waiter approached with their meals and after a quick grace they began to eat. For the first couple of minutes, they ate in semi silence until Tekena decided it was time to lay everything out in the open. He lifted his hand and brushed a loose tress out of her face. Isoken sucked in a breath under his touch. The way she responded to him caused a stirring in his loins. Under different circumstances he'd have no problem pulling her to him and exploring her lips, the feel of her body next to his. But there was much more at stake. His future. Their future.

"Tex...we—"

Tekena reached across the table and placed his hand over hers.

"I can't do this friend thing anymore. When I asked to be your donor, I really thought that having you in my life in any capacity was okay. I signed that contract when in the back of my mind, I knew it could backfire." He sighed. "In under four months, it already has. Despite what I told myself, some of you is not better than all of you. I know you feel the same or you wouldn't be fighting me this hard. I'm crazy about you and I need you. So, let's fight this thing that's keeping you back, together."

His chest tightened waiting for her response. He needed her to at least admit to herself that they deserved a chance. Then he'd move mountains to give her what she needed.

"I need you too," she spoke softly. "The love I have for you is deep. But the thought of losing you... I'm petrified."

"You won't lose me." Tekena moved his seat closer to her. He took her trembling hands in his. "I'm not going anywhere."

"But you can't promise me that!" Her voice cracked.

"No. I can't, but neither can anyone else." He stroked the back of her palm with his thumbpads.

"But everyone doesn't do something to intentionally endanger themselves. With Frank, I knew there was a possibility, but with rose colored glasses, I ignored it."

"Baby, I'm so sorry you had to go through that. But I'm not Frank. Our destinies aren't the same." Logically, Tekena knew she wasn't comparing him to Frank, but the circumstances, so he pressed. "Driving is a lot safer than it's ever been." Tekena went on to describe the measures that have been introduced to reduce accidents in the sport. He watched as the crease on her forehead straightened with his explanation.

Isoken removed her hands from his. "Babe, I hear you. But you drive at speeds of close to three hundred and fifty kilometers an hour. There's nothing they can do to make that safe."

"Who told you that?"

She shrugged. "Eze mentioned it in passing some time ago."

I'm going to strangle him.

"Isn't it true?"

Tekena nodded.

"The way I feel about you terrifies me. With you it's different. Tekena, I won't survive if anything happens to you. Do you understand me?" Isoken covered her face with her hands, then looked at him again. "I fought like mad to stay away from you. That's why I was mean to you from day one. But here we are."

Tekena laughed. "You scare me too. I've never felt this deeply for anyone, but I can't have you pushing me away anymore. I can't Goldie, I can't." He kissed the back of her hand. "We'll work through this together. Promise me we will."

Isoken nodded her head.

"I need to hear the words, baby."

"I promise."

Tekena wasn't sure what the future held for them. But he was determined to fight with all he had for their love to trump her fears. One thing he did know was that he wasn't willing to live without her and his child being active parts of his life.

THREE DAYS LATER, Tekena walked the red carpet amid camera clicks and screams for his attention. It was the grand opening of the Gidi Motor Speedway. The red carpet had never been his thing. He hated explaining who he was wearing or what his relationship was with the woman who adorned his arm. In this moment however, he took his time as he wanted to cherish this moment and the woman by his side.

Isoken's one condition for walking the carpet with him, was that they didn't answer any relationship questions. He was okay with that, especially since anyone that had eyes could see what it was. She needed to make up her mind on what they were going to say because he knew that after this, her sister and his boy would be waiting in the winds. Either way, he was okay with what Isoken wanted to do publicly.

"You good?" Tekena squeezed Isoken's hand to get her attention amongst the frenzy.

Isoken's eyes shifted from the photographers to him. "Yes, I'm fine." Moving her body slightly, she posed for another picture. "You know I have to get to work after this."

"We'll talk about that when we get inside."

She gave him a warning look and he knew he'd lost that battle.

For the remainder of their stay in Ghana, the cloud of gloom lifted, and they enjoyed each other and the views of nature. There was no doubt how beautiful Isoken was, but what drew him to her the most was her mind. They talked for hours about books, politics: foreign and local, faith and how they wanted to raise their kid. Every evening, she would fall asleep while he massaged her scalp.

In six short months, he had gone from "she's not that bad" to "I'm feeling her" to "I need her to survive." There was no doubt in his mind that he wanted them on the road to marriage. He no longer wanted his child born out of wedlock, but also knew that was a steep hill to climb.

A few hours later, the opening ceremony was winding down. The festivities had run into the early evening, but he was done. The project he'd been working on for close to three years was finally functional. The place was packed with politicians, dignitaries, and top celebrities from the major Nigerian industries. Kamal Danjuma and Abayomi Rice were also in attendance. Both men were with their wives. Kamal also brought his twin and his wife.

Upward Solutions and the event coordinators had done an amazing job. The turnout was great, and some local races were already booked. His school's registration had spiked almost ninety percent. Tekena was proud of Eze and his drivers/instructors because they represented TSquared well.

He turned his head trying to locate Isoken. True to her word, the minute they got inside the venue after the ribbon cutting, she'd disappeared. He knew she was working, but he still missed her.

His heart leapt as Isoken approached. *Yep, I'm not going to make it.* Tekena closed the gap between them and pulled her in for a hug. She rested her head on his chest and he planted a kiss on her forehead.

"I'm exhausted. Are you ready?" She whined.

"Waiting on you to say the word."

She lifted her head, and her eyes met his. "Okay let me get my stuff. I'll meet you near the car."

Moments later, they were seated in the back of his SUV as the driver navigated the highway. In palpable silence, they both attended to messages on their phones. Tekena responded to his last email, then glanced over at Isoken who was still buried in her device. On impulse he took a picture of her side profile. He posted it to Instagram with the caption *My Preferred Speed*. Turning off the comments, he set his phone to the side.

"Is Gambo one of the people you're texting?"

With a puzzled look she faced him. "My boss?"

"Yeah."

"No, why would I be texting my boss?"

"I don't know, maybe because you've worked on three major campaigns back-to-back and could use a little break."

"Huh? I'm fine."

He turned his body to her. "Come back with me."

She narrowed her eyes. "Is that a question or a demand?"

He moved his stare to her phone then returned it to her face. "Whichever one will get you to say yes."

"I have a job I happen to like."

"And I'm not saying you don't." He raised his index finger. "But I have two more weeks off and I want you in my world. You don't have a major campaign so you can work from anywhere. You can Zoom, call, and email. Whatever you need. I got you. Come back with me." He clasped his hands together. "I'll beg if you want me to. Please don't want me to."

Isoken's lips turned up in a smile. She tugged on his beard gently drawing his face closer to her. "You're lucky I love you." She brushed her lips against his. His hand went to her nape as he deepened the kiss.

Victory!

CHAPTER 30

With her towel tied around her growing bosom, Isoken examined her bump. The steam from the running shower fogged up the mirror, but she could still see her seventeen-week-old pouch. Except for the morning sickness which came in the afternoon and her ever changing cravings, the pregnancy had been easy. Most days she had to pinch herself to ensure she wasn't dreaming. She was writing poems again, her relationship with God was so much better and Mr. Gambo had offered her a full-time position. She still had her sights on opening her own agency one day, but that was way down the line. Her only focus right now was bringing a healthy baby into the world. Tekena supported her decision and reminded her that whenever she was ready to take that plunge, he would be right there by her side.

Tekena.

Her relationship with him was another thing that had her on a constant high. They'd reached a level of intimacy she never would have thought was attainable without sex. The emotional and mental connection between them sometimes shook her to her core. They still teased each other, were quick on the comebacks and clap backs, but since they decided to be together, something she couldn't quite articulate had lifted. Their willingness to go the extra mile for each other was mutual, hence the reason she was currently in Milan.

Isoken loosened the towel and stepped under the hot jets. Mr. Gambo was more than willing to give her time off. Although she had warned him not to, Isoken was sure Tekena had something to do with his enthusiasm. When they left Lagos, they flew straight to New York. For the first couple of days, they lazed around his penthouse condo. On the third day however, she wanted to go out and he obliged. They got in a picnic in the park, play at the theater, museum tour, and a spoken word performance. They ended most evenings with a romantic dinner or something simple in her hotel room or his condo. On the tenth day, they boarded a flight to Italy. Here, Tekena refused to have her stay in a hotel. He claimed the ones that were reputable were too far from where his apartment was. So, her present accommodation was his guest bedroom.

Tekena was in training for his race in two days while she was going shopping with Elle, Andreas's wife. The day after they arrived in Italy, Elle came over and welcomed them with stuffed meatballs. Her husband was doing much better but was out of commission for the season.

With the weather still a little bit chilly, Isoken dressed in a brown cashmere sweater and black jeans. Her phone rang and she smiled. She'd wondered how long Osaro would be able to keep her sister from calling.

"Hmm *na wa o*. You got a man and abandoned me," Itohan whined.

"Really? Says the woman who shut off her phone for a week because she was on her honeymoon."

"It's not the same. This is you and Tex...Tekena Tamuno!"

"Yeah, that's bae." Isoken took off her scarf and brushed her hair.

"Ha! Hold on let me check if the sky has turned purple."

"My dear *left matter*, the sky is intact. We thank God for giving me sense."

Itohan laughed.

"How are you? How many more weeks?" Isoken asked.

"The doctor says three more weeks. But him and the devil are liars. I'm trying to get Osaro's big head son out of me sooner than that."

"You know your husband can help you with that. Tell him to—"

"Must you always be nasty?"

"Nasty? I'm trying to help your life. Talking about popping out my nephew."

Itohan giggled. "So? How did this happen. Is he willing to accept your child?"

Isoken's stomach fell at the reminder of the secret she was keeping from her sister. Despite the change in their dynamics, she and Tekena still wanted to keep the baby's parentage under wraps.

"Yes, he's good with it."

"How are you though? Are you now okay with his career?"

Isoken shuddered. She grabbed her purse and left the bedroom. "To be honest, no. I only know that I don't want to be without him."

"But you have to have peace."

"And I do when I'm with him. I've been trying to ignore the nagging voice in my subconscious replaying tragedy." She opened a jar of nuts and poured some in a bowl. "I've been trying to hold my thoughts captive. You know, as the Word says."

"But sometimes we need to acknowledge them first. I asked this years ago, so I'm asking it again. You look so happy and I'd hate to see this blow up. Do you want to go to therapy? I'm all for needing Jesus, you know that. But we sometimes also need therapy to help us through stuff."

Isoken thought about it for a minute. "I don't know if that will help me."

"But you have to try. I did right after Osaro, and I got

engaged. The hurt over my abandonment ran deep. Even now, I still see my therapist, but not as much."

"Hold on." Isoken removed the phone from her ear to look at the text that came in.

I'm here, getting on the lift now ~ Elle

"Sis, I gotta go. Elle is here. I'll call you later."

"Aww, look at my Keni, inviting her man's friends into her heart."

"Please, this is about food and retail therapy. She's cool *o* but you know I don't do new people." They shared a laugh before Isoken disconnected the call.

As she walked to the door, she remembered her time in Ghana, desperate to recall all Tekena told her about the safety of racing. His plea and the love she saw in his eyes cracked the foundation of the wall she had carefully erected over the years. Logic wanted to keep fighting him, but love won. The feelings she had for him were here to stay, no matter how hard she tried. In that moment, she knew she had to try. If she didn't, she'd spend her life mourning what could've been.

THEY WALKED into L'immagine Bistrot Ristorante, which was Isoken's favorite restaurant any time she was in Milan. The lunch time crowd had yet to gather so they were seated immediately. After ordering drinks, Elle pulled out the matching earring and necklace set Isoken had encouraged her to buy. When they left Tekena's house, they visited many small shops before ending up in Galleria Vittorio Emanuele II, the oldest shopping mall, and a major landmark of the city.

"I can't wait to try this on."

"It'll look great on you. If I'm not here, make sure you send me a picture. I wanna see how it looks." Isoken picked up her menu.

Elle did the same. "Sure." Then she sighed.

Isoken lifted her eyes to Elle, her brows knit together. "You okay?"

"Oh yes. I'm happy. Although we just met, it's nice to have another woman around and not those groupies that follow the men everywhere."

Isoken's brow raised. She hadn't attended a race yet, but she didn't know that groupies surrounded them. She made a mental note to discuss that little tidbit with Tekena later.

T2: Hey, I miss you.

As though he knew he was the center of their chat, his text message came through. She picked up the phone.

"Give me a sec Elle."

I miss you too. U betta not hv any groupies next to you.

T2: LOL. Tell Elle I said she talks too much

I'm serious

T2: And I love you. No groupies. Be safe and feed my child good food.

Love you too. Bye.

Isoken put the phone down and looked up to see Elle staring at her with a wide grin across her face. "What?"

"Your smile was so big as you were texting. I'm so happy for Tex...and you, of course."

Heat prickled Isoken's skin like the sun was shining directly on her. Was it that obvious? Before she could respond, the waiter came back with their drinks and they placed their orders. When the waiter left, Isoken decided to shift the conversation. They discussed family, the racing circuit, and them one day visiting Nigeria. Elle shifted to the topic of love and marriage when the waiter returned with their food. Isoken was glad for the interruption as this wasn't a topic she wanted to discuss. They said grace and began to eat. Isoken had spent the last two hours on her feet with only those nuts for a snack, so she was starved.

"I really feel like I'm right on this; a proposal is on the way. Soon," Elle said.

Isoken shifted in her seat, her lips turned up in a weak smile. "We'll see."

Elle however didn't seem to get the message because she continued, "Behind all the bravado is a sensitive and incredibly good man. But ever since I've known him, he's avoided relationships like a plague. Then he introduces you and I can see his world light up. Someone who accepts him for who and what he does. On top of that, he's walking with God. I can only imagine what the future has in store for you two." She twirled her pasta.

Isoken put her fork down in her plate, her appetite fleeing. She looked at the woman opposite her who was concentrating on her food totally oblivious to the weight of her words.

Someone who accepts him for who and what he does. Was that really her? She'd never let him quit for her, but wasn't there something deep down that wished he did? Since she had decided to give them a chance, they'd watched a few races together. Even with his hand in hers, watching him on the screen still caused her heart to thump in fear and trepidation. She chided herself at not being strong enough to overcome the emotion.

"Did I say something wrong?"

Elle's voice brought her out of her thoughts. She must have been wearing her emotions on her face. "Oh no you didn't."

"The upcoming race will be your first one. I'm so excited for you."

"Yeah, me too." Isoken picked up a slice of lemon and squeezed it into her glass of water. "Me too."

There was no part of her future where Tekena didn't play a leading role, so he better be as good as every sports channel said he was and come back to her in one piece or she would hurt him herself.

ISOKEN GRIPPED the mug in her hand with more energy than necessary, but it was all she could do to stop her fingers from shaking. It was close to two a.m. and she couldn't sleep. The soft melody to "My Prayer" by Called Out Music spilled from Tekena's room to the balcony. She swayed her head back and forth, remembering the day he told her he needed music to sleep. She leaned against the rails.

The beauty and serenity of the city's skyline was a sharp contrast to her raging mind. Logic had been in constant battle with emotion since she got back from lunch. She'd occupied herself the best she could. Even did a little work to distract her until Tekena got back. They talked a little bit over a light meal.

She could feel him studying her from time to time when she would disappear into her head. She must have done a good job at pretending to be fine because after asking what was going on a few times, he dropped it. Although his lingering skeptical stare told her that he doubted her. She quickly changed the topic because the thought of him climbing into a car with any kind of discord between them petrified her. Besides, she didn't want to keep sounding like a broken record.

It was a routine for him to retire early the day before a race and she was all for it. She needed to be alone with her thoughts. Retiring too, she'd prayed and pleaded with God to keep him safe. She had talked to God so the only thing to do was trust that He wouldn't do her wrong twice. Running out of words to say, she'd drifted off to sleep.

A day later, amidst the loud screeching of tires, squealing breaks and blaring screams by adoring fans, Isoken strolled hand in hand with Tekena from the garage. The atmosphere was electrifying, and she could see the appeal for adrenaline rush. Tekena had introduced her to his crew and showed her his car. His cherry red, sleek Ferrari stock car was a beauty on the outside and had a beast of an engine on the inside. He took his time reiterating and showing her the additions to the car that made it safer. She knew the time he spent making sure she was comfortable, was probably time he needed to do some pre-race stuff.

"Why was there only one mechanic with your car? There

should be more than one, in case one person missed something," Isoken said.

Tekena stopped walking. "There were two. You only met one of them. Listen baby, they've done all the checks and re-checks." He rested his forehead against hers. "Please don't worry. I'll be fine."

The pleas in his voice made her want to kick her behind. She was doing the exact thing she promised herself she wouldn't do. Worry him.

"Okay, I'm good." The false words came out so effortlessly. A moment passed between them with him trying to read her and she, putting on the performance of a lifetime.

He escorted her into a suite. There, she would watch the race on the screen. Tekena introduced her to a few people. Elle and her husband were there along with his management company representatives, some guests, and the team owners.

"Tex, it's time." Axel, the man he'd introduced to her as the head of his crew walked up behind them.

Andreas walked up to meet them. "Ready?"

"Yeah, man." Tekena kissed Isoken with so much passion, despite their audience. He bent and kissed her stomach then whispered, "I love you."

"Love you too. Tekena you better come back to me *o*."

"Always." He grabbed his helmet and left with some other men behind him.

Take control God.

Tsoken's eyes followed every move Tekena made. Her eyeballs were dry and hurt because she refused to blink. Isoken put her hand over her mouth as she watched Tekena put on his balaclava and helmet. After he got in the car, was strapped in by Axel, and his steering wheel fixed, he drove onto the track. Elle kept trying to talk to her and she had to control the reflex to seal the woman's mouth shut. Isoken rubbed on her stomach to settle it. Her baby for sure could feel her anxiety.

Tekena had gone a few laps. So far so good. Isoken felt her heart thumps dissipate and she relaxed in her seat. He was going fast, but he was driving well. A couple of cars got in his way, trying to block him and she could hear his team telling him to veer in another direction to outsmart them. They were approaching a bend and, in that moment, she stood. It was a controlled track but what she also knew was that turns were tricky. Especially with the cars in front of him.

She prayed he would take it easy, but she also knew this wasn't a hobby and he was in it to win. As they approached the corner, Tekena was able to go wide with another car. However, she could hear his team murmuring about him being on the outside. Isoken lifted her hand to cover her eyes when she saw his car and another driver's car so close that their tires were almost touching. Soon, Tekena was in the clear and they were in the fourth turn when the circuit marshal raised a flag. Isoken dropped back in her seat and shifted to Elle, without taking her eyes off the screen.

"Thank you, finally!" Elle shouted.

"What does the flag mean?"

"Oh, the marshal is letting those cars know to get out of the way."

Isoken half listened as Elle explained that those cars were driven by racers who ranked poorly. Why they were even allowed to drive didn't make sense to her, but she wasn't here to rewrite Formula One rules. All she wanted was for her man to be back by her side. Isoken waited for the cars to comply. They did and the race continued. They were now in the sixth turn, and Tekena's car was on the outside again. Her eyes darted to Axel, who was speaking to Tekena. Isoken returned her gaze to the screen and in that split second, her world stopped.

Tekena's car was clipped by another driver who made an aggressive turn at the bend. He was on the outside and at a disadvantage. The next moments played out like a movie, except this was her real life.

It all happened so fast. Tekena's car went straight through the barrier. One of his tires came off, and his car broke in half and seemed to become a huge fire ball. Isoken was frozen in place. The medical car was at the sight in seconds with the fire extinguisher. Other personnel rushed to the sight, but she couldn't see Tekena. Axel threw his headset across the room and rushed out of the door.

Tekena hadn't come out of the fire.

One hand flew to Isoken's mouth while the other went to her stomach.

Her scream was halted by the lump in her throat.

He hadn't come out of the fire.

Her eyes stretched wide in fear.

Her chest tightened, pressured by the vice around it.

She couldn't breathe.

God, please deliver him. Please let him move. Don't do this to me.

Isoken felt Elle's arm around her, but she shrugged it off. She didn't need anyone's touch but Tekena's. Her heart thudded in her chest. Oxygen eluded her. The ringing in her ears got louder. She closed her eyes, struggling to steady the pace of her heart. Sweat trickled down her back.

"Oh, thank God. He's jumping over the barrier."

Isoken's eyes flew open at Elle's scream. Isoken watched Tekena climb over the metallic partition and his feet were doused with the extinguisher. Only the bottom part of his suit was on fire. She could hear the commentators saying it was a miracle he walked out of the fire and credited his safety to the halo.

He was alive.

He's coming back to me. But he almost died. He could be dead right now.

"Keni, he's okay."

Isoken turned to Elle. She couldn't form the right response, so she stared at the woman. How could she do this week after week?

"You don't look so good. Are you okay?"

The tears she'd held now blurred her vision. Her head spun. Her hands shook as the realization of what could have happened sunk in. She struggled to fill her lungs with air. She heard loud talking as Tekena neared the room. Blood rush to her head and pounded in her ears. Of their own accord, her feet moved in the opposite direction as she darted out of the room.

She ran.

Isoken had no idea where she was going, but she needed to get far away from the roaring engines. She took the corner down a hallway. The air was more palatable. She took in a couple of breaths, then saw the restroom. Rushing in, she headed for the sink. She ran some paper towels under the cold water, rubbed them against the back of her neck and dabbed her face. The bile that threatened to erupt from her stomach settled.

She stared in the mirror, closing and opening her eyes several times, hoping the black spots disappear. Every possible scenario for disaster played out in her head. With shaky hands, she struggled to get her bag open. She pulled out a bottle of water, twisted off the cap and drank. Her chest heaved, and the tears began to fall. No matter what she did, she couldn't get the intense crushing pain in her heart to stop.

Who was she fooling? She couldn't do this. There was no way she could go through this again. She would be doing him, herself, and their unborn child a disservice. Tekena deserved someone who'd support him wholeheartedly. Their baby deserved to be properly nurtured while in her womb. And she deserved a peaceful, stress-free existence. The three of them deserved better and if she had to shatter her heart to give it to them, she would.

"Goldie, you in there?"

His voice caused her to shut her eyes and take a deep breath.

"Baby, come out please."

She still didn't respond.

"If you don't come out, I'm coming in."

They had enough to deal with, without him being seen in the women's bathroom. Isoken washed her hands and walked out. Tekena was leaned against the opposite wall with his head back and eyes closed. He stood up straight when he sensed her presence. He tried to close the gap between them, but she widened it by stepping back.

"Are you okay?" Her voice was shaky.

"Yes, I am. Are you okay?"

"You almost died."

"But I didn't."

Panic and frustration slipped over his face and he stepped toward her again. She stepped back. His flippancy annoyed her.

"Baby, I'm okay. Limbs and hands intact." He turned around showing her evidence of his comment.

"But one wrong move and it would've been over. I can't do this Tex. I can't." She shook her head.

"And by this you mean?" His voice shook.

"Us. You. Me," she cried. "You came into my life and became the reason I breathe. You've become what I didn't know I needed, but I now must live without. Several lifetimes flashed before my eyes as I watched you out there today. The same breath you gave me, you almost took away."

Tekena moved toward her. "Bab—"

"Please don't touch me." The hurt in his eyes pierced her heart, but she knew that his arms around her would shatter the little resistance she'd built.

"I'm not Frank!! I am not him. You're afraid, but I'm not Frank. I don't plan to die!"

"He didn't either! And how dare you?" His words sliced her. Over the past few months, her love for him had grown so deep that she wondered if what she felt for Frank could even be categorized as love. She had survived Frank, but with him, she wouldn't make it. And there was their baby to consider.

"I'm sorry. I love you. Please don't do this..." His shoulders slumped.

"I love you too, but I can't be with you. I can't. I can't."

"Are you kidding me? So, you're just going to walk away? After everything?"

"Do you think this is easy for me?"

"Then don't do it!"

"Tekena—"

"Nah, don't do us like this." His eyes darted toward her stomach. They lingered there a few seconds before traveling back up to meet hers. The hurt was replaced with disbelief. "So, what's your plan? To walk off with my child? You can't keep me out of my child's life."

His tone was harsh as he spit out words that punched her chest. She knew he didn't mean them, but that didn't make it hurt any less. She desperately wanted to reach out to him. To hold him. She wrapped her arms around herself and lifted her eyes to his. She wanted him to hear her clearly.

"I never intended to. I just can't be in yours." She turned away. No need dragging this any further.

"Isoken. Keni. Baby, please wait. I need you."

The desperation in his voice froze her in place. Isoken hung her head but kept her back to him. "If I stay, you still won't have me, because I feel like I'm dying slowly."

She heard him moving toward her. The anticipated agony from his touch propelled her forward. One step after the other until she was out of the building. Grateful he didn't follow her, she leaned against the wall. Moments later, her phone rang.

"Oh my God. I've been trying to reach you. We stayed up to watch the race. Are you all right?"

Her sister's voice pushed the floodgates open and tears streamed down her cheek. "I need you."

"Come on. I'll be waiting."

CHAPTER 32

A month later, nothing Tekena did filled the void Isoken left behind. He threw himself into practice, work and anything that freed him of his memories of her. Even if it was temporary. It was the only way he could preserve the part of his mind that remained intact. His time with Isoken was the best and most painful experience of his life.

It produced heartbreak from a love he was sure he'd never find again. It also produced his princess. Tekena looked at the sonogram on his phone. They'd found out they were having a girl. The burn from the treadmill he was currently on mirrored the sensation from the day Isoken walked out of his life. Regretting letting her walk away from him, he'd rushed back home. Instead of her, he met a note with profuse profession of love but notifying him she'd left Italy for the US. She promised to let him know when she arrived. That promise, unlike the other, she kept.

Tekena couldn't bring himself to hear her voice in the days that followed. Instead, he kept up with her through Osaro. After praying and pleading with God to bring her back to him, he resigned to praying for God's will. He sent his usual morning and evening text to keep himself updated on her health and the baby's but refused to answer her calls.

He needed to keep his head clear. His career was the only thing in his life that had ever been stable. For a few idyllic months, he'd thought Isoken could be that too. She made her position clear and he had no choice but to accept it.

Tekena got down from the machine and took a drink of orange Gatorade. This was his last night in Spain. He hadn't done as well as he expected in Azerbaijan, the city after Italy. However, he had done better in the previous day's race. By morning, he'd be headed to Montreal before he got another two-week break. Taking in the lyrics to "Deep End" by Lecrae playing through the gym speakers, Tekena sat on the bench to read the Bible verse of the day. The best way he'd figured out to get his prayer time in was when he worked out.

Yet I am not alone, for my Father is with me. John 16:32

He reflected on its relevance in his life. The thoughts were still swirling in his head when his phone rang.

"Hey man. Is she okay?" His heart thumped.

"Wow. If I weren't the one that called, I'd have thought I had the wrong number."

Tekena let out a sigh. "Ro, answer the question man."

"Chill, she's fine. I can't call you no more?"

"You never call this early." Tekena threw his towel on his shoulder. "Besides, since OJ made his appearance, you ain't been calling me. I've been calling you."

Tekena couldn't believe his boy was now a father. He'd seen him do the uncle thing with his niece, but hearing him talk about his son, Osaro Michael Ikimi, Jr, was a whole new experience. He was born a week after Isoken arrived. Visa issues with their mother and Aunty Lizzy being ill caused Isoken to remain behind to help her sister. She and her boss worked something out and she was afforded additional time away. Tekena had been concerned since she was also pregnant. His insistence on her resting and taking it easy caused a text war between them. He didn't want to keep fighting with her, but he wasn't letting her put herself at risk either.

"Yeah, whatever—"

Tekena chuckled. "Wassup?"

"Man, when you coming to get your girl?"

Tekena's head fell back as laughter rippled from his stomach. He wondered how Osaro lasted this long. The Adolo sisters were no joke together. Now add a baby and a pregnancy. "You okay over there?"

"Nah, I ain't okay. Between OJ, Baby Cakes and now your girl, I can hardly spend time with my wife."

"You sound needy."

"Shoot, I am. I need you to come and get your girl. She was already mean, now on top of that, I'm dealing with a broken heart and pregnancy cravings."

"Ro, that was one time." Tekena remembered the day Osaro called to report Isoken had him in Walmart at one a.m. He'd gone downstairs to get something for Itohan and met her in the dark crying over a hotdog. He went from asking her what was wrong to the aisle of Walmart, looking for relish.

"What happened? I mean I know what happened, but how are we gonna fix this?" Osaro asked.

Tekena scoffed. "We?"

"Yeah, we. I'm suffering too."

Tekena ran his fingers through his beard. "I can't keep chasing her if she doesn't wanna be caught. I can only take so much rejection."

"You know she's not rejecting you."

"Tell that to my heart and ego."

"So, that's it. You just gonna let her go?"

"Yeah, man. She must want to be with me as bad as I want to be with her. If not, I'm gonna always have the uncertainty that I'll wake up one day and she'll be gone."

Osaro exhaled. "Yeah, I feel you."

"Besides, she's carrying my child. I can't have—"

"Your what? Nah man, walk that back. For real? That's you?"

Tekena bowed his head. Osaro's reaction reconfirmed he and

Isoken made the right decision of secrecy. Their families and friends would've been too much to handle, especially with the way they came together.

"I can't believe y'all didn't say anything. Why though?"

Tekena explained what happened and the reason behind their silence. "Don't say anything. I don't know if she's told her sister yet."

"She better. I refuse to sleep on the couch if Itohan finds out I knew and didn't tell her." Osaro chuckled. "Somehow I knew it. The minute Itohan told me she was pregnant. I told Mac that had to be you. He owes me five K."

"Man, y'all some gossipy—"

"Call it whatever. I knew you were feeling her when you first got to Lag and your confused, gotta have it your way self wouldn't let her get pregnant by anyone else."

Tekena remained silent because his friends knew him so well. He smiled at the thought. "I can't believe y'all bet on me. But I'm more disappointed Mac don't know me better."

Both men laughed. After a beat of silence, Tekena spoke. "But for real though, I can't have her stressed out. So, I'll back off."

"And you think that's the best thing to do? Space?"

"She did that, not me."

"But—"

"Let it go Ro. I'm good."

"No, you're not, but I'mma drop it."

"Take care of her."

"I got you."

"Bet."

Tekena disconnected the call and he felt his mood sink.

Lead me, Lord. Lead me.

ISOKEN PLACED the last bottle in the sterilizer. She smiled as she absently rinsed out the kitchen sink. Her sister's milk wasn't coming in enough to sustain the baby, so she was substituting with formula. Isoken had watched in admiration as Osaro encouraged and tore down her sister's doubts of her being inadequate because she had to give their baby formula.

Isoken dried her hands, then rubbed against her stomach as she watched Osaro play soccer with Baby Cakes in the backyard. He was a great father, and she was so happy for her sister. She wiped a stray tear. Too bad her situation had to be so complicated. She was tired of crying.

"Ouch, all right," Isoken murmured at her daughter's kick.

Tekena must have put a hex on her. Any time she had a negative thought about him, her daughter responded with a kick. Over the past several weeks, her emotions had swirled in one vicious cycle. Logically, leaving was the right thing to do, but that didn't take away her anger at having to do it.

Anger.

Hurt.

Longing.

Regret.

These were the reactions to the separation from him. On arrival, she'd cried in Itohan's guest room for five days straight. Her life was like one giant fog after a rainy day. With the passing of each day, little by little, the fog lifted. She could now see the damage the torrential rainfall left behind. But before she could really assess the damage, her nephew decided to make his appearance.

Since they'd been back from the hospital, they'd settled into a routine and Isoken had time to dwell on her feelings. It sucked. She thought with fear and distance, she'd be able to start healing. But instead, her love for Tekena intensified like a consuming fire.

Hence the regret.

The feeling she had in that garage after Tekena's accident was nothing compared to what she felt now without him. She began watching his races. She was still scared, but not terrified. There were no more panic attacks, but that could be because she was watching in an emotionally relaxed environment. When it became too much, she detached, turned off the television and prayed. After every race, he sent her a text.

I'm back and safe.

Those four words every time. And she responded with two of her own.

Praise God.

She wished she had done things differently, but the decision had been made. And she wasn't still sure if she could do the live racing circuit. What kind of woman doesn't show up for what's important to her man? It also wasn't fair to him to keep popping in and out of his life. Her decision was like sinking sand. One day she was firm in it, the next day, not so much.

"Finally, he's sleeping." Itohan's voice pulled her from her thoughts.

Isoken lifted off the kitchen counter and turned to face her sister.

Itohan strolled over to her. "What's wrong? Why are you crying?"

Isoken sniffed and wiped her wet face. When did she become a cry baby? She pulled out a chair and sat. In silence, Itohan followed suit. In all the craziness, they really hadn't had a lot of time to talk.

Isoken looked down at her hands on the table. She interlocked her fingers. "You know no matter what you read or see in movies, you can never be prepared. Nothing prepares you for the loss of a loved one. The day Frank was buried, the last bit of hope I had was destroyed. Until then, I had hoped someone would jump out and tell me I'd been punked.

"Leaving for South Africa was my way of cushioning the shock and mourning. All of those years in the air were me in denial and taking back some control of my life – a life I knew would spiral out of control if I stopped. The minute I let my heart catch up with my head and face the reality of what happened, I knew I was for sure going to sink so far in a sunken place that I wouldn't have been able to survive. I was good...okay, until I had the very thing I'd used to cope taken away from me."

Isoken lifted her head and met her sister's teary face. "Please don't cry for me." She grunted. "You know, I wish as women we weren't held to an unattainable, sometimes toxic standard of strength. Because then I would've been comfortable in my weakness and vulnerability and asked for help. But you know me, I didn't. Instead, I bargained with God and decided to have a baby."

Isoken rubbed her stomach. "With the joy of my life also comes the pain of my life. But this time a million times worse. How much does God think I can bear?"

"I still can't believe you're having a baby with Tekena." Itohan rubbed her temple. "Up until recently. I thought he was only your man, but him being your baby's father puts a new perspective on things. I'm still hurt you kept that from me, but you're suffering enough so I'll let that slide."

Not having the energy to explain her decision, Isoken ignored the statement and Itohan continued.

"God never gives us more than we can bear. It's us that choose to bear it alone, so it's heavier. I can't begin to understand how you felt losing Frank, but God has given you a second chance. You've bottled up your feelings for so long. Now you must let the process run its course so you can be accepting of God's plan for you. I want you to remember that no matter what you decide, you have no control. I repeat, no control over your life or Tex's. So why not enjoy what you can while you can? Your grief is showing up as fear and that is paralyzing your move forward. You must tackle that with someone, sis. I know an exceptionally good therapist in Lagos."

Itohan grabbed Isoken's hands, her eyes pleading for the right response.

"You can't have love and easy. I'm not talking about suffer head love. I'm talking about taking a chance, risks and commitment through thick and thin."

Therapy was something Isoken had begun contemplating. She believed in God's healing power but was now convinced that she could benefit from a specialist. "I'll think about it. I need to get back to Lagos anyway. I'm surprised how generous Mr. Gambo has been with my absence."

Itohan gave her an incredulous look.

"Why are you looking at me like that?"

"Don't tell me you don't know your man called and threw his celebrity weight around."

Isoken shrugged. "I don't know. He's not talking to me."

"So, what are you going to do to fix that?"

"I love him so much but, in my dysfunction, I'm only causing him pain. I have to fix me first." Isoken stood.

"The sooner the better." Itohan walked over to the fridge.

Isoken strolled towards the kitchen exit but stopped short of leaving. She turned to her sister. "Look at you, giving big sister advice. I'm so proud of you."

Itohan's brows came together. "Uhm, I am the big sister."

"I know but you were slacking for a minute. Living like a stalker hermit." Isoken raised her hands to the heavens. "We thank God for Jesus."

Itohan laughed. "You still have no sense."

Isoken giggled. It was the closest to a laugh she had come to in a while. She might be able to salvage her relationship but first she needed to work on her. She prayed that when she was ready, Tekena would be willing to give her another chance.

A WEEK LATER, Isoken hugged her sister, kissed her nephew and Eseosa, and got in the car with Osaro. She was headed to the airport for her flight to Lagos. She had run away from her life enough. It was time to tackle her issues. She insisted an Uber was fine but like his bull-headed friend, her brother-in-law ignored her like she wasn't even speaking.

Since he found out about her baby's paternity, Osaro had teased her relentlessly. She retaliated by crying about needing something when he least expected it. He was really the big brother she didn't have. Thinking of brothers, she made a mental note to call hers when she got to the airport. Zogie came over when Itohan gave birth and stayed for a couple of days before heading back to school. During that time, they'd talked, and he gave her the same advice Itohan had. Not to let fear rob her of her happily ever after.

"Sis, I'm sure your sister has told you everything you need to hear from a logical standpoint. If it makes a difference, I do understand where you're coming from." Osaro glanced over at her.

Isoken furrowed her brows. "You do?"

Osaro chuckled. "Don't sound so surprised. But yes, I lost a sister, remember? It's not the same as losing a lover, but the effects are similar. I almost let my guilt and need for control keep me from your sister. She's the best thing that's ever happened to me and I almost lost out." A beat passed. "I know my boy can be a handful..."

"Who are you telling?" Isoken folded her arms across her chest

Osaro grunted. "And, so can you. You're made for each other."

Isoken cut her eyes at him. He laughed and shrugged.

"Don't give up living for today because you're scared of tomorrow," Osaro said.

"I'm realizing that now. But he won't talk to me. He declines my calls and sends me a text instead."

"If anyone can make him do anything, it's you."

Osaro's words sat with her. After her talk with her sister, she'd returned to her room and called him. She wanted to beg for his forgiveness and tell him she was going to therapy. But no answer. Instead, moments later, he texted asking if she was okay. Once she responded in the affirmative. He gave her some story about not being able to talk and never returned her call. She tried two more times before she realized he really didn't want to talk to her.

"Where is he?"

Osaro pulled into the parking space at the airport. He turned to face her. "You know you're my sister, but he is also my brother. Don't reach out if it's not permanent. You'll agree with me that we can't have him distracted."

Isoken sighed and nodded her head. "Yeah, I know."

For a fleeting moment, she allowed herself to dream of winning the fight for her fairytale.

BREATHE

When you left, a part of me went with you
I followed you but I went astray
Dark clouds engulfed my perfect view
What once were bright blue skies, now turned gray
I didn't let anyone outstay their welcome
I barricaded all the doors
I should've taken these shackles off sooner
'Set me free' my heart implores
Love, a familiar feeling, this time more intense
I held him at a distance, but now he's become my whole view
He worked his way into my heart, tearing down my defense
Now my heart knows it's time to start again and embrace the new
Not everything in life can be good
That's one tidbit I'll never forget
But the Lifter of my head is always good
So, I don't want to look back and regret
This is me, putting fear aside
Claiming the best is yet to come
I refuse to keep my breath inside
Instead, I'm committed to allowing this love blossom

CHAPTER 33

"Zogie, are you sure man?"

Tekena glanced at the GPS and grunted when it announced that he'd been rerouted. "I talked to Ro after he dropped her at the airport." He made a sharp U-turn, and headed to the hospital.

"Tex, I wouldn't call you if I wasn't. Osaro did drop her. Then she called me, and we got to talking when suddenly she decided to change her flight."

"And she was coming here? To Canada?"

"Yes, she wanted to surprise you. Unlike Itoh, Keni makes a lot of spur of the moment decisions." Zogie tittered.

"Yeah, don't I know it."

She's going to be the death of me. Lord, I've survived the roughest racetracks, how am I about to die in the hands of this hard-headed woman?

"I was going to call Itohan, but right before Keni was taken to the hospital, she said not to. But now I can't reach her, so I decided to call you first."

Tekena had tried to get in touch with her too but couldn't. "Yeah, good looking out. Hold up on that. Once I see what I can find out, I'll hit you up."

Tekena disconnected and overtook the car in front of him. The last thirty minutes was like being swallowed up by hell. The thought of anything happening to Isoken and his baby suffocated him. On her way to Montreal, the plane ran into some turbulence. The chaos on the plane was so bad that it caused four passengers and one crew member to be taken to the hospital. Isoken happened to be one of them. Why didn't she head home as planned? Why had he let anger and hurt rule him to the extent that he hadn't talked to her in weeks? What if he never got the chance again? Zogie said she sounded fine, but Tekena needed to lay eyes on her.

Fear.

Panic.

Guilt

Regret

Those were the emotions that had been running through him like a freight train. Moments later, Tekena parked the rental and rushed into the hospital, making a beeline to the reception.

"Hi. Hello." Tekena drummed his fingers on the counter.

"Hi, may I help you?"

"I'm looking for a Ms. Adolo. She was brought in from an airplane." After giving the nurse additional information, he waited for her to check something on the computer.

"Ah yes, hold on."

It was like *déjà vu* for Tekena, but this time, his world was on the line. After waiting for what seemed like an eternity and explaining his relation to Isoken, he was directed to her room.

Tekena trotted to the elevators and took the short ride up. His steps slowed as he approached. He knocked and entered. The log in his chest disappeared as the sound of his daughter's heartbeat boomed from the monitor.

Tekena strolled over to Isoken, who was asleep. With his hand over her stomach, he gave thanks to God. Tekena moved a chair closer to the bed and sat. Picking up her purple poetry notebook that lay open face down across her chest, he brushed his lips against hers. He attempted to put the placeholder on the opened page when he saw the word, "Broken."

He saw that it was a poem entitled "Broken Things." He was caught up in the ease at which she expressed feelings she hadn't fully expressed to him. Before he closed the book, he had read other poems titled, "Blink," "Sweet Mist" and "Breathe."

Tekena lifted his eyes to her. He understood her so much better. Now that he knew the extent of her pain and love for him, he kicked himself for being so dismissive. It was uncanny; but Isoken being in a potential plane crash gave him a better understanding of her perspective when he had his accident. Even though her brother said she was okay, he had died a thousand deaths until he saw her. In his case, she had to watch the horror happen with no comfort until he moved. He couldn't put her through that. It might be better for them to go back to their original plan of co-parenting.

Tekena rested his head on her bed and prayed. Moments later, he felt fingers move over his head.

"Babe..."

He shot to his feet and peppered kisses all over her face. "How do you feel? What happened? What are you doing here?"

"The plane ran into some turbulence. It was really bad. Stuff was being flung around and everything. Because I'm pregnant and had some discomfort, they brought me here. I should be discharged soon."

"Is the baby okay?"

"Yes, she's fine."

"Okay...why are you here?"

"I wanted to surprise you,"

"Yeah, you did that, but why?"

"Are you not happy to see me?"

"You left me, so again...why are you here?" He leaned back and folded his arms across his chest. He was glad she was fine, but if she had gone home as she was supposed to, she wouldn't have been in danger. So, he really needed to know why she was here.

He read her thoughts, but he wanted to hear her say them. He was unsure if he could trust her love for him.

Isoken sat up in the bed and lowered her eyes before lifting them to meet his. "To tell you I'm sorry. To tell you I'm ready to stop running from my fear. To tell you I can't exist without you in my life."

"You're going to have my child. I will be in your life."

"I don't mean only as my child's father, but as my man."

"How do I know you won't up and leave me again? I'm still going to be a race driver next year. Nothing has changed."

"I know that." She let out a heavy sigh. "Why are you making this so hard for me?"

"Hard? Do you know what it feels like to have your heart ripped out of your chest, but you have to do everything you can, not to lose focus, so you won't make a mistake that might cost you your life?"

Tears rolled down her cheeks that he really wanted to wipe away, but his frustration got the best of him. "Look maybe you were right. We should just—"

"Don't say it. I wasn't right! I'm sorry for hurting you, but you must look at it from my perspective. I'm terrified of losing you."

"Then we should've worked together. You promised me that, but at the first sign of trouble, you ran. I told you I can't play these games with you. I love you very much, but I like my sanity."

"Tekena, I can't change the past. I can only acknowledge my mistake and ask for you to trust me. Trust this. Everything was theoretical until I actually saw you in a car that caught fire...do you know what that did to me? But when the plane started shaking, all the weeks away from you seemed like a waste of time. My love for you runs deep. I can't deny it, neither do I want to anymore. But in order for me to give you my all, I have to deal with this fear." She exhaled. "So, I'm going to talk to a therapist."

A few moments passed between them. Tekena sat at the side of her bed. He caged her in with an arm on each side of the bed.

"I'm happy you are going to get help. And I'm going to be with you every step of the way."

She sniffed. "I'd like that." Isoken cradled his face in the palms of her hands. "I love you, Tekena."

"Forever?"

"To infinity." Isoken drew his face closer and poured the passion behind her words into a kiss, one he had no problem deepening.

***

"Hello Isoken."

Isoken adjusted herself on the sofa and returned her therapist's greeting. She had been a patient of Mrs. Bolaji for the last eight weeks. She now had a deeper understanding of herself, fears and self-erected roadblocks that had hindered her. The biggest lesson she had come away with was that her grief for Frank wouldn't go away with time, but she could live and love again with skills she's been taught to cope.

"Today will be your last session, but you don't seem happy."

Isoken let out a sigh. "I'm happy you've helped me to see things clearer. You've been terrific but all the work I have been doing seems to be for naught."

"Why?"

"My baby's father—"

"Tekena? I thought he was more than that?"

"I don't even know what he is anymore. Some days he's my man, some days he's my baby's father...It just seems like he's holding back. I know I broke his heart. But I had my reasons and I have been trying for two months to show him that I'm fully committed." Isoken raised her hands and slammed them on her lap in frustration. At seven months pregnant, she didn't think that the relationship between her and Tekena would still be surrounded with such uncertainty.

"Did you come to therapy for him or you?"

"I came for me...us...but..."

"From what you told me, Tekena fought for your love, but you pushed him away at every turn. I'm sure you can understand his hesitancy."

"Yes, and I have tried to get him to trust this. I've been more involved than I used to be. I'm better at communicating my feelings. But..."

"All you can do is work on you, which you have done. The ball is now in his court. But you must also have the courage to set boundaries for a defined relationship. Gray areas are never a good thing with matters of the heart."

Isoken nodded and talked to Mrs. Bolaji for the remainder of her one-hour session. Their eight-week intensive sessions were over, but she promised to keep in contact.

Isoken walked to the parking garage. The scorching sun prickled her skin. She lifted her attention from her phone and halted her steps. Leaned against her car was Tekena. He sauntered toward her.

"You're supposed to be in Belgium."

"True."

"So why are you here?"

"My heart is here." He grabbed her hands and stared at her. "I've been waiting for this day since you left Canada. I didn't want to pressure you about us until you took care of you."

"Why didn't you tell me? You've been driving me crazy." Isoken placed her forehead on his chest.

"Yeah, watching you squirm was fun. You shoulda known you can't get rid of me that easily." Tekena cackled.

Isoken lifted her head and rolled her eyes. Tekena kissed her lips and got down on one knee.

"Goldie, you're it for me. My now and my future. Marry me. Please?"

Isoken's hands trembled at the sight of the ring in the red velvet box he'd pulled out of his pocket. She took in a couple of quick breaths to control her breathing. Their journey flashed before her eyes. With him it was different; she didn't need a plan or a buffer. He came in and helped her let go. Now she could breathe.

"Yes. Yes. Yes."

Tekena slid the ring on her finger and rose to his full height. He circled his arms around her and drew her in for a kiss.

The End

EPILOGUE

Two years later.

ISOKEN BELLY FLOPPED on the bed and pulled out her phone from her robe. They were at the Zimbali Resort in South Africa to celebrate their one-year wedding anniversary. They had a quick registry wedding before their daughter was born. The main ceremonies, however, took place immediately after Tekena's final Formula One season. Tekena moved back to Lagos but they made New York their second home. He didn't win the championship but came in second in the standings. She and their daughter were waiting in his Monaco hotel room to celebrate.

Tarila Tiana Tamuno made her debut at thirty-seven weeks and she was the center of their world. Although she wasn't a boy, she was still T3 to her father who she had in the palm of her hand.

Isoken looked at the time. Her husband wouldn't be back from the golf course for another couple of minutes, so she had time to watch her favorite video. She opened the video clip of their wedding reception and forwarded it to her and Tekena's first dance as husband and wife. Her eyes watered as she watched them sway to "For You" by Kenny Lattimore. An oldie but goodie with lyrics that expressed their hearts.

Her ivory wedding dress was a take on modern Hollywood glamour. The lace mermaid gown with off-the-shoulder sleeves and a sweetheart neckline fit her form perfectly. She'd worked hard to get back to her prebaby size although it wasn't something she'd obsessed too much about.

Initially Tekena was worried that preparing for a wedding would put her in a bad space but she reassured him it was okay. When she recognized the onset of negative memories, she used her coping skills to get through. Besides, Tekena was an only child. She knew his mother had looked forward to his wedding day for years and Isoken wasn't about to take the fanfare and experience away from her. And what a fanfare it was. Celebrities from Tekena's world, family and close friends stormed Benin Nigeria in style for their wedding.

"Goldie baby, we got dinner reservations. How many times you gonna watch that video?"

Isoken was so engrossed in her thoughts that she didn't hear Tekena enter their hotel suite. He plopped down on the bed with her and pulled her on top of him.

She kissed him. "Hey babe. I love watching our special day. How was your game?"

"It was fine. Why you gotta watch it when you live it every day?"

"And I'm having the time of my life." She pecked his lips again. "Okay let me call your mom to check on Tari, then we can hop in the shower." Isoken attempted to dial but Tekena took her phone.

"No. My daughter is good. You've talked to her three times today already. I'm trying to give her a baby brother and you playing around."

Isoken laughed, remembering their honeymoon. They had called to check on their daughter. Tarila had cried on the phone and Tekena cut the honeymoon short, talking about she needed him.

"Nah, homie don't use me as an excuse. You're just afraid to see those pretty eyes. Then she'll pout and shed that single tear she uses to get you every time and you'll go running."

Tekena rolled her over and got on top. "She got it like that. But so do you. I love you Mrs. Tamuno."

Isoken exhaled. "I love you too." His love gave her the strength to breathe again. "Okay, let's go shower and see about this son you're talking about."

GLOSSARY

to khian gbe mwen wa ah ~ **Do you want to kill me. (Bini. Isoken's native language)**

Lamogun- **Royal Greeting. (Bini. Isoken's native language)**

D'evbin ne vbe rue ~ **Why will I want to kill you? (Bini. Isoken's native language)**

Oyese o, we vbe vbo ~**I'm fine. And you? (Bini. Isoken's native language)**

Vboze ~ **Why? (Bini. Isoken's native language)**

Ciao ~**Hello (Italian)**

mio figlio ~ **My son. (Italian)**

Tesoro **(Term of endearment. Italian)**

I ba te ~ **Greeting (Kalabari. Tekena's native language.)**

FINAL NOTE

Thank you for reading Isoken & Tekena's story. Just in case you haven't read the first book in the series, I have an excerpt for To Live Again. But first...***please consider leaving me a review.*** If you liked this story, I trust you'll like some of my other titles. But before we get to those, never miss sales, new releases, or freebies. You can ensure that by joining my mailing list. I'd love to stay connected.

ALSO BY UNOMA NWANKWOR

Now to those other titles

Stand Alone Books

An Unexpected Blessing, August 2013

He Changed My Name, February 2016

When You Let Go, May 2014

The Ultimatum Series (Complete Series. Listed in Book Order)

The Christmas Ultimatum, November 2013

The Final Ultimatum, October 2016

Sons of Ishmael Series (Complete Series. Listed in Book Order)

A Scoop of Love, January 2015

Anchored by Love, December 2015

Mended with Love, October *2017*

Redeemed Through Love, October 2019

The Invisible Shackles Books

To Live Again, March 2018

To Breathe Again February 2021

The DuBois-Arazi Family Novels (Uncompleted Series)

A Promise Fulfilled, November 2019

Collection of Short Stories & Flash Fiction & Sweet Romances

Vegas Nights, August 2020 (Sweet Romance)

Second Shot, August 2020 (Sweet Romance

TO LIVE AGAIN EXPERT

"Now I see where you came up with your outlandish assumption."

His voice caused her to stop digging in her purse for her keys and returned her gaze to him.

"May I?" He gestured toward the drawing.

She nodded, and he removed the tack that held it to the corkboard. She watched as he sauntered toward her. He stood before her. Any closer and his body would touch hers. She moved back, but he moved closer, until she was backed up against the Smart Board. Itohan decided right there and then, she was having a heart attack.

He stared down at her and she accepted his challenge holding his gaze. A vision of him taking her to the morgue because she'd died under the intensity of his gaze flashed through her mind. That could not and would not be her portion, so taking him on wasn't in her best interest. He was testing her, and she was bound to lose. She should be running and not entering the ring with him. Warning alarms went off in her head. This was a dangerous game, so she gave in. With nowhere else to go, she stepped aside.

"Did that feel like I play for the other team?"

She was stuck. When she told her brother the story, he told

her she had inadvertently questioned Osaro's manhood. Right now, he was trying to prove a point and with the way her breath caught in her chest, he had accomplished his goal.

He bent down, putting his ear at the level of her mouth. "I didn't hear you, Ms. Adolo." His tone demanded an answer.

"No," she whispered.